QUEEN
OF THE
NORTH FOREST

BOOK ONE OF THE LIN BEIBEI TRILOGY

ROBB MASON

Published in Australia by
Newbattle Books
Melbourne Australia
newbattlebooks@gmail.com
ABN 40851248439

First published in Australia, 2019

 A catalogue record for this book is available from the National Library of Australia

MASON, Robb
Queen of the North Forest
Book One of the Lin Beibei Trilogy

ISBN: 978-0-6482732-0-2 (paperback)

ISBN: 978-0-6482732-1-9 (epub)

Cover layout and design by Alfred Obare
Typesetting by Sophie White
Printing by Ingram Spark

Disclaimer

This is a work of fiction. All of the characters, places and events portrayed in this novel are either products of the author's imagination or are used fictitiously.

*This book is dedicated to all
creatures in danger of extinction
– and to the people working
to prevent it.*

CONTENTS

1	The Disc in Granma's Closet	7
2	Disc Daze	14
3	The Disc Delivers	19
4	The Accidental Tourist	24
5	Into the Void	32
6	A White World	35
7	Granma's Vase, Mother's Broom	44
8	Meet the Locals	56
9	Friends with Benefits	67
10	The Second Day	72
11	North Forest Saviour	82
12	Meet Other Locals	92
13	Say Hello to the Family	108
14	The Decision	120
15	'Marsupials March'	132
16	Away from the Hill	145
17	Monkey and the Dragon	154
18	Once Bitten	168
19	Enter the Dropcat	177
20	Walking with Granma	192
21	Roughed-up and Rescued	203
22	Back with the Herd	219
23	Battle the Bandarken	226
24	The North Forest	252
25	Atop the Bigbirds	265
26	Fire Mountain	279
27	Lin and Arben	295
28	Beibei and the Beast	309
29	Farewell	323
	Acknowledgements	331
	About the Author	333

1

THE DISC IN
GRANMA'S CLOSET

Pots and pans clattered and the smell of steaming noodles drifted through the house. Morning was the best time. Mum was up and busy; no pressure, no talk, just ten more minutes snug and warm before she had to get up for college. Lin Beibei rolled over, hit the snooze button on her mobile and looked at the time: 6.50am.

"Mmmmm," she murmured as she woke slowly, sheet rumpled around her chest, sleep fugging her brain.

Daylight glimmered around the edge of the blind, the dark slowly yielding to grey. Lin thought about the day ahead. Was everything sorted? She ticked off stuff in her head: no assignments due, the accounting test was next week, and she'd done her homework in the library yesterday. Everything was okay. Today would be another ordinary day – get up, wash, dress, get her gear together, say 'G'morning' to Grampa, have breakfast with Mum then meet her best buddy, Song Qili, at the bus stop. On the rattling coach to college they'd have a 'goss and a giggle'; a morning like so many before.

Lin took in her room, as ordinary and organised as ever. Gauze curtains hung around the window. Pop posters clung to the walls, photos of pretty-boy singers she'd loved as a young teen and didn't want to let go. Not yet anyway. The floor lay bare except for a small, patterned rug. A tall, wooden closet that was her granma's stood parallel to the bed, the only heavy presence in a light, bright space. Next to the closet a chest of drawers held her clothes. On top of the drawers sat her make-up and mirror.

Set apart on a plinth atop her bedside table stood Lin's one treasured possession, a parting gift from her dying grandmother... a small, crimson vase. She woke every day to that little red urn, a container that held the sweetest memories. A small vase, such a simple thing – they could be bought anywhere in China – but nothing could replace the love, laughter and life held within it, memories of an old woman whom Lin adored. That little red vase meant everything.

Granma had been with Lin throughout her childhood, bringing warmth and joy as she'd shared skills and wisdom. It had been seven years since Lin last held her granma's hand and she'd wept for days when those kind eyes closed for the last time. Lin's grief had been total. Nothing could replace Granma, and the vase was her one memento. 'It'll be with me forever,' she'd promised. 'Forever.'

She looked at the vase and smiled. *G'morning, Granma.* The old lady's presence filled the room with love as it always did.

Lin smiled, stretched and rolled over.

"Just ten more minutes. Please."

It was then that a strange blemish edged into her drowsiness, poked her sleepy state like a gentle push-in-the-back. The gap between the bedhead and the closet – a space she'd peered through sleepily on so many mornings – looked different. Something hung there. Or did it? Whatever might be there didn't bounce out like an ad on her iPad; it edged into existence like the faint clang of a distant alarm. And didn't go away. Lin blinked, and tried to focus. It looked like a foggy spot. Maybe it was her eyes. She rubbed them. *Naah, there's nothing there.* Lin rolled over. Perhaps she was dreaming, maybe she was still asleep. *Sleeeep, please. I need ten more minutes. Mum'll be pounding on the door soon.*

Yet she was drawn to look again. Okay, it was different. And it hadn't been there when she went to bed; she would've noticed. But an odd aberration dangled in that space now. It must have arrived in the night. Lin closed her eyes. *What? That can't be!* Her head snapped clear as if slapped. She sat up, surprised and curious.

C'mon. Things don't just arrive in the middle of the

night. This isn't a train station. Front on, she could barely see the odd arrival. But when she lay back and looked at it, the shape took form; a convex oval of fuzzy space about 75cm wide hung like a ghostly jellyfish, a half metre from the floor. A shadowy border rimmed its edge like singe marks around a burn hole. Two darker lines jagged across the middle. It looked like a bubble of lava. *Yeah, sure, and there's a volcano under my bed. I'm not gonna look.* A moment later Lin thought it resembled a big baby's navel. She smiled. Maybe she was dreaming.

"Time to get up," a no-nonsense voiced barked outside the door.

The handle rattled.

"Wakey, wakey! Breakfast's ready. Get moving or you'll miss the bus."

Lin was awake now, and definitely not dreaming. Her mother commanded serious attention. Ignoring her didn't work. Lin tried it as an infant and was quickly brought to heel. Wang Mei wasn't big, just bossy and brusque. Crossing her was like tackling a tsunami with a sponge; the deluge would wring you out every time. Wang Mei brooked no challenges, took no prisoners. Village shop-owners ducked under their counters as she walked by; the family stepped around her carefully.

Lin got out of bed, walked towards the door, paused, thought better of it and called, "I'm up, Mum. I'll be there soon."

As she turned to stare at the strange newcomer, a shaft of sunlight slipped by the curtains and grazed its edge.

The odd arrival shimmered gently then exploded with light like a fireworks festival. A myriad of silver beams no thicker than a hair's breadth flickered from its edge, striking out from each other, lightening, brightening, radiating in a dazzling arc to the bedhead, the closet, the floor, the walls. Lin's room erupted like a starburst, filling with light, blinding and brilliant. In the centre, like a squat spider in a sparkling web, hung the silent, grey disc.

Eyes wide and hand to her breast, Lin rocked on her heels. Her breath caught in her throat. "Omigod! What is that?" She groped blindly for the top of a chair and lowered herself onto it, staring open-mouthed.

"Mum, come and... ", Lin called, then paused. "No, it's okay, be with you in a minute."

She had to know what this was before anyone else saw it.

Lin moved to the edge of the bed, reached out a hand, hesitated, and pulled back. Then, holding her breath, she stretched out her foot and nudged the closet door. It wobbled shut. Nothing else moved, but threads of light now hit the wall.

Lin shook the bed. The disc stayed steady. The light threads slipped past the bedhead. Lin pursed her lips and her eyebrows lowered as she gazed at the kaleidoscope of colour. It was amazing. What was it; maybe a secret portal to somewhere? Where? *Wow. Gotta know more.* And her dad had to see this. He'd know what it was. But he was away working, and Lin had to get to breakfast. Now. Or Mum'd kill her.

She couldn't show her mother. There'd be security around so fast Lin might never know what it was. And if her mum saw the intruder it could be all over for the disc. Her mother wasn't much for mysteries, but brooms were lethal weapons in Wang Mei's hands. Lin wanted to know more about the anomaly, not mull over its shattered remains.

"I'll be two seconds, Mum," Lin called, and turned to inspect the invader.

As she did the sunlight faded, and so did the disc. The light that made it explode like a starbust disappeared, leaving the disc dull and dreary.

Lin decided to hide the visitor. She didn't want to touch it; she thought the strands would anchor it where it was, near the floor by her bed. Granma's closet had two doors at the bottom closing off a copious interior. Lin reckoned the space would be big enough to contain the disc if she swung the closet around. After dumping last year's textbooks, an old bumbag, a bunch of plastic flowers, broken umbrella, pair of smelly gym shoes and her dad's ancient Walkman, Lin took hold of the closet with strong arms. She had to shift it around and sideways.

With some sweating, swearing, heaving and grunting Lin manoeuvred the closet from one wall to another. The disc filled the space behind the lower doors, hanging there like a plastic, see-through wall clock counting out time. Lin closed the doors and smiled, satisfied the disc wouldn't show. Moving the closet wouldn't be noticed. She often shoved stuff around from wall to wall or to a different place in the room. After putting the other stuff away, Lin dressed quickly, gathered her school gear and hurried to the kitchen. *I'll put my make-up on later, or Mum'll have a piece of me for letting brekky go cold.*

2

DISC DAZE

College turned out tough. The work wasn't hard; Lin liked her classes, even some teachers. But the disc continued to bother her. Oval holes in old closets, dimpled discs and babies' navels, light pockets and skyrockets messed with her head. She fidgeted and wriggled, adrift on a sea of wonder.

A teacher asked if she was okay as she wasn't her usual self. Lin fobbed her off and tried to concentrate. It didn't last. The disc held her hostage. She'd seen nothing like it and had no idea of its purpose, or even if it had one. Lin had her mother's dislike of uncertainty; she preferred things clear, simple, and straightforward. Like the accountancy she was studying. But the disc seemed light years beyond any bottom-line balance.

Song joined Lin for lunch in the canteen. More than once Lin opened her mouth to mention last night's arrival but closed it each time. She'd done the same on the morning bus ride. Song and Lin had shared everything from crèche to college; they were as close as sisters. If she couldn't talk to Song about it, who could she talk to? *She's my bestie.*

Still, the idea of discussing a bizarre object in the closet next to her bed was... well, bizarre. Embarrassing even. What could she say? How could she bring it up? Lin pictured the conversation. 'Song, I have this strange, dull thing sitting in my room, and it's supported by lines of bright light, and... '

Lin paused. They shared a similar mindset. How would that sound?

She pictured the rest of the chat. 'Oh?' Song would respond with that uplifted, questioning tone Lin knew so well. 'Oh?' Again, higher this time. She would have one eyebrow raised now and probably say something smart. 'So, there's a dull thing squatting in your room, eh? It's probably your brother.'

Song liked Lin's brother, she just had a different way of saying it. But it made Lin's point, to herself at least. The disc wasn't something you could talk about unless you'd seen it, and Lin wasn't sure she wanted people to do that until her father had. No, it was all a bit much. She couldn't tell Song, and they were best buddies.

The more the day moved on the messier her mind became. Was the disc a doorway to somewhere? Where? What could've put it in her room? Why? Why not in Tienanmen Square, the Forbidden City or in Xian next to

the Entombed Warriors? Anywhere for that matter?
What is it and why's it in my room?

* * *

The next morning, bright sunshine poured through Lin's window. Damn. She'd forgotten to pull down the blind when she went to bed. Only half awake, still dreamful and drowsy, Lin remembered it was 'sleep-in Saturday'. She could spend more time in bed. The sleepy scholar pulled the sheet up and buried her head in the pillow. *Mmm, wonderful! More bed.* She needed it. Late Saturday morning there was a supermarket job to go to but that was hours away, almost a lifetime. Bed was better, so much better.

Work was far from Lin's thoughts on a soft and balmy Saturday, a peaceful morning of an early summer day. The house lay still and quiet, the air mild and sweet. Outside, a bird trilled peace and contentment. Like the bird, Lin was at ease; nothing bothered her. She yawned and rolled over for another hour's snooze...

And smacked her nose.

The closet's bulk blocked her view. That was different. So was its occupant. Yesterday's static crackled in her brain. Lin sat up and rubbed her nose.

"Ooooh. That hurt."

She wondered if the thing was still in there.

Lin reached out her arm and opened the closet. The reaction was instant. Only an edge of the disc was lit but the response was stunning. Silver threads flooded the room with light. Lin's pulse raced; her mouth fell open. She closed it and the closet, and the room felt dull and ordinary.

This was too much. Lin had to know more, and she couldn't wait for her dad. She didn't know when he was coming home. Anyway, she was a big girl now and this wasn't a beetle or some coloured thing like she used to bring him as a kid. This was weird and strange, and Lin wanted to know more. Now. Maybe it *was* a portal. Her shoulders trembled with excitement. Thoughts of fantastic flights into mystery and magic crowded her mind. *Maybe it could mean a romantic adventure. Wow!*

Lin hopped out of bed and opened the closet. Whatever this dull, grey shape was, whatever it was doing in her room, Lin sensed the answer lay in the disc not the light ring; that was simply a scaffold. She picked up a pencil and pushed the point into the disc where two dark marks formed a shadowy Y. The disc resisted; a return force pushed back, not much, just a gentle pressure, like prodding a down pillow with your finger. She pushed harder. The pencil went further and then without Lin's help slid into the disc and disappeared like a snake down a hole. Lin grabbed at it, but the shaft slipped from her fingers and vanished.

What! Lin threw back her hands. *That's silly. Pencils don't disappear! It must be stuck.* She put her index finger into the same place and probed. Her finger slid in until the face of the disc edged against her in-turned fingers and thumb. Lin waggled her pinkie around but couldn't feel anything. She pushed again until her fist slid behind the face.

An alien force grabbed her hand and dragged it into the disc.

Lin jerked her arm back, startled. Her limb came out, but the suction was scary. She shuddered, looked at her trembling hand and resolved to be more cautious. What was this thing, and what did it do, except eat pencils? It was a puzzle. But, she needed to get ready for work. The disc and its pencil-snitching power would have to wait.

Lin closed the doors, wagged her finger at the closet's contents, and said, "I'll get back to you, don't leave."

3

THE DISC DELIVERS

Lin woke suddenly in the pre-dawn hours of the next day. The room lay dark around her, and it took a few moments to focus. She peered through the gloom seeking anything different. Nothing seemed out-of-the-ordinary. So, what'd disturbed her? It was only then she noticed scratching coming from the closet. *What the hell is that?* The noise couldn't be the disc; it had sat silent since it arrived. Something else was in there. Maybe it was a rat. That was possible. The scratching sounded like one. The noise stopped.

Lin steadied herself with the idea that it might be just a common pest. There were millions of them. Rodents suicidal enough to risk an assault by Wang Mei's broom sometimes came up from the river and sneaked into the house looking for scraps. They were harmless, if dirty. Lin had dealt with them before. They didn't scare her.

The scratching started again, this time accompanied by an odd mewling, a desperate, squeaky sound. *That's so not a rat.* But if it wasn't, then what was it and how did it get into the closed closet? Lin switched on the bedside light and looked at the closet doors. They trembled with pressure, pushed to the limit of the latch. Should she open it? Whatever it was, it couldn't be very big as the closet was small and the disc was in there too.

Lin reached down, opened the latch then snatched back her hand. The doors stayed shut; the mewling and scratching stopped. Maybe it was waiting to see her. Taking a ruler from the bedside table she pried open the door. It swung away then stopped. A hairless tail lay curled against the side of the closet wall. It had to be a rat; it had that long, thin tail. Damn.

Lin swung her legs over the bed, grabbed one of her mother's brooms and locked the door. She looked back in time to see a small, pink nose poke around the other closet door and push it open. Lin stopped. *That's definitely not a rat.* A long, pointed snout, moved slowly forward to let two bright eyes stare at Lin from under a pair of decidedly un-ratlike ears standing erect on a furry forehead.

Lin liked animals, but this wasn't one she knew. It wasn't a civet cat, panda or fox, or any Chinese animal. It's kinda cute though. Suddenly the creature hopped out of the closet, knocking the door as it scurried under the bed. Lin could see the still-suspended disc. She bent to look at the visitor. It was the size of a small cat but not the same shape. Its back legs were bigger than the front ones, and it had a striped rump. The animal stayed crouched and quivering, big ears, pink nostrils and sharp eyes taking in everything.

Lin sensed no threat. The tiny creature didn't appear hostile, just scared. It looked at her and blinked. She returned the look and smiled. An odd sense of relief, and curiosity pervaded her mind. Whatever it was, the little critter touched her being. Its plight – small, scared, and alone – was enough to melt the coldest heart, and that wasn't Lin's.

More than once her father had returned animals to their owners after his kind-hearted daughter had brought them home. 'Aw, Dad, can't we keep the duck, please?' His daughter might be grown now, but Lin Xia's baby still had the same feelings. *Awww. It's so sweet.* What could she do for the little mite? It might be thirsty. Lin left to fetch water.

When she returned, water bowl in hand, she heard the little invader before she saw it, scrabbling around on top of her chest of drawers. It knocked over a perfume bottle. When the little creature sprang onto her bedside table and threatened the red crystal vase, Lin screamed,

"Nooo! Get away from that."

The visitor squealed in fright, jumped to the floor and scrambled under the bed. It was terrified. Lin felt the fright as if it were her own. She also sensed a purpose as though the creature wanted to pass something onto her but couldn't overcome its fear. *Don't be silly. That's not possible.* It was an animal, she was human. What could it tell her? Lin scolded herself for shouting at the terrified critter, which scared it even more. But she'd sworn never to lose Granma's vase.

Lin's mother chose that moment to intervene. Wang Mei rapped on the door and with voice raised wanted to know what the racket was about and if Lin wanted breakfast. If that wasn't enough to scare the visitor, she rattled the door handle and, when it wouldn't open, demanded to know in a louder voice why her daughter had locked it.

"Wait a minute, Mum, I had a bad dream and locked the door. I'll be there in two seconds. How about breakfast in twenty minutes?"

Lin pushed the water bowl under the bed then stood. *What'll I do with the beastie under the bed?* Her mum would take to it with a broom. The problem sorted itself. In three hops the little invader made it to the closet. In another bound it was into the disc, rear legs twisting the rim out of shape like a young kangaroo diving into a pouch. The tail was the next to last thing to go.

The last thing seemed like a plaintive plea, an unvoiced appeal in Lin's head that quickly faded. The folds on the disc settled and it hung undisturbed once more. Lin closed the closet and, with the room back to normal, opened the door and tried to appear casual and unconcerned to her mother.

The room returned to normal; Lin didn't. She remained confused. Had the critter gone through the disc? *Was it really here?* Maybe she was dreaming? Lin wasn't sure of anything. Finally, pebbles of poop under the bed convinced her. She definitely hadn't put them there. She saw again the legs and tail vanishing through the disc. It must have arrived that way. The small animal came through safely, so the other end was wherever it came from. The disc was a gateway to somewhere; maybe a zoo, a fauna park or somewhere different. None of this settled Lin's mind and none of it helped her understand what the creature was and why the disc hung in her closet.

4

THE ACCIDENTAL
TOURIST

It was late Friday when Lin trudged home from the bus stop, tired, and more than a little pissed off. The week had been so tough she'd largely ignored the disc. Her teachers had been demanding, building the pressure prior to exams and they wouldn't let up. And she knew the house would be empty. There'd be no-one to talk to. Her father was supposed to be home this weekend, but he'd made different plans. He was taking Grampa to Suzhou to visit his sister instead.

Lin couldn't be angry as Grampa seldom saw the rest of his family. But she so wanted her dad to see the mystery in the closet. And if her father's absence weren't enough, her mother was away taking clothes and cash to Lin's brother at university. Wang Mei wouldn't be back until Sunday. Lin had two whole days to herself. She didn't mind really as the quiet was welcome and she'd work to do. Some company would have been good though. Maybe she'd call Song later.

Lin got through the door, slumped on the couch, flicked on the TV, opened a textbook... and nodded off. She didn't know how long she'd dozed but it was dark when her head bounced off her chest for the umpteenth time. Maybe it was bedtime. She had the weekend to study. The weary scholar switched off the TV, tidied up, drank a glass of water and headed to her room.

As her hand touched the handle a spike of unease pricked her senses. Something was wrong. No smells, sights or sounds bothered her. But something was amiss. She just knew it. Lin opened the door quietly and hit the light switch.

The little critter was back.

This time it was on the floor in front of the closet with Granma's vase grasped in its paws.

Lin took it all in fast, yelled,

"No! Give me that," and lunged at the creature.

The startled animal squealed, scrambled the short space to the closet and leaped into the disc still clutching the red vase. Lin was too late. The last thing she saw was the creature's feet and tail vanishing through the portal. The critter and Granma's vase had disappeared.

Lin flopped on the bed with an arm over her eyes, her body suddenly racked with sobs. The stress of hiding the disc, the invader and the loss of Granma's vase overwhelmed her. She wept. Lin lay on the bed for long minutes, shaking and sniffling, distraught over her loss. *Not the vase. I promised you I'd keep it, Granma. I promised.*

Slowly her poise and purpose returned. *C'mon girl, get a grip.* Granma's vase was gone; so, what now? The answer came quickly. The idea rose fast and bright as a lightning strike. She'd go through the disc and get the vase. The vase was Granma and her. She had to have it back. If that meant going through the disc, then that's what she'd do.

A voice of caution surfaced, the voice of her parents: *Don't be silly, Beibei. You don't know where the disc goes; you don't know if it'll hold you. How will you get back? What will you do? It might be dangerous. You can't do it by yourself. You're a girl. Let others look after the disc. You could be hurt or killed. Let the police deal with it.*

The clamour continued until an adamant voice cut across the blather.

'Do it, Lin Beibei. Do it now! Get my vase.'

Lin heard Granma's voice rise above the babble in her brain.

'Do it. The vase is you and me, Beibei. Get it back. What's life without excitement or risk? As tedious as those millions of people wasting their lives chasing money in boring jobs. Go through the disc. Get my vase. *Now.*'

When Lin understood this, she knew it had to be. *Okay, Granma. I'll do it.* Her mind settled in deadset determination. If she waited for her parents they'd have security swarming over it in minutes. Then she'd never get the vase.

And what would she tell the police? This thing arrived in the night. It shines like a sun and sucks like a vacuum cleaner. First it took her pencil. Then it delivered a rat-like alien. She'd got it some water. The creature returned and stole Granma's vase.

And I want it back.

They'd think she was crazy. She'd not be allowed anywhere near the disc. With such a wild story she mightn't be allowed near anyone for a while, or sharp objects. And the vase would be lost. She couldn't have that. The creature came and went through the disc... why not her?

She'd get the vase and come back. How long could that take? The little critter visited twice so it can't be far. The opening was narrow but it went through, and the portal stretched. It'd stretch for her. She wasn't that big. *Yeah, it's possible, and I've gotta do it. I've got to get the vase. It's Granma and me. I'm going after it. I'll be back before Mum and Dad get home.*

She'd do it now. That way she'd be back by morning and no-one would know. Lin quickly assembled things to take. Her mobile phone, of course, couldn't go anywhere without it. She'd want a selfie. A small container of food, probably dumplings in case she got hungry. Lin picked some from the fridge and put them in a plastic box. Some tissues and a water bottle were next. The pile on the bed grew.

Perhaps one of Grampa's cigarette lighters? He wouldn't know one was gone and it could be useful. She'd need her crushable, cotton hat too, the one her father gave her to protect her skin from the sun. She didn't want to end up looking like a farmer's wife. Lin retrieved it from the chest of drawers; that and a small bottle of antiseptic handwash. The pile was getting larger. A toothbrush and cosmetics were next. Toothbrush? Cosmetics? How long was she going for? She always took a toothbrush and a small cosmetic supply when she travelled. They'd go into her over-shoulder carry bag.

Lin worked on the plan for the trip. One of her mum's brooms would be good as a brace across the opening in case she got drawn through before she was ready, or if it was too tight and she needed to get out. The kitchen broom would do. It was long enough to span the opening with some overlap on either side.

The plan moved on. Lin decided against the shoulder bag as the strap might get caught. All she needed would fit in her old bumbag. They were so out of fashion now, but it strapped close and would be easier in a tight place. She'd only be away a few hours. Perhaps they wouldn't notice the fashion blunder where she was going, wherever that was. Besides, the bag was a a better match for her jeans, sneakers and sweatshirt. You never know who might be at the other end – could be a cute boy.

Lin got the broom and readied the gear on her bed. The mirror embedded in the bumbag lid would be handy, as would the comb she'd left there. She let it lie on the bottom of the bag and neatly packed the other stuff on top. The bag closed easily. Lin swung it behind her, caught the flying, free end of the belt and snapped the buckle in front of her belly. It felt snug.

Bag organised and on, Lin was ready to go.

'Do it!', Granma's voice echoed in her head. 'Get our vase. Now!'

Lin sat on the bed with the closet open and gazed at where the small creature had vanished. *I wonder where it went?*

She'd find out soon enough.

The strange, grey density seemed as ever, a drab, forlorn ring hanging in her closet. But she'd seen the dazzling display and watched it swallow a small creature. It was in her room for a reason. But what? Lin knew such questions were like asking a teacher about an upcoming test; the questions were clear and straightfoward, the answers were vapid and vague.

The disc was a riddle. Moreover, it was a riddle tricky to get into. The disc hung above floor level, a little to one side of the closet space. The creature had dived through headfirst. Lin wasn't about to do that. Headfirst seemed claustrophobic at best, suffocating at worst. She didn't fancy either. *And I can't hang onto the broom that way.* She'd put her feet through the disc and ease the rest of her body after them. The inner drag would help. As she went through she'd roll over and use her hands to push backwards along the floor. That'd be the best way. She could use the broom to stop her if it got too tight.

The clock by the bed read 10.20pm. Time to get the vase. Lin placed the broom on the floor parallel to the bed, at a right angle to the closet then sat on the floor beside it. Raising her knees to her chest, feet together and toes pointed, she wiggled on her bum towards the disc.

The surface trembled slightly when her toes touched. Lin pushed. Her pointed feet penetrated the disc's surface, which immediately resettled around her vanished toes and feet. Easing her body to the left, she edged a little further. As she rotated Lin transferred more of her weight to her left arm, steadying herself on the side of the bed with her right. The ring sustained her weight and began to drag on her legs as she slipped into the portal.

The pull was strong, the suction constant. Lin had turned so that her chest was facing the floor and she was supported by her two hands. The disc continued to drag. By now it had swallowed up to her knees.

It works all right. The pressure on her legs was constant. She tried to move but couldn't bend her knees. She couldn't move her lower limbs at all. Now breathing hard, her face flushed, Lin gripped the side of the bed with both hands to stop being dragged into the disc. *I'm not going; this is too tight. I'm too big for this. I've got to get out.*

But removing her hand from the floor made the force more powerful and she was in to her waist. Hanging onto the bed was not enough; she was being sucked further. With heart pounding, Lin grasped the broom and held it at head level. It'd reach across the closet space and rest on the frame and stop her moving. It had to. The strength of the wood and her arms would hold her. *Omigod, this has to work or I'm gonna be crushed.*

By the time she'd slowed, Lin was almost into the disc. Her mother's broom lay athwart the doorframe. She tried to turn onto her back to grasp the closet drawers above her and pull herself out. The broom shifted in her hands and when it settled again the handle no longer spanned the frame; the brush head was next to the door's edge.

The bristles bent.

The broom couldn't hold her weight.

The disc kept dragging on her body.

Lin Beibei disappeared.

5

INTO THE VOID

Hauled into the suffocating crush of a tight, dark space, Lin screamed. Thick blackness muffled the sound as if she'd yelled into a cushion. Her legs and body were held hard, arms pressed to her head and elbows jammed against her ears. She wriggled and strained but could change nothing. She could flex her body but not move a limb. Her frantic writhing neither dented nor deterred the smooth, cool interior; she was held wrap-bandage tight in a cold, clammy embrace.

Lin still held the broom. She let it go; it stayed put. The handle was in reach of her fingers but she couldn't grasp it. The broom was coming with her. *Gotta get outa here. This was so stupid.* She clawed at the stifling mass. It gave slightly under the pressure of her touch – like pushing into putty – but stayed firm and resistant. She could not move. Pressure grew. Lin could feel her heart drumming.

The heat of her breath condensed on the slick blackness and dripped, cold and slimy, on her head. Sweat squirmed down her back.

Slow rhythmic pulses raked Lin's body, forcing her through the darkness, squeezing her along like toothpaste in a tube. But where it was pushing her she had no idea. Lin wanted out but the hard hold drove her on in absolute blackness, heart hammering, sweat greasing her skin. Lin's breathing got harder, shorter; her lungs strained with the effort. All the oxygen she had lay in a tiny pocket formed by her elbows jammed hard against her head. It would last a short time before it ran out and she suffocated.

What was the stuff that held her? It was soft yet solid, as though she'd been buried under bodies. Her nose sucked in the stench of fear and sweat, and her panic grew. She gagged. Her chest heaved, and the breath wheezed in her lungs. Was there enough air?

There was no sign the ordeal would end.

If this is what the tiny mite had gone through to get to my room, no wonder it was terrified. Poor thing. This out-of-place thought flashed through Lin's brain just as the pressure lifted from her legs. She could wriggle her toes and flex her feet.

The portal's interior kept forcing Lin along. Her knees released, then the length of her legs. She kicked out to warn anyone who might be there. Finally, her bum cleared the exit and her lower body sagged like a bent pillow. Lungs and chest aching for air, Lin knew she'd be freed. *Hang on, girl. We're gonna get out of this. Just a few more seconds.*

The disc was about to release her feet first and on her stomach. Maybe she was still in the village, at school or even just outside her room? It had only been a short trip. Yet she was coming out feet first, bum up and exposed. What if someone's there? This was so not a good look. And what about her hair and sweaty eyes? Her mascara must look terrible.

Lin's upper body arched out of the disc and she flopped onto a soft, cool base sucking air like a landed fish. Her hands brushed her clothes and checked her bumbag before she rolled over and looked around.

There was nothing to see.

6

A WHITE WORLD

The once-dense blackness was now cool light. Lin propped on her elbows, gasping for oxygen in the thin air. The unwilling voyager rubbed her eyes, squinted and looked about. Around her – like peering through clingwrap – spread a hazy, grey-white world with no silhouettes, no shadows... and no support. Lin stiffened. *There's nothing beneath me!* She lay suspended in space, not falling but not supported by anything she could see. When she pushed her forearms down pressure built on them. Something held her up; it just wasn't visible.

There was nothing else to notice; the little critter wasn't around, neither was Granma's vase. Red would stand out like a traffic light. The broom slid out to lie beside her. Beyond the broom the abyss of white blurred into nothing.

Maybe if she sat up. It worked, even as her mind fought the notion there was nothing to sit on. Lin swivelled slowly.

"Aah," she breathed. "There's the disc."

It looked familiar, even friendly. It wasn't quite the same; it was the other end after all, but it looked like the one in her room. At least it was something familiar. Maybe it'd take her back if she needed.

Lin thrust her hand into it. Nothing. No pressure, no pull. It wasn't taking her anywhere.

"Shit! What do I do now?"

She dragged her feet beneath her and stood up to wobble on her toes. The nervous adventurer took two halting steps, her arms waving for balance, and, encouraged, shuffled two more. It was like walking on a trampoline. The pressure built against Lin as she moved. There was no way forward. She tried leaning into it, thrusting her arms like a breaststroke swimmer. Nothing. She couldn't push past the invisible resistance.

Lin moved her right arm sideways, pushing to explore, bouncing on the balls of her feet as she shifted position. Every forward push met pressure. Sideways movement was difficult but possible. She gasped and panted, her chest heaving irregularly. Lin turned in a tight circle. Finally, she understood; she was trapped in some sort of spacepod. There was air, but not much; her lungs wheezed like an old bellows.

Lin was adjusting to life inside a clear-gel, ping-pong ball when she fell, backwards. She didn't trip; there was nothing to trip over. But she dropped on her bum in the cushion that held her. As she sought a reason, Lin noticed the exit disc shrinking, disappearing. *Omigod, I hope not.*

Maybe it was getting smaller as it moved away. But if that's happening then she must be moving. It didn't feel like it. Lin struggled to stand but found herself pinned.

The exit portal scaled down to a tiny crooked mark, then disappeared. Now she felt the pod accelerate; it pinned her with powerful G-forces as adrenalin coursed through her body. The module hurtled on, holding Lin fixed, panting and trembling. Her eyes switched from side-to-side looking for anything familiar to allay her fear. Then for the first time since she'd been pitched into her circular space chariot, Lin noticed something that wasn't grey, pale and wishy-washy. Odd images of a world flickered overhead, streaking beyond the confines of the pod like the tag end of film through an old projector or a bad upload on YouTube. Blurred visions streaked around her, fleeting and flimsy but continuous.

She recognised the soft, rounded mountains and waterways of southern China. But these looked different. She understood soon enough; the scenes were running fast-backwards like a reversing DVD.

The vision vanished to be replaced by velvet darkness that washed around the capsule like ink buoying a pearl. Suddenly cold, lonely and afraid, the import of what she'd done hit home, and Lin shivered, violently. *Omigod, where am I? This was crazy. I could be killed.* Mugged by reality, the wayward wanderer hugged herself for warmth and comfort as anything familiar sped away and left her breathless, chilled and afraid.

The dark held terrors for Lin. It could have been a

childhood thing; she wasn't sure and didn't care. The fear was now. As a small child she'd gone down a mineshaft with her father. Deep in the mine's dark and stretched capillaries, the power failed. Darkness descended like a closing coffin. A miner stumbled into her and cursed; she fell over and lost her father's hand. Alone and terrified in absolute blackness, Lin could see nothing. Fear welled in her chest as tears coursed down her cheeks. It seemed an eternity before power was restored through one small light and her father's caring face loomed above her. He picked her up and spoke comforting words as she'd wrapped her arms around his neck in relief.

Lin wished her dad was with her now. But no such reassurance offered; no father, no warm voice or hug came to ease her fear, just the cold, the quiet and the menacing mantle of black. *I wish I hadn't done this. It was stupid. What did I think I was doing? If I'm gonna survive this trip, Granma, I'll be doing it by myself.*

The darkness had turned the capsule into a shadowy sarcophagus. Lin pushed her hands down against the cushion of air that supported her. She could sit up. The pressure that pinned her had eased. As her eyes adjusted to the gloom, the traveller found it wasn't completely dark. A flush of pale light washed one side of the pod. It came from a small yellow ball, a round haze in the far distance. Lin didn't recognise it at first. Was that the sun? If it was, then she was somewhere in space. Lin closed her eyes and her chest heaved as the enormity of such an idea played with her mind. She couldn't be in space, could she? Slowly she accepted the reality even if part of her remained unconvinced.

For if it were the blazing centre of the solar system then it wasn't the football-sized heat source that glared through the industrial haze of a Chinese summer and turned Lin's home province into a furnace. This was a wan, weak pretender, a pale orb hanging in infinite blackness, a 5-watt bulb in a desert at midnight. It emitted light enough for Lin to notice, but not much more. It wasn't warm either. She slapped her arms across her chest to keep out the cold, then hugged herself. As her eyes adjusted, Lin took in the pinpoints of light surrounding her. If she was in space and that was the sun then she should see a small blue planet, or maybe a red one. She could find neither.

Lin teetered upright in her wobbly cushion. A myriad stars smeared a milky arc above her, the stars so close that Lin felt she could reach out and cup her hand behind one, like cradling a jewel in her palm. The awesome sight overcame her. Lin's jaw dropped as her eyes opened and her heart soared. *Oh my God; this must have been what Yang Liwei felt like on his first space mission.* What would the Chinese space authorities say if they knew a young citizen was trapped in an airlock on the edge of the galaxy? They wouldn't believe it. She wasn't sure she did.

Lin lurched backwards.

What now?

She wasn't hurt, just confused. Her heartbeat sped up as her hands sought support in the invisible pillow that surrounded her. Maybe the pod was slowing, or even speeding up. But nothing inside or out helped her judge its speed. The sun, the stars and the blackness remained. Lin's body held rigid as she struggled to breathe. The wheezy work of her lungs rasped through the silence. She held her breath. *God, it's quiet.* There was no noise, no creaking or groaning as with a ship at sea, just an all-embracing, absolute silence.

I could die out here... I wanna go home. Tears spilled down her cheeks, the moisture freeze-drying instantly in the chill oblivion. It was then the visual images started anew. The first vision reared around the pod threatening to swamp it, a sensation so real that Lin flinched. An enormous seascape loomed around her, an expanse of ocean rolling to the horizon, wave after wave of cobalt blue with only an occasional white cap breaking the sameness. The spacepod sped through spindrift so close Lin felt she could touch it. Was this real? How would she know? She lay spellbound by the rolling repetition.

And then, drifting long-winged and low over the water was what looked like an albatross. Perhaps it really was the ocean! If it wasn't, her dreams were getting extremely detailed. Lin's mind and confidence were shaken. She couldn't tell fantasy from reality. The earlier scenes of China seemed uncertain, time-shifting visions of what was. Maybe this was what is.

As though in answer, the sea angled away, and the breakers got smaller as the pod reared and banked. A volcano loomed beneath her, smoke billowing from its fractured peak, lava steaming into the sea. There were no people anywhere, no villages, towns or farms, just the lone albatross gliding like a shadowy spectre over the ocean's extremes.

Smaller islands came and went. Tropical lagoons, clusters of palm trees, an occasional mountain arrived and disappeared. Was this ever going to end? As Lin searched for an answer, a tiny spot like a beckoning finger appeared on the leading edge of her shooting sphere. It grew larger. At about the time Lin realised it was the portal reappearing, the blue water yielded to a drab land of brown and green.

This was different to the water world that had come and gone, and so unlike the warm and wet side of China. Below her spread an arid world of plains and low, rolling hills with tall, dry forests cut by an occasional stream. This had to be a dream. And a bad one at that. There were no signs of life, although at such a height anything but a dinosaur would be hard to see.

As Lin pondered a moment on dreams and dinosaurs, the disc expanded to its full size, the pod returned to its grey-white interior, and everything was still.

Lin had landed; the broom by her side

She peered at the disc. It returned the same deadpan look it'd worn since they met. Okay, this end did look different. The shape and size were the same but the lines across the entry were askew. They gave the portal an odd look as though it was saying, 'End of the line, the bus stops here, time to get off, why are you still here?'

Lin didn't want to get off. She didn't know what lay outside. Here in the spacepod it was quiet and safe, safer than the wild ride she'd just been through. She hadn't had such a bizarre trip since an amusement park ride at the Shanghai Expo. At least she hadn't thrown up this time.

Lin was not without courage. Right now, however, her courage was tempered with caution. That's no bad thing, her father would've said. But it was her grandmother's reprimand she heard: 'Do it, my child. Get my vase!'

Her family seemed far away. Maybe they were, perhaps they were outside the portal. Lin didn't know. For a girl who's supposed to be bright, she didn't know much about what had just happened. Some things were clear; she was dumb to get herself into this spot. What made her think entering a weird blip beside her bed was a smart thing to do? Why any of this was happening was guesswork. Exiting the pod was the way to find out.

Granma would agree. Besides, if she stayed too long maybe the pod might reverse and she'd end up back in her room. Without the vase. Or just maybe she had no choice. For Lin suddenly sensed the pulse that forced her through the portal was edging her towards the exit. The broom was heading that way or was the pod shrinking, squeezing its contents towards the exit and out?

Lin had similar feelings at college when people shoved her forward to 'volunteer' for something she didn't want to do; 'You do it, Lin; you're good at it. You do it.' The force was unwelcome but unstoppable. If she stayed in the pod she was pretty sure it'd turn itself inside-out and heave her out. Staying inside wouldn't answer any of her questions. It was time to go.

But this time she wasn't going out backwards and bum up. That was gross and so not cool. Headfirst sounded better. Lin fumbled through her bumbag, found the comb and pulled it through her hair. Appearance in order, she picked up the broom and inspected the head and handle. Just one of her mum's brooms. But a new plan surfaced. If she poked the handle through the disc first she could hang onto the broomhead and let it pull her along like hanging onto a waterski rope. She hoped this plan was better than the last.

Lin approached the disc, the broom held tight in her hands. She looked around at the only thing she knew right now – the interior of the pod. *MyPod.* She smiled, then pushed the broom handle tentatively into the disc. The cross-beams dropped the quizzical look and sucked avidly on the wooden shaft. Lin yanked it back. She took a breath then pushed the broom forward once more. *Okay, you're ready; am I?*

7

GRANMA'S VASE, MOTHER'S BROOM

Lin struggled to her feet, shaky and subdued. The disc had dumped her in a copse of dull-green, spiky scrub. Strange trees rose behind her... scraggy, almost sinister. She didn't recognise the place. It certainly wasn't home, and she didn't like the look of it.

I want outa here. She hoped the disc went backwards. A small branch lay at her feet. Lin picked it up, broke off a fragment and jammed it into the disc. The portal swallowed it. Lin's breathing eased, and her mind settled. There was a way back. *I can go home. But where's the vase and who's here?*

She looked around. No-one. Just trees. Dammit. No boys. Her worry about coming out sweaty and soiled was pointless. That was a shame; a bit of romance might've been fun. Lin smoothed her clothes, got out the mirror, combed her hair and checked her mascara. *Looking good.* She was relieved; it'd been a rough ride.

The broom lay at her feet, as did her pencil, the one the disc swallowed. Next to them, an arm's reach away under a short shrub sat Granma's vase... bold, bright and unbroken. Lin gasped in delight and dropped to her knees. She picked up the little red urn and clasped it to her breast as tears of relief slid down her cheeks. *I've got you back. I love you, Granma. Thank you. You're the reason I'm here... wherever I am.* Mission accomplished. She could go home.

But where was she? It certainly wasn't Shanghai; she couldn't see a car or a building, and it certainly wasn't near the Great Wall. There was always a crowd there. Wherever she was, it didn't look like China. Lin could see no tracks, fences, houses, high rises, roads, shops, rice fields, veggie patches, noodle wrappers, Coke cans, cars, cycles, KFC boxes, cigarette butts, old newspapers, nothing. Not a thing that suggested home. The place seemed people-free. Where *was* everybody?

Lin could just make out the disc; its blurred shape hidden among branches on top of a scrubby ridge that fell away to a narrow, sluggish watercourse. The ridgeline finished behind her at what might be a plateau. In front of her, occasional craggy rockfaces stood bare and bold along the valley's edge. Small trees and scruffy shrubs grew haphazardly on a valley floor made rough by water flow.

A spray of leaves fluttered down to land at her feet. Lin picked up the sprig of long, slender leaves and put them to her nose. The smell was distinctive; she knew it well. Gum leaves, for sure. During middle school an Australian teacher had taught her English class for a term. He'd smuggled in some leaves to give the students practice with scent and taste words. The smell was astringent, sharp, and hard to forget. Lin studied the nearby trees but there were no signs of koalas. To Lin, koalas were to gum leaves as pandas were to bamboo.

Am I in Australia? Come on, don't be silly. It couldn't be... or could it? If the spacepod had dumped her in Australia, then it was a place she'd wanted to visit. She liked koalas and kangaroos. The idea that this could be the land 'down under' amused Lin more than convinced her. She wondered how far from Melbourne or Sydney she might be. If Australia was really where she was. *Naah, it couldn't be. Too weird.* Gum trees grew in other places, even China. It was more likely she was at home, although in a place she didn't know. She'd gone somewhere... and it felt distant, old, and worn out.

Lin got out her mobile phone. The location device might tell her where she was. A selfie would be good too. *Me and the gumtrees.* Lin pressed the 'on' button. Nothing. She pushed again, again nothing. She even held it down a while and peered hopefully at the screen. Zero. For the first time since her dad gifted it to her, the phone didn't work. *Okay. No photo shoot today.* The phone went back into her bumbag.

A line of sweat broke on Lin's forehead, and damp trickled down her underarms. Wherever she was, it was hot. Like Wuhan in August. Lin reckoned it had to be 35–40° C. Still and stifling air hung around her like a cloak. Leaves drooped limp and listless from the trees. It felt like a high-summer day and past mid-afternoon. She took off her sweatshirt and tugged the t-shirt away from her body to let in air. It was *hot,* the only relief lay in shade as no buildings or bus shelters broke the bush panorama. No sign of life showed anywhere. She'd have a quick look around before heading back through the disc. There had to be people here who could tell her where she was.

Lin clambered up the slope behind her. A broad, tree-dotted plain rolled on towards the horizon and a cloudlike haze. Smoke? Or a mirage? Lin couldn't be sure. A flock of white birds pecked at seeds on the ground. That was all? Smoke? Birds? No people. Apart from the birds, nothing moved. The heat continued to beat down. As Lin turned away, a brightly-coloured bird flew across the valley, noticed her, squawked in surprise and baulked away to roost in a tree and peer at her warily. Lin felt like an alien; this wasn't a place she knew and not one that seemed to care. *There are only birds here, and even they don't like me.*

Maybe a walk would give her a better idea of where she was. People were sure to ask later, and she had no photos. After wrapping the vase in her sweatshirt, Lin put it back under the shrub, jammed the broom-handle into the ground as a marker, then walked down to the stream. Her mum would be impressed with her broom skills. *Yeah, sure.* Lin thought it better to walk down the waterway and then return back along it to find the broom. If there were people here, they'd be near water and this murky brook seemed the only source.

The heat grew as Lin walked and flies swarmed around her face. She picked a switch to swat them away, but it made no difference. They didn't let up; they were as pesky as telemarketers. The sluggish stream flowed along a shallow, pebble-strewn course. Now and then a fallen tree blocked its flow forcing the rivulet to find a new way around. Jumping over or crawling under trees didn't slow Lin as she walked on.

Still no signs of people. No roads or paths cluttered the view, no old fences or buildings and no derelict bikes or abandoned houses. This wasn't China; there was always a reminder of people somewhere. There wasn't even a Macca's box.

Lin picked her way through the stream's clutter. Around one bend a rocky outcrop jutted from the valley wall to form a small pool with a smooth, sandy beach. Rushes grew around the marshy edge and tadpoles flitted through the water. *Frogs. Hmmm.* Frogs and birds might be the only critters around.

Except for the pond – pretty, damp and green – the country was dusty, rough and boring. Lin stopped. There was nothing she hadn't seen in the first few metres. The country was the same, everywhere... and *hot*. As much as she tried to walk in the shade it wasn't possible, and her soft hat gave little relief. Lin turned around, stepped over the stream and walked back along the other bank.

She picked her way carefully until a fallen tree

blocked the path. Clambering over it might be difficult; walking around looked the better move. At the butt-end of the fallen giant, next to the stream and close to where the exposed tree roots pointed upwards like stiff, arthritic fingers, a series of flat stones pushed up rough steps. *I'll run up the stones and leap across the trunk. I don't want to get my feet wet. This'll be easy.*

Lin bounded from rock to rock but slowed before taking the final leap. She hesitated. Something held her back. Then she saw it, coiled on the rock ahead.

A snake.

Lin's face drained of colour as the hair lifted on the back of her neck.

"Omigod, I could've stepped on it," she whispered as her gut clenched.

Snakes were Lin's ultimate dread. They repulsed her. There was something slick, shiny and evil about them that made her flesh creep and her bowels heave.

"Uuurghh." Lin's hand went to her mouth. She kept her innards in place except for a silent retch.

The reptile made no move. It remained coiled, low and lethal, like a spring about to snap. With its small head poised slightly above the coils and the forked tongue flicking in and out, the serpent stared fixedly at Lin. The snake was as thick as Lin's upper arm, slate grey-black and shiny with a ribbon of red running low along its flanks like a warning flag. There was no way forward. She jumped back and clear.

When she found her feet – mouth open, heart in

her throat – Lin stopped and looked back. The snake lay hidden behind the tree roots. She picked up a branch, mumbled a strangled, "Shoo, shoo," and threw the branch at the rocks and reptile.

She then leapt across the creek and stumbled along it before looking back. The rock was bare. The snake had gone. It had probably slithered into the grass.

Lin's shoulders shook, and her breath ran ragged. *God, how I loathe snakes. That's it. I'm going home. Now.* If the vase was brought here as a trick, and her with it, then so be it. But she had the vase and had taken a look around. And as well as the heat and the nothingness, there were snakes. She'd seen enough. Time to get to the disc, and home.

The portal was easy to find. The broom handle stood vertical against the scrub like a square in a room full of circles. Flagging the spot had been smart. Everywhere looked the same. The same ragged bushes surrounded the same muddy pools; identical trees grew around similar bends. Lin found her way into the shade and slumped by the shrub that sheltered the vase. She was hot, bothered, and not a little let down. But she'd got what she came for and it was time to go. She turned to pick up the bundled vase.

Movement flashed in the shrub.

Lin leapt to her feet, eyes wide and heart racing.

Omigod. Not another snake!

The young visitor peered at the bush, her body tense and hands trembling. Was it a snake? *God, noo!* She expected to see a lethal length of grey scales and sinew slither away. But no serpent lurked in the scrub. Something else crouched by the vase... a small, striped animal, half-hidden among the grass and branches. The creature perched on its hind feet, front paws tucked against its chest. It looked at Lin with its head cocked. She'd seen that pointed snout, berry-like nose, sharp eyes and angled ears before. It was the critter that pooped under her bed.

You little cow, you stole Granma's vase! But she felt relieved. At least there was something she knew. *It's here.* Of course, it was here. Wherever 'here' was. It was just good to see something, anything, that didn't scare her witless.

Lin reached to pat the animal. It sprang away faster than she'd jumped from the snake. Instantly the creature was deep in the scrub, nose twitching, ears turning, eyes fixed on Lin. *Ah yes. I might have seen you before but you're not a pet.* How could she encourage contact? The same problem presented when it arrived in her room. What had she done then? Water. It wouldn't need that as it could drink from the stream. Not that she'd swallow such murky muck. But she had her mum's dumplings and they were to die for. They'd be worth a try.

After slowly easing her bumbag around, Lin reached in, unclipped the food container and pulled out a dumpling, all the while keeping an eye on her new-found buddy. Moving slowly and deliberately Lin pulled three broad leaves together on the ground as a rustic platter. She dropped the fragrant dumpling into the middle, rose cautiously and tip-toed back. The tiny creature's eyes shifted from her to the food, its nostrils twitching. The little animal liked the aroma for it hopped to the platter, ripped off a piece of dumpling and stuffed it into its mouth. Then it took some more. Crumbs were soon flying around like a Cookie Monster skit. Lin grinned. It might not be big on table manners but it sure was big on dumplings.

Lin leaned against a tree and watched her companion demolish the food. It *was* cute. How come she'd not seen sign of it when she took a walk? Maybe there were other things she hadn't seen. She smiled as the pint-sized predator finished the last crumb and looked at her. The human being and the undersized animal locked eyes for a moment. Then it looked away. An image of forests flashed through Lin's mind. *Why forests?* She smiled and shook her head. It was such a wary, little fellow. But they were so, so dissimilar. It wasn't just that it was little and she was big; the tiny critter seemed at home in this bleak and boring place. And Lin had no good feeling for it at all.

Lin smiled; but she was taking her vase and going home.

"Sorry, my little friend. The vase is mine not yours, and it's precious."

The traveller looked down at her striped pal to say goodbye. It was late afternoon with but a few hours until dark. She didn't want to be here at night. There'd been blackness enough in the spacepod and she didn't feel like sharing a night with snakes or any other animals that might be lurking about. She looked at her new buddy. *I'm sure you're okay though.*

The small creature looked at her, its head tilted. Not for the first time Lin sensed it was trying to share something. She couldn't be sure how she knew this or even that she did. Yet whenever her little pal looked her way, strange tree scenes flickered through her mind.

Are you doing that? Don't be silly. Of course not. Lin knew that couldn't be. Perhaps she just linked the little critter with forests. Or maybe she was sensing things that weren't there, like old folk who think their pets talk. It could be that her over-heated brain was trying to find calm by thinking cool and serene. There was nobody here and it was lonely. She'd been stressed; it had been a big day and wasn't getting easier.

Still, Lin couldn't escape the feeling that this timid animal was trying to tell her something. And a particular vision persisted. She'd sensed the same scene when it visited her room. But she knew little about forests, and the trees she was seeing didn't look like the ones in Szechuan when she'd gone on a childhood trip to look for pandas with her dad.

The Szechuan forests had been wet and dense, filled with tall, slender trees, moss, mud and bamboo. The images invading her brain now were different. Taller, thicker trees with heavy ruffles of brown bark stood close together, striving towards the light. At their base, fallen branches, creepers and ferns braided a matted mass. The forest looked gloomy and forbidding and, in her mind, Lin was walking towards it at the head of a host of strange beasts.

The scenes she'd viewed from the spacepod were

external. This was different. These were dream-like visions that invaded her mind with reruns she couldn't control. Lin hadn't known anything like this before and could only think the trip had affected her mood and mind. She looked again at the little creature.

A crash shattered the silence.

Lin swung around, ready to run... then stopped.

A large branch had broken from a tree ten metres away. Leaves, dust and debris swirled like a small cyclone before settling into the wasteland. The tree's wound gaped raw and bloodless. In the moments it took Lin to take it in, the dumpling devotée had gone. Lin searched for her little buddy, but it had disappeared. All that took her eye was the open gash, exposed and sallow against the trunk, like skin stripped from flesh. Within moments the valley resumed its numb silence, the hush more vivid because of the din that had gone before. Even the birds stayed hunched and huddled, not daring to squawk.

Lin looked at the branches above her. She thought they were safe but how would she know? One had just broken away. It could've killed her if she'd been under it. This was another warning, like the snake. This place was dangerous. But she'd retrieved the vase, reconnected with her little visitor and said some sort of goodbye. There was no reason to stay.

Lin scanned her temporary homesite and gathered her belongings. The sweatshirt she put on, despite the heat. It was easier than carrying it and part of the return journey would be chilly. The vase went into her bumbag, and the broom she kept to hand. Putting it through the disc handle-first was a good idea. It had worked well.

Gripping the broom tight, Lin moved towards the disc.

8

MEET THE LOCALS

The disc didn't alter whichever way Lin looked at it. The phenomenon stayed fuzzy, oval and enigmatic. But it'd take her home because that's what she wanted. *Let's go. Time to get away from snakes, flies, heat and this horrible place.* Lin picked up the broom and glanced around to say goodbye. The valley hushed as if holding its breath. Lin hesitated. Something was wrong. She knew it. But nothing moved.

Lin shrugged off her unease and shaped to enter the disc. She placed the tip of the broom handle on the lined, oval face, hunched her shoulders and pushed.

Pain seared her skull.

A bellow of anguish ripped through her brain.

Lin reeled in shock, dropped the broom and clutched her head.

No physical hit took place; just an intense, negative

bellow that rattled her brain from the inside. The pain ebbed leaving a dull throb and a sense of calamity.

"What was that?", she whispered, clutching her head.

Lin didn't know what caused the pain but there was no stopping her now. Home was the target. No sudden headache would get in the way.

Lin picked up the broom again, placed it on the disc face, murmured, "Let's go," and pushed. The next jolt – an intense, aggressive thump of denial – dropped her to her knees. She let go the broom and grasped her head.

"Oh, shit!"

Pain throbbed in her brain.

Lin rose unsteadily to her feet and retrieved the broom. She made as if to approach the disc then stopped and leant the broom against a tree. This was so not working. Maybe it needed a bit more thought. She didn't know what just happened but, hey, she was a smart girl, and having her head bashed was so not a good plan.

Lin needed time to look at her options. They were few. She wanted home; it wasn't happening. Staying the night looked likely. She had water and food and could survive the night if she had to before trying the disc again tomorrow.

Water bottle to hand, Lin sat on the grass with her back against a tree. Anxiety rumbled in her belly and she forced down the fear fomenting in her gut. *I don't like this. Not a bit.* Sure, she could stay here, but there was something strange going on. Why wouldn't the portal accept her when it had swallowed a branch she'd pushed into it not long ago? What if it didn't take her back tomorrow? What then? How was she going to get home? *Okay, girl, worry about that when you have to. First, where are you going to spend the night?* If she had to stay out all night, then that meant a place away from snakes. Okay. Up a tree, under a bush, in a cave, anywhere, as long as there were no slick, shiny serpents. Lin sussed the area slowly, looking for a likely campsite.

Then it slipped into view, staring at her, stiff and stationary like a statue carved out of earth and fur... the most bizarre animal Lin had ever seen. She did a double-take then stiffened in fright. *What is that?* The huge beast – a brown behemoth with dark, doleful eyes – didn't move; it just looked at her from its place down the slope.

Omigod, is that brute for real? Lin leapt to her feet, eyes wide, ready to run. The brute didn't budge. Where had it come from? It hadn't been there a minute ago. Maybe she was seeing things.

The landscape blurred into a grey-green curtain as Lin stared at the intruder. Nothing moved. The two stood frozen in time and space watching each other as if paused on a screen. *Am I dreaming?* Maybe it was the hits in her head. Whatever it was, the thing in front of her was weird; it couldn't be real. It had to be a nightmare. Ignore it and it'll go away. That's what Granma said. If she closed her eyes and didn't look, maybe it'd go away.

Lin closed her eyes, massaged her scalp with her fingers and looked up. The beast still stood there, peering at her. The creature bobbed its massive head, and blinked. *Omigod. It's real all right.* Lin scuttled behind a tree to check out the mega-monster from a safer place. The creature stared at the spot where she'd disappeared. Lin glanced up to see if there were branches she could climb. There were. She could clamber to safety if needed. The beast was too bulky to be a tree climber. Lin hoped so anyway. Hidden behind the trunk, she stuck her head out occasionally to look at the weird creature, wanting it to disappear. So far Granma was wrong. It wasn't going away. The big brute continued to blink but made no other move and Lin slowly relaxed. It didn't look deadly or dangerous; it did seem sort of dopey.

This was one unlikely animal. It looked to be taller than Lin at the shoulder and had to weigh a tonne or more. Brown, large, and stocky, the beast was as big as a rhinoceros but lacked the menacing horn or body armour. Large teeth jutted from the upper jaw, two prominent teeth protruded like ivory chisels beneath. From where she stood it looked thick-skinned and probably covered with hair like a doormat. The stare said, 'Don't even think about wiping your feet.'

The creature crouched bear-like but its legs were thicker and wider apart, the front pair tipped with massive claws. Inturned forefeet made it look pigeon-toed. The large head had a long muzzle and a rounded, bulbous nose, all supported on a thick, heavy neck. The prominent teeth gave the animal a buck-toothed beaver look. The head was balanced by drooping jowls and pointed pig-like ears. Part bear, pigeon, beaver, rhino, pig; it was the most bizarre animal Lin had ever seen... unsightly and gross, a lumpy tank with an overshot jaw problem no orthodontist could fix.

Images of a forest flooded Lin's mind, stronger than before. A vision of green and moody treescapes returned, short dark trees scattered among tall, wooded spires. *Great. I'm in a place I don't know looking at the weirdest animal I've ever seen, and my brain's in the woods running fantasies. This's stupid.* Was she going crazy? She had to get home.

The huge, hairy beast didn't move; it stayed where it was, staring glumly and dumbly. The forest was still in her head, and the creature looked as though it expected something. As if it wanted to talk with her. Just like the little guy. Could these creatures put stuff in her head? Was there something they were trying to tell her about this forest? *Come on, this Dumbo-sized derelict? Get a grip!* This was too much for Lin but judging herself in no danger from the docile Dumbo, she sat again at the base of the tree to think some more.

Entering the disc got pushed to the back of Lin's mind as other matters crowded in. Another image came to her. This time she was on her knees on the ground in front of the disc. The only time that happened, Lin knew, was scant seconds ago. Could the creature have been watching? Lin wondered again if an animal was capable of puting images into her head. It didn't seem likely, especially not from the goofy gargantuan staring at her from down the slope. *Get real. Animals can't put stuff in human brains. They can't 'talk' like that. What am I thinking?* More importantly, how was she going to lose the leviathan and find a place to sleep? Lin thought about her options. Maybe she'd spend the night up a tree.

The vision in Lin's mind shifted. From nowhere, the image of a small band of these large brutes came to her. She was walking among them. The group approached an overhanging rock outcrop by a small stream in country much like that around her now. They stopped, and Lin walked toward the overhang to be met by another creature of the same type, smaller in size and with a baby by its side. The dream-like vision faded to be repeated, almost identically. Lin regarded the images, the ideas, and the incongruous animal facing her with new respect. If she took these images as an attempt at contact, this unsightly oddball was inviting her to go somewhere with him. Was this for real? What else could be putting such stuff in her head? But had she 'talked' to it too?

Ideas about safety suddenly clouded Lin's mind. She didn't know where she was and wasn't sure if she was awake or dreaming. She did know that however she got here and whatever crazy state she was in, this was one mysterious wilderness. Sunset wasn't too far off, and a bizarre creature wanted to take her home to mother. *Yeah, right! Just like the Greataunt Tigress in the fairy story where the big cat dresses up as an old relative so she can eat children.* This critter had the teeth, hopefully not the temperament. This was madness, probably more stupid than going through the disc. 'Take a chance, Beibei,' she heard Granma say. 'Take a chance.'

Before Lin could decide, a small creature emerged out of the brush and hopped over to sit beside the big, hairy beast. Her little striped buddy? By the way it looked at her, its head cocked to one side, Lin was certain of it. The two creatures stared at her as if they wanted something. She'd never had reason to distrust the little creature; it had never done her any harm. Well, except for taking the vase. As far as this world and its weirdness went, however, Lin thought she could trust it. She had no way to get into the disc, and no safe place to stay. Granma's voice said, 'Go for it!' She pictured herself walking among these creatures and, somehow, they seemed content.

A language teacher once explained to Lin the meaning of the English saying, 'In for a penny, in for a pound'. As Lin got up to walk towards these strange animals – the mighty and the miniature – she couldn't help but think that this was as close to the meaning as she was going to get. But Lin was uneasy. Was she really safe with these creatures? The creatures in question waited, shifting side to side, their ears twitching, eyes blinking. Lin sensed fear in their wary stances and jerky movements and wondered how that monster could be afraid of her. *It's ginormous!*

Lin paused, then turned away. Even if she went with this weird wildlife she'd have to return here. The disc was her way out. And it was here, among the scrub in this valley. She put the vase under a small bush, waved a finger at it and promised she'd be back to pick it up tomorrow. *I've got leave you this one time, Granma.* Lin then stuck the broom firmly into the ground as a marker. She combed her hair and checked her makeup. The familiar ritual eased her fears and, feeling presentable, Lin joined the pair of oddly-matched animals. As she neared them she'd even more reason to wonder why the larger one was agitated; the top of her head barely came up to its shoulder. It was about three metres long and nearly two metres tall. It really was huge. On the other side, the little hopper came up to her shins.

The two creatures turned away. The large beast led the way and plodded up the valley past the fallen branch in the opposite direction to the one Lin had taken on her walk. Lin followed; the little guy bobbed along behind – busy it was, so BiZi she named it. Its short legs made it hard to keep up with her longer steps but BiZi skip-hopped quickly enough. Fortunately, the colossal critter was slow. Lin would have smacked into his broad backside more than once if she hadn't been watchful and slowed.

Lin especially kept an eye on his rump after he dropped a large pile of steaming, smelly dung on the trail, manure she almost stepped in. Her nose wrinkled in disgust.

"Eeuugh!"

For a while the young walker contemplated what size diaper would be needed to clothe the huge arse bumping along in front of her. When she got to whether it'd need velcro or a half-metre-long safety pin to hold it together, she gave up.

The valley was much the same either way; fallen trees and branches, wild and unkempt scrub each side of a sluggish stream. More than once the animals splashed through the water. Lin found narrower points and jumped over the waterway. She didn't want to get her feet wet, sneakers dirty or mud on her jeans. There might be a boy, you never knew. *Just no more snakes, please.*

The mismatched trio continued this way until the leading member clumped up a long incline towards the plateau edge. When it reached the top after a laboured climb, the large beast stopped. Lin drew breath and looked for her little pal. He wasn't there; BiZi had stopped by the last patch of scrub and stood, head cocked, watching her. He wasn't coming any further. Maybe this wasn't his territory; perhaps he was a citizen of the scrub and not a prairie dweller. Lin could see a shared image in her head. BiZi was going to stay in the valley and Lin was to go on with the big creature, alone. It looked safe. She lifted her hand in salute, the little fellow didn't move.

Lin reckoned it might be an hour off sunset as she followed the large one onto the plain. The sun was slipping behind wispy strips of grey cloud, the light playing with their edges as the colours went from pink to orange to red. Brown, tussocky grass spread ahead of them; the same rough clumps of trees – some taller than others but all dry, drab and coarse – dotted the land ahead. The air held the fragrance of sun on grass. Their walk took them clear of trees, but there was no track. The unlikely duo walked single-file through the dry grass skirting thick, clumpy patches of scrub. Lin couldn't see where their destination might be... her view was blocked by a huge bum.

They plodded on.

After a while Lin tired of the trek. It was boring stuck behind a large arse. The view was limited and unappealing, like getting stuck behind a bus in Shanghai except the exhaust fumes were solid, and just as smelly. She'd detour and have a look at a clump of trees. Her big buddy would plod on and she'd catch up. She couldn't lose him in this country. He was too big.

Lin hadn't strayed more than a few metres towards the trees when a sharp alarm cracked in her brain. The pain was nothing like the hit she'd had trying to enter the disc, but it was bad enough. The toothy beast had stopped, head turned, staring at her. A vision of the tree she'd been walking towards slid into her brain, a pig-sized animal grazing quietly around the trunk. The scene was pleasant, rustic and rural. Lin wondered what it was all about and where the image came from. The answer came, quick and chilling. A large, cat-like creature dropped onto the smaller animal, ripped its belly open with one swipe of a clawed foot and bit savagely into the neck, clamping the animal's throat so that it died wrenching and squirming, choking in its own blood.

The scene was brief and brutal. Lin flinched as if struck and gaped at her heavyweight companion. He peered back, impassive and unmoved. The meaning was clear. She didn't know this world; he did. There were dangers, don't wander off, avoid trees!

It spelt out something else for Lin. It was this bus-sized beast with the dopey demeanour that had stopped her from entering the space portal. It'd prevented her going towards the trees in the same way it'd stopped her going home. It was this creature who'd given her the thump in the skull when she'd tried to enter the disc. How had he done that? Maybe he wasn't so dopey after all.

Lin stared at the beast with suspicion, and respect. He returned her stare with his usual morose look. She'd thought him a bit slow. That was wrong of her. *So, who's dopey now?* But how did he do it? And why did he want to keep her here? And would the disc and Granma's vase be there when she wanted to go home?

The two trudged on – the lumbering giant and the slim, slight girl – Lin tucked behind the ample arse of her large leader. She pondered the wrinkled rump as it swayed gently, the short, tufted tail swinging a slow half-beat behind the measured pace of its owner. It'd take a barrel of Botox to smooth out those wrinkles. It was no Kim Kardashian, but there was a grace to the walk despite the backside bulk. Lin watched on, fascinated. So much so that she didn't notice company until another five minutes had passed.

Three other dentally-challenged denizens of this land had strung out behind, moving to the same slow, rhythmic beat as the leader. None of them looked like passing; none of them looked capable of any burst of speed. They rocked along in a stately, measured tempo, huge bodies rolling side-to-side as they headed towards whatever rendezvous the evening held.

9

FRIENDS WITH BENEFITS

The plateau angled up. When Lin puffed to a stop beside her colossal consort, a shallow valley spread before them. Lin took in the view and snorted.

"This place sucks."

There was nothing different, just the same-old, same-old... grey-brown, dry, and boring. The arid hollow was like the one she'd dropped into on her arrival, maybe wider but with fewer trees, certainly none that could hide a deadly 'dropcat' like the one her companion had pictured.

More big beasts scattered across the valley. They were mostly smaller but definitely the same species as her new acquaintance. There were compact versions among them, the size of large, stocky dogs. Lin reckoned these might be females and their calves. If this valley was home for the night, then okay. It just wasn't the Shanghai Sofitel.

A narrow waterway threaded its way through the valley, muddy waterholes dotting its length like stains on a grubby tablecloth. The valley floor had been disturbed in places, the grass stripped as though cut by a plough. With Lin in line the large beasts trundled down a grassy track beaten flat by weight of numbers. None of the assembled animals took particular notice of her, although some lowered their heads as she passed.

Lin had taken to thinking of her big-bummed buddy as BeBe, only to herself, of course, lest she make a mind picture and have him take offence. Not that it seemed likely. He didn't seem the overly-sensitive type given his dung-dropping displays.

BeBe plodded towards a rocky overhang that Lin recognised as the place pictured in the vision-shifting. Another of the beasts broke away from a group as they approached and plodded towards them accompanied by its offspring, a cute copy of the parent. The female – Lin assumed it was anyway – lumbered up to her and lowered her head. The small one mimicked its mother, very seriously it seemed. Lin could see nothing in her mind but somehow recognised a form of greeting and bobbed her head. They all lifted their heads and eyed each other. They didn't seem suspicious, just watchful and wary. Lin needed to be careful. *God, they're big.* Even the little one was as sturdy as a short sheep.

Eventually, the female turned away and Lin saw an image of her following along. So she did. How did they do this vision-shifting? And how did Lin receive it? Who knew? She just went with it.

The female walked to the far end of the outcrop and looked glumly at a ledge that rose towards the back of the recess. The ledge was longer than Lin was tall, a bit wider than her body and covered with matted grass. It was certainly too small to fit any of these bulky beasts. If she lay down on it, however, she would be protected from wind and rain, and the grass was dry, soft and thick to the touch. Lin nodded her thanks, and the cow plodded away, the little one wobbling at her heels.

Lin sat by the rock-couch and looked over the valley. *Well, here I am, Granma. I hope you're happy. Sucked down a spacepipe to a place I don't know, to spend the night with a bunch of weird and wild critters I've never seen before. I've taken a chance, and here I am. What next?*

Behind her the sun was setting, in front of her the animals were settling for the night. Some found space under the ledges protruding from the valley's edge; others trampled spots under the few trees that grew. The beasts paid her little heed. Lin felt no threat from this pack of peculiar pachyderms. She was also tired and hungry. Two dumplings and a sip of water went in a flash.

Luckily, Lin didn't eat much. But she'd have to find food and water before long. The shadows lengthened but the valley stayed visible in the evening light. Going for a short walk didn't seem a problem. Lin formed this action in her mind and tried to transmit it by thinking of BeBe. He swung his head to look at her but made no move from his resting place. Lin explored around her perch without wandering far. A small crevasse hidden from the rock ledge ran off the valley wall. She investigated. Everything seemed safe, although food wasn't obvious, water likewise. She rinsed her teeth with a dash of water from her bottle, took a piss, then made her way back to the ledge. As night fell she crawled onto the thick grass matting, cradled her head on the bumbag and fell asleep.

Sleep lasted but a few hours before Lin awoke to an icy chill. Her teeth chattered, and her body shivered in the frigid air. Even drawing up her knees and wrapping both arms around her chest didn't help. *It's freezing.* She'd nothing else to wear; all she had were the clothes she had on and hugging herself wasn't working. Desert landscapes could do that. It was just like in Xinjiang province... hot during the day, very cold at night. *Very clever, girl. You know your geography. But what about the cold? What are you gonna do about that?* Lin longed for the comforts of home and the cosiness of her warm, soft bed as she tossed about, her crossed arms desperately trying to hang onto any warmth.

A bulky shape lurched out of the night and slumped by her ledge. The dumpy frame of the female blocked off almost the entire space while the little one wedged in by her rear. Lin was at first startled, then appreciative. The closeness of the large, hairy bodies brought Lin warmth and yet let in fresh air. The large creature must have grasped her frozen anguish and chose to respond. Lin was grateful for the fresh air. She needed it. The smell was ghastly. Whatever they rolled in, they didn't wash off. Of that she was certain. Lin's nostrils crinkled in disgust as the smell filled her nose and mind. An image returned to her wrapped in a thought that suggested: 'Yes, you are smelly, but we will put up with it.'

What! Me? People don't smell. But Lin couldn't take offence, for she was warm. She scratched the huge, hairy back in gratitude and did the same to the little one with her foot. It was like rubbing an animated emery board. The creatures grunted and squirmed in pleasure. These happy thoughts came to Lin before she closed her eyes once more and slept, comfortable and warm, until morning.

The early rays of the sun shone into Lin's sleeping recess. She opened her eyes to notice, first, that her enormous eiderdown had decamped taking the little quilt with it. The air felt full of frost although the vicious chill had lifted with the light. Lin stretched, and found she'd survived the cold and discomfort. Her back was a little stiff but not nearly as bad as she'd thought it would be. She blessed the soft grass and the wild and woolly warmth of her night-time visitors. Now for a wash, breakfast and water. Then what?

Please.

I've gotta go home.

10

THE SECOND DAY

Lin rolled off her ledge, stretched, wiggled to ease the stiffness and took in her new world. Two of the big creatures were moving up the valley's edge while more stayed around the muddy waterholes and grazed on the reed beds. Some tore at the ground with clawed forefeet, ripping up tree and shrub roots that they sheared off with their teeth.

One of BeBe's big buddies hoisted its front legs up a tree trunk to feed on leaves. It clung on with a daintiness that seemed impossible to Lin given its girth, like a circus elephant balancing on a stool. Another of the herd had a rounder shape than the others. Lin thought maybe it was pregnant until she spotted a small, blunt head peering out from the underbelly. These creatures were pouched! Just like kangaroos, although the pouch faced the rear! How did that work?

Lin pursed her lips as her brow furrowed. This place was bizarre, but it had to be Australia. The only pouched animals she knew were marsupials, and the only country where lots of marsupials lived was Australia. But these huge creatures weren't ones she'd seen on that country's tourism ads. They didn't look like present-day creatures. So, if they weren't current critters, when did they exist? Or how did they get here? The female that kept her warm during the night was nearby ripping leaves from a tattered shrub, the calf by her side. Theirs was clearly a vegetable diet. Lin had no need to worry about a Greataunt Tigress gobbling her up. Forget the fangs; they're vegan.

When it noticed Lin was afoot, the bulky creature plodded over and lowered her head, as did her trailing calf. Lin responded with a courtly bob of her own. Lin had given them names. The female was Ida as in eiderdown; the calf was Little Quilt. Her dad would love that. Whoever made up the phrase 'Dad jokes' was thinking about Lin's dad. Of that his daughter was sure. Her father's corny sense of humour often caused her finely-arched eyebrows to rise and her eyes to roll back in dismay.

"Oh, no Dad, puh-leeze!" she'd said more than once. "No more dad jokes. They're so not funny."

Ida was also the name used by a friend of hers in English classes. She had a big bum but in no other way was she like these odd creatures except, maybe, she could use some dental help. *I wonder what she's doing now while I'm waking up in a world so different to anything either of us could know?* China seemed so far away.

Lin showed Ida her near-empty water bottle and shook it. No response. Of course, when would Ida have seen a metal container, or know what it was for? Lin developed an image of herself splashing water from a pool then looked at Ida. That worked. There was no recognition of these exchanges, no widened eyes, no nods; just an image flashing in Lin's mind of Ida walking, Lin following. Ida clumped off, Little Quilt bobbing at her heels. Lin followed hoping they weren't heading for one of the mucky sludge-pots in the middle of the valley. She couldn't drink from those. No way.

The walk didn't take them far before the valley wall cut back revealing a broad gully. At its head lay a murky pond, edges muddied by the big feet of the creatures that had plodded there to drink. Ida looked at the water and then at Lin. The visitor was having none of it, although she tried to keep her mind clear of criticism. If Ida could pick up feelings of disgust with smell, she'd sure understand criticism of the water supply.

"Urrgh! That's disgusting," Lin muttered.

"I'm not filling my water bottle from that. That's gross."

But Lin found a way to get hydrated. The pond was spring-fed. Water trickled from under a rock layer about two metres above the pond and cascaded over a ledge. She filled her bottle from the mini-cataract, splashed her face, then dried her hands by flapping them like flippers. That was one problem solved this morning. What about breakfast? She needed something. Roots and leaves may be the local diet, but it wasn't hers. *Where are you with the noodles, Mum?* Lin shook her head and looked around.

On a rock layer above the cascade, a short shrub with red berries eked out a tough existence. Lin peered at the tiny fruit clusters; maybe they'd do for breakfast. The bush grew too high to be stripped by the creatures, even balancing on tippy-toe. But the tallest had eaten some of the lower branches. The remaining berries looked okay. Lin signalled her eating interest to Ida. No response. *That must mean okay.*

Lin scrambled up the ledge, picked a berry and ate it. It tasted tart and had a pulpy texture, but it was edible. She ate enough to fill the gap in her belly, then put as many as would fit into her food box and kept three or four in hand. The dumplings were running low and any food would be useful. If the berries were harmful she'd know soon enough, but right now they sat easy in her stomach. Another problem solved. The day was going well. So far.

She jumped down onto soft ground a little way from Ida and her calf. Lin showed the handful of berries to Little Quilt. He looked at the food and Lin, then backed up behind his mother. Lin placed a red berry on the ground and stepped back, mumbling encouraging words. The stocky little creature poked his head out from behind his mum's ample rear, looked at the berry and again at Lin. He shuffled forward until he reached the red fruit, sniffed it, sucked it up and retreated.

Lin crouched, open hand extended, red berries bright in her palm. She smiled and made encouraging noises.

Little Quilt edged out from his cover and sidled forward. He stopped, eyed Lin warily then started forward again. He wanted the berries; Lin could tell. She stayed as still as she could. Finally, the little critter reached her outstretched hand, drew lips back over large, projecting teeth, pushed out a purplish tongue and knocked the berries from Lin's fingers. Then he sucked them off the ground. Lin's hand felt like it'd been savaged by a kitchen scourer, but it was the first real contact she'd had with the calf and she treasured it. *He's a funny little fellow.*

The threesome ambled back along the ravine to enter the valley proper, Little Quilt now trotting between Lin and his dam. Lin had made some progress; at least, he wasn't hiding from her. Food sharing would do that for you. As they plodded around the bend the trio surprised a kangaroo. The long-legged creature had been balanced on its hind legs and tail, cropping leaves from a tree a few metres in front of them. Lin paused, surprised, but no more so than the kangaroo, which bounded away. The tall creature stopped and looked back once before hopping out of the valley.

It was definitely a kangaroo; there was no mistaking the big hind legs and smaller forearms. The forefeet were longer than Lin recalled, and finished in long, strong fingers. The creature was huge, bigger than kangaroos Lin had seen at the zoo. From the tip of the swivelling ears to the toes of its giant feet, it was almost as high as an apartment ceiling. The face was wide and blunt, the muzzle short and strong with the eyes facing forward giving it an 'old man' appearance, a bit like an ewok from Star Wars. But much larger. It was a kangaroo, no doubt... another mega-creature.

This growing gang of outsized animals – particularly the kangaroo – confirmed for Lin that she had to be in Australia. Where else? It was the only place she could be unless she'd stumbled into a remake of Jurassic Park. If so, she'd better watch out for raptors as well as dropcats.

That disturbing feeling returned, the one nibbling at the edge of Lin's awareness since she'd been dumped in this place. These weren't modern animals; they looked like megafauna – giant, ancient creatures – and, if that was so, they'd been around a long time before Lin's ancestors, even before her ancestors' ancestors. These animals were supposed to be extinct... dead, gone. Yet here they were, alive and kicking. And here she was. Where?

Lin knew she'd travelled through space. But maybe she'd travelled through time too. She might have gone backwards through the centuries, maybe even millennia. So, the question was not only where she was, but when? Where was here and when was now? Or when was then? She had to think about that.

The trio trundled back to the ledge where Lin had spent the night; it looked home for now. Lin was reflective and quiet as ideas buzzed through her mind, not the least being what she was doing in this ancient time zone with these primeval creatures and, more importantly, when was she going home? She'd have to sort it out with BeBe.

Her thoughts were interrupted by a brawl that broke

out among these placid pachyderms. BeBe bellowed at a large male that'd been hanging around his harem. The sound joined the gravelly growl of a tiger with the high honk of a goose. It impressed Lin. The noise had to be hard to make. It was probably BeBe's funny-shaped head and puffy nose that did it; like he was blowing his nose and roaring at the same time. What was he up to? Whatever it was, Lin was staying out of the way. The critters were big, and ugly. She retreated under the ledge.

BeBe's bellow rolled around the valley. The challenger roared in response. Lin flinched. Frightened birds squawked off in surprise. BeBe the bull lowered his head and attacked.

This was a different BeBe. Head and tail lifted, he charged at the interloper with the percussive power of a belligerent bulldozer. The trespasser was blind-sided. BeBe smashed into the enemy's flank knocking it off balance and slashing an ugly wound down its side. Grunting loudly, breathing heavily, he stood back, then charged again. The challenger backed up, turned, and ran. BeBe gave chase, buffeting the interloper's side and slashing at its rear. Finally, they halted, facing each other. BeBe snorted, then charged, pulling up short of a head-on collision. He glared at the challenger then roared again, the sound thundering around the small valley like an oncoming storm. The intruder hesitated, shook its head and backed up. BeBe bellowed once more, and the challenger dropped his head.

That was it. Lin knew the battle was over. The challenge

had been seen off, the old order restored. BeBe had his cows back.

The big beast snorted loudly, whether in disdain or pain Lin didn't know. More likely gallumping that massive weight around had sapped his energy and he was gasping for air. He didn't look very fit. Although how Lin could tell the aerobic health of a beast that weighed over a tonne, moved with the pace of a glacier and survived on tree leaves, she wasn't sure.

BeBe roared again, and the intruder backed off before hobbling away. The dust settled, animals took up grazing, birds returned to their perches and the valley assumed its usual peace. All was as before... except for Lin.

BeBe turned and lumbered towards her. Lin stepped back a pace, her mouth open, hand to her breast, eyeing him in a new light. *Omigod, what a brute.*

Ida had watched the battle impassively. She'd probably seen it all before, and Lin knew enough about wild creatures to guess that Ida's future with one large bull would be much the same with the next. A younger, stronger challenger would rise and take BeBe's place – maybe even Little Quilt one day – and BeBe would be banished to the fringes of the herd to languish like an old elephant. But not today. This morning he'd triumphed and there'd be no more conflict for now.

BeBe lumbered towards Lin and lowered his head, she returned the greeting. No vision-shifting took place. BeBe seemed relieved just to stand, collect his wits and gather his energy.

This was not the time for Lin to find out what was happening or when she was going home. The barn-sized behemoth's sides heaved from effort, and Lin let her questions lapse. She'd 'talk' to him later.

There were other things to do, although choosing her best outfit wasn't one of them. She was wearing it. Initially happy with her travel kit, Lin could now list its shortcomings. Clean underwear ranked high on the missing list. So did soap and a towel. Any other clothing would have been useful. Still, she could clean her teeth, comb her hair and touch up her face.

Lin was fastidious about grooming and hygiene. Leaving her cosmetic kit at home was her idea of a day gone very wrong. The idea of personal body odour appalled her. Now, she was in a wilderness with stinky company, no change of clothes and precious little to pretty herself up with except a comb, hand-wash, perfume, a small container of tissues, facial make-up and lipstick. It'd have to do. A boy might just show up although she now thought this unlikely unless it was Jackie Chan looking for a new beast to reprise his *Beauty and the Beast* role.

"Hmm. I've plenty to show him."

Lin made her way to the crevasse to clean her teeth, comb her hair, and give herself what her mother called 'unders and overs' – a small wash. Or a lick and a promise as her granma used to say. *That's much better*. She felt human again. Lin sat on her sleeping ledge and stared out across the valley. She could no longer see BeBe. Maybe he'd gone to deal with other problems. *I wonder where I am really? And when?* Lin pondered the questions as she watched the bulky creatures resting in the morning sun. Finally, BeBe returned. Now to talk to him, if talk was the right word for the vision-shifting ordeals. He'd be ready now.

11

NORTH FOREST SAVIOUR

Take me back to the valley of the disc. Now! I want to go home. Lin conveyed the message to BeBe as vividly as she could, picturing the place where they'd met and the two of them returning there. Vision-shifting was tough, exhausting work done more in hope than certainty. Was Lin getting her message across?

Apparently not. BeBe showed no interest whatsoever. The toothy titan kept pushing his own images; a forest and a strange creature a little like himself but standing on two legs and with dark hair and wild, strange eyes. It was leading a group of large and small creatures towards distant woods. BeBe's visions were persistent and powerful but when they finished Lin had no idea what any of it had to do with her. She wanted out. Now. Her family would be frantic. *Gotta go home!* BeBe ignored her messages, continuing to recycle the forest pictures.

Finally, Lin understood BeBe's images as a history.

The saga came to her like images off a story-board. It was an Attenborough wildlife documentary without the ads... or Attenborough. At first Lin found it hard to follow; she couldn't absorb the stuff as fast as BeBe delivered it. And she struggled to find a meaning. The story swept into her mind as a melange of moving images to be interpreted and woven into a story. But the longer it went, the better Lin got... and the wearier. The exchange was gruelling.

The saga began after the demise of the dinosaurs. Lin watched on, eyes closed, as BeBe's kind evolved and spread throughout a cool, green land, generation after generation, along with a variety of creatures living with and off each other. No rose-coloured world this, no fantasy fable of love and harmony. BeBe's ancestors struggled with brutal reality; one animal's death meant another might live. Blood, injury, death, destruction, and life flowed endlessly. Lin winced and squirmed as BeBe pictured what that meant. Individual creatures came and went but life continued. It was all connected even if the large weed-eater could never have known as much.

Lin's strength flagged after only a small stint of vision-shifting. Her head hurt. She reached for her water bottle. Keeping up with BeBe was like sitting through a sad movie on repeat without the comfort of Coke, popcorn, and a soft cinema seat. She could use more tissues, too. Lin called interval by opening her eyes, raising her hand, and turning away. She shut down her concentration. BeBe's brain could cope with vision-shifting; her grey matter wasn't up to it.

As she took a break Lin wondered anew how this vision-shifting worked. As BeBe's tale unfolded she'd been taken by how it was run together and stored. It was if his species' history was imprinted in his DNA and he could replay it through the mental projector of his mind. But none of that explained how Lin received it. Nothing like this had happened before. She had no psychic skills. She was practical like her mum. After a short break, BeBe started again. The mood had worsened; the pictures more sombre. Lin braced herself and wondered what this was all about. And when it would end.

I wanna go home.

The landscape had dried; grass had shrivelled into dirt, waterholes shrunk to muddy bogs and trees stripped to leafless skeletons. BeBe's kin struggled on, looking for food and water, tongues lolling and their ribs sticking out like pickets on a fence, their world broken by drought.

Then wildfires appeared. Roiling infernos driven by searing winds reduced whole forests to blackened stumps and smoking earth. Animals died in agonisingly vast numbers, their burnt bodies stiffening in the blackened landscape that had once been their lush home. Starved and parched survivors stumbled on through the gaunt forests, past the charred bones of their kin, scavenging food and water wherever they could. Marauders stalked the herd, taking a toll on BeBe's kin and culling their numbers further as they fought for survival.

BeBe's story went on, harsh and compelling. Lin looked on as the images rolled unbidden through her mind.

Violent images of a volcano startled her, the pictures close and vivid. The spacepipe had taken her near an eruption but it hadn't threatened her life. It'd been colourful, entertaining even. Now she witnessed the devastation close-up through the eyes of the terrified animals. First, a small lava flow, then a massive firestorm of blistering ash and flaming debris that blocked the sky, smothered the earth and poured death, pain and misery on the animals trapped within its fiery field.

The land was left grey, smouldering, and desolate. Lagoons were clogged with layers of muddy ash, the water undrinkable; trees were decimated, no grass grew. Those animals that survived were forced to flee both volcano and predators.

Finally, images of humans, small bands of nomads arrived in Bebe's images. *What?* Lin's jaw dropped. *There were people here?* She hadn't seen any.

Few at first, their numbers grew. BeBe's forebears tried to 'talk' with them, but it hadn't worked. The newcomers could not or would not see. The new two-legged occupants slaughtered what they needed. They killed to eat. They killed to live. Their spears and clubs cut a bloody swathe. The invaders torched the land for easier hunting and gathering. BeBe and his kin were no match; they had no answers to this fast-changing world of drought, fire and menace. Danger threatened them from all sides. Their very existence was at stake.

The creatures had one chance, an ancient bond, a covenant that whenever their world was threatened a strange, dark-haired creature would arrive to take them to a forest of safety. They understood this implicitly. When their kind was on the brink of destruction, there would be a saviour. BeBe was unclear about who or what had made this vow to them. Where the forest was, he couldn't say.

The giant herbivore and his kin believed this unquestioningly. The saviour leading them to safety idea was a constant meme in their store of images; like those that appeared in Lin's mind when she first met these creatures. It was the same for many animals – as Lin found out later – from the large kangaroo down to her tiny, pointy–eared buddy, BiZi. His kind, too, believed the saviour to be truth. It had always been with them... an image of a strange, dark-haired creature that would lead them to safety.

Saviour, covenant, vow, promise, bond and pledge; Lin turned the words over. Those were her words, her way of understanding BeBe's vision-shifting. Lin knew they were fraught with religious meaning, and she wasn't religious. And BeBe didn't look the devotional type.

Like her practical parents Lin believed science and reason would shed more light on life's mysteries than faith and belief. Yet BeBe's images kept repeating this primeval theme and Lin had no other way to say it. There would be a deliverer, a champion, someone or something to lead these creatures to safety. That had been promised.

The saviour was pretty much a dark-haired version of BeBe walking on two legs. Other creatures had similar pictures; the deliverer looked like a modified version of their own kind standing upright. No consensus existed. The saviour was a chameleon that changed colour and form with each believer.

One thing they all agreed on; the creature would come to them through a new sun, odd, disturbing, and mysterious as that image was. A new sun? That's what they knew. That's what BeBe's images showed. The new sun would last from a new moon to an old moon and after that the chance for deliverance would be lost. The spacepipe with one end in Lin's room and the other in this land was the new sun to BeBe. He'd seen its glory when sunlight caressed it.

It was the disc that told them of the possible arrival of the saviour from the North Forest. BiZi had seen it first. The slanted rays of the late afternoon sun had found their way into the bower where the disc was located and lit it up like a brilliant star. Initially shocked and then excited, BiZi had taken this find to BeBe, scampering the length of the valley to 'talk' with him.

Could this be the new sun? Was this to be their way out of the dangers that faced them? They didn't know, but they were full of hope. The situation had never been as dire but there was nothing to guide them. Nothing like a new sun had ever been seen before; they'd never had to make such decisions before.

BeBe and BiZi came together to look at the disc. Mindful they only had a moonspan for the saviour, they waited, fretful and impatient. More time went by and finally a strange broken piece of coloured wood arrived.

Then nothing. BiZi decided that the suffering their clans had already gone through and the prospect of more fires and more predators – human and otherwise – made it important to find the creature and bring it back to do its job. The wood came through the disc; he would go back through it to find the 'saviour'.

The middle of the sun was the only way BiZi could see to go, and there was no way BeBe would fit. But the little creature did, negotiating both portals and the pipe. The creature they wanted was not there; the sun led to a small, pale, dark-haired, two-legged creature in a square space full of hard edges, smelly stuff and no trees. Their images were clear, however. A new sun would bring a saviour, and it had dark hair. The small creature had to be it. BiZi returned to take something to force it to follow him. It worked, although the creature didn't seem to know its part in this story.

BeBe was looking directly at Lin. The vision-shifting was done. The curtain had fallen. Now was the time for a response from the audience of one... Lin. Ida was looking at her; so was the calf, their gazes intense and steady. There was something they wanted: 'Will you take us to the North Forest?'

What? Me? Lin stepped back in shock. For all the experiences she'd gone through, for all the vision-shifting that'd taken place, Lin's idea of herself hadn't changed. She was an ordinary Chinese girl who'd strayed down a spacepipe looking for a vase, and now wanted home. She'd never imagined anything like this. *Me? A large mythical creature? Hardly. A saviour? Not likely.* To think she could lead them on a trek to somewhere was just crazy. She wasn't Mao Tsedung leading the people on the Long March. He was a military hero, she was a college student, and so not the saviour they sought. What did she know of such a forest?

But BeBe's vision was firm and fixed. They were in crisis; she'd come through the sun as foretold. They'd known that would happen. She was the one; they knew it. It had to be her. Her hair was dark. *Well, yes! But most Chinese have black hair.* And wasn't she from the North Forest? *Well, no, she wasn't,* conveyed Lin. *I come from a town,* although this was lost on BeBe who'd never seen houses and never would.

And then it hit her. It should have been obvious from the start. Lin's scalp prickled, and her face flushed. It had to be a coincidence, surely? *Come on!* Her eyebrows lowered as her lips pursed.

Lin was her family's name – her father's, and his father's name for generations. It was a name shared by millions. It wasn't extraordinary, just a simple family name. It also happened to be a Chinese word for woods or forest. It depended on how you said it. Same with Bei. It meant north as the Bei in Beijing made that city the northern capital. So Lin Beibei could be the North Forest. *C'mon, this has to be a fluke.* Or did it have a meaning? Lin didn't know. Just like she had no idea why one end of the spacepipe ended up in her room and the other in this land.

Lin Beibei, the north forest; all this could morph into the strange creature from the North Forest. Lin could see that, even if she wasn't happy being called strange. *If you think I'm strange, guys, well... hey, take a look around!* But she couldn't see what any of this had to do with her. She'd got herself into the spacepipe chasing a vase, she hadn't come here to save the world, or any part of it. Why she could vision-shift with these creatures, she didn't know. It was baffling and bizarre. But it didn't change a thing; she was so not the person BeBe sought. She couldn't lead them to wherever they wanted to go. *I can get lost on the way to college.*

The unwilling traveller made it as clear as she could. She wasn't their hero. Lin signalled the same to BeBe as well as indicating she wanted to return to the disc. Now. BeBe's features didn't change; he kept the same glum look. There was no appealing nor cajoling. They knew Lin to be the saviour. If she wasn't, then the new sun would bring them the champion they expected. BeBe signalled it was too late to take Lin back today. The heat was building, and he couldn't plod through it. He was weary from the battle to save his cows. In the afternoon, slow as he was, he wouldn't be able to take her to where they'd met and return to this valley before dark. He needed the protection of his kin when the sun went down. Predators wouldn't challenge a group at night. It'd be early tomorrow before he could start.

Lin was worried. She didn't want to be here another day. What would her family be thinking? But she wasn't going cross-country without help. Not with her navigation skills and drop-cats around. She'd wait.

Lin turned away, hand to her forehead, her face strained with pain she didn't want BeBe to see. Her chest tightened, and tears welled. Remorse tugged at her heart. She didn't want to disappoint these animals. They were simple and sweet, and they desperately needed help. She'd love to, but she couldn't take them on a trek to a place she didn't know, a place they didn't even know. This was their country, not hers. What did she know about it? Nothing. *Blindfold me and spin me around in Shanghai and I might find my way home, eventually. But here I'm alien... and lost.*

The creatures' needs were beyond Lin. The dry harshness of the land confused her; its empty plains and vaulted skies made her shoulders tremble. The noisy birds made her jump; its serpents chilled her blood. The creatures' vision-shifting had been powerful and BeBe's story had wrenched her heart. These creatures had been kind and she felt safe with them. They were different and unique.

But she could only wish them well and hope they survived the changes that threatened. She couldn't help. Her job was in an office as an accountant, not head of a wilderness expedition. She couldn't be their leader, their saviour.

I just want to go home.
I just want to go home.

12

MEET OTHER LOCALS

Okay, nothing to pack, nothing to do; just wait for BeBe to walk me back. Lin had the rest of the day to herself. A walk might clear her head as the morning had been tough. The sun was well up, and its rays warmed Lin's shoulders as she gazed over the valley. No threat loomed. Her hat was on and she checked her bumbag and water bottle. Yep, both in place; time to stretch her legs and put the worry of the morning behind her.

Lin turned to go, then stopped. *Stay still. Don't move.* She didn't know why. A gut instinct, sure; but something was wrong. The valley had fallen silent and still. An eerie hush spread over the land. The air felt... electric. Lin's eyes flicked from side-to-side as the skin on her neck prickled and a hollow sensation gripped her gut. Animals stopped grazing and lifted their heads. BeBe and Ida hesitated, their eyes wide and ears swivelling. No birds chirped, no insects jumped. Even the trees seemed to hold their breath. Everything waited. *For what?*

The earth jolted.

Violently.

The world wobbled as though massive feet had stomped on the planet. Trees shivered and shook. Lin froze like a tense tight-rope walker, her breath ragged and her heart pounding. A growl rumbled through the guts of the trembling earth. Eons of subterranean discomfort belched molten magma along the collapsing caverns of the underworld. The air crackled with static. A faint reek of sulphur spewed from the pores of the earth and floated in the eerie atmosphere.

As suddenly as it started, it stopped.

Trees stopped shaking. The horizon stilled. The earth settled.

Lin did not.

The tremor might have quit, but her terror didn't. Finally, after a few deep breaths, she found a fallen log and sat. Lin needed calm, a pause to recover. China had occasional massive earthquakes and this one wasn't big, but it was scary. And if it scared Lin, then it terrified the animals.

BeBe and Ida were horror-struck; fear had broken out on their usually fearsome features. Images of red-hot rock blistering skin off their kind, and blackened carcasses contorted in death flashed through their panicked minds and seared into Lin's. She witnessed the terror and despair of their past as they dug through depths of desolate ash-grey landscape trying to unearth something, anything they could eat or drink. Lin was drawn into their despair. They had no way of coping with such havoc. All they could do was move on, seek safety elsewhere and put drought, fire, earthquakes, volcanoes and marauding humans behind them. It seemed futile. They had no secure home.

The land settled, and the animals eventually returned to grazing. Birds took up their calls and flew swift and low along the valley to bank in sweeping unison and land chattering among the trees. A silver-black lizard slid ground-low through the short grass. Darting grasshoppers jackknifed into each other and the earth. A beetle climbed to the tip of long grass stem and peered at Lin. A lone butterfly cartwheeled in eccentric circles pausing occasionally to muse on its next magic move. The rumble had retreated but the fear stayed, growling gently in Lin's gut. She sat for a long time on the fallen tree trunk gathering her wits, looking at her surrounds, wondering again where she was... and why.

Finally, with her fears eased, Lin got ready to continue her walk. The subterranean stirring scared her, but it was over. She could do nothing about it and there was no-one to talk to. A stroll would be good. First, she'd check it out with BeBe.

Lin stared at the mammoth marsupial and pictured her purpose. He made no response, good or bad. Satisfied for her safety, Lin made her way slowly to the small ravine and the spring that trickled from the rock. It was cool and quiet in the gully. She refilled her bottle, trapped a small amount of water in her cupped hand and splashed it onto her forehead and neck. *That's better.* Lin combed her hair and checked her face in the bumbag mirror. Satisfied her appearance was as good as it was going to get, she looked for food. The small shrub still had berries on it and Lin gathered and ate a few. *I'll take a few more for Little Quilt. He likes them.*

Lin sat on the ledge to finish eating and gazed back along the ravine. Everything lay still, so unlike the harsh and jarring tension of the quake. She soaked up the stability but eventually jumped down and walked back along the ravine, hoping to see the mega-kangaroo again. When she arrived at the bend where the ravine joined the valley, Lin rose onto the balls of her sneakered feet and crept alongside the wall. She didn't want to disturb the animal if it was grazing. Lin peered around the bend. Nothing. No sign of life. Just the valley and the tree the animal was browsing the last time.

Damn! She'd so looked forward to seeing that kangaroo. The tremor probably scared it. Or maybe it wasn't time to eat. Whatever, there was nothing here. She'd head back to BeBe and the gang. As Lin turned, a movement caught her eye. She looked again. A baby kangaroo, maybe two-thirds of a metre tall stood near its reclining mother under the branches of the tree. The creatures had rested in the shade, their coats blending with the colour of the grass and the shadows. Great camouflage. Only the movement gave the little one away.

As Lin watched, the young animal idled slowly around

the tree, keeping an eye on its parent, not venturing far, just moseying about. The mother kangaroo lay raised on a foreleg, head elevated, ears alert... quiet, watchful and wary. The young hopper went on a ragged circuit tugging playfully at an occasional leaf stem. Lin smiled at the movement. First the forepaws went to the ground and the creature took its weight there as well as on its tail. Balanced on this front-feet-to-tail tripod, the hind legs swung forward to retake the little critter's weight and allow it to rise and repeat the rhythmic pattern. Lin was enthralled. *That's so cute.* At a point near the valley wall a large branch swept close to the ground. The little hopper chose to go around it rather than duck the low-hanging bough.

As the young kangaroo moved around the branch it turned its back to the valley wall and lost sight of its mother. A man emerged from behind a rock, club in one hand, spear in the other. The hunter reared back to heave the club at the small kangaroo.

"What? No!", Lin yelled, bolted out of hiding and ran at him, arms lifted, hands clenched into fists.

If she was surprised at seeing another human being, she was appalled at his intentions.

"No! What do you think you're doing? No! No! Don't do that!"

In an instant the mother kangaroo swept the young one into her pouch and bounded away, the baby's feet sticking out like crooked sticks in a vase. She never looked back. The hunter had thrown the weapon, but it went astray. The spear, which he'd dropped, lay on the ground. He stepped clear of his hide, a slender, near-naked figure with only a belt and wrap to cover his groin. He looked at Lin in what seemed complete amazement, maybe fear.

As the echoes ebbed and the valley returned to quiet, Lin peered at the newcomer, her thoughts swinging between revulsion and curiosity. Another person! Okay, a cruel thug but, hey, another human being. Maybe this club-toting barbarian could tell her where she was. And when.

She'd talk to him. Lin approached slowly her hands palms-up, a sign she carried no weapons. It didn't work. Her attempt at peace must have alarmed the hunter because he backed up against the rock and tensed, ready to run.

He was young, maybe her age. He had a nice body too – lean, tall, and muscled. Pity he was a thug. The newcomer wore his long, dark hair pulled back behind his head. His cheekbones were high and broad, with well-marked eyebrows over round, brown eyes. His nose was broader than hers and longer, while his mouth had a slight tug on one side that might give him a quizzical expression when he wasn't terrified.

The young man was built more like Liu Xiang, the lithe hurdler, than Yao Ming, the giant basketballer. He was kind of nice-looking for a monster that threatened helpless babes. The most obvious feature about him – apart from his near-nudity – were thick welts carved across his chest. The scars were bold and looked like they'd been cut not long ago. They stood out from the smooth line of his pecs and the gloss of his skin. Maybe they were initiation scars, cuts made to heal in a raised pattern. Lin had read about that sort of thing. What they meant, though, she didn't know; but they must've been painful.

She wondered what he thought of her as she approached...

*   *   *

He stepped back as it neared him; a ghost-like, pale creature with dark, straight hair and covered in strange, coloured hides. It had a funny lump on its lower back and the blue and white feet had no toes. The walk was human-like, but it was nothing like he'd ever seen, not even in other clans. Strange creatures featured often in his people's stories, but no tales told of scary things such as the one approaching him now. The screaming beast had emerged from the water valley and scared off the kangaroo he'd stalked all morning. Food wasn't easy to get. First the shaking earth drove the animals away and then this monster ruined his only chance at the hunt.

And now it was coming for him...

As it got closer he noticed the smell, as if the creature had rolled in flowered grass. It would make a bad hunter smelling like that. The creature showed its teeth, extended blue arms and mumbled noises that left his ears and mind confused. The hands reaching for him were pale and thin with long nails, like the claws of a dead seagull. He needed his spear to defend himself but when he bent to pick it up the creature stepped on it. He stammered a welcome to his land and hoped his death would be painless and do honour to the legendary bravery of his forebears...

*　　*　　*

Foot planted firmly on the spear, Lin sighed inwardly; she'd given it a good shot, tried to make peace with the near-naked neanderthal. But it wasn't happening. He seemed terrified, as though she was about to hit him. *I scare him? Omigod, why?* She was small and slender while he was tall, strong, and obviously capable, even if his hunting habits were gross.

The hunter remained aloof and alert, eyes suspicious and watchful, stance tentative, poised to flee or fight. Lin stared at him while the pair remained unmoving. The uncertainty got to Lin. This couldn't go on. They couldn't stand there looking at each other like bad actors who'd lost their lines. Something had to give.

Lin chose to risk everything, smiled her sweetest smile, took her foot off the spear and motioned for him to pick it up. She walked away to pick up his club and brought it back. *Whoa, that's heavy.* Holding it in her hands as if a gift, Lin proffered the weapon, handle-first.

"Take it'," she said. "Go on, take it."

She smiled. He caught her eyes, suspicious. Lin continued proffering the club, gently poking the handle at him until he reached out cautiously and took it. Lin smiled again and stood still. The visitor shifted the club to his right hand, hefted it, then let it drop to his side with the spear.

Lin continued smiling at the young hunter. *At least he doesn't want to whack me with it.* That was a start. But what now? He was staring at her; she was looking at him. Lin's body buzzed with excitement, every sense alert and tingling like when she'd played in the college table-tennis final. But this was going nowhere.

She tapped her finger on her chest and said,

"Me, Lin," like Jane in a Tarzan movie.

Then she reached out to touch his chest.

"You...?"

He leapt back, startled and wary. His weapons rose, then fell as Lin did nothing more. He obviously wasn't ready for first contact. Undeterred, she tried a few more "Me, Lin" taps on her chest and more gentle points at his.

At last he grasped what she wanted.

"Aah," he muttered, pointed at his chest and mumbled something that sounded like Arben.

He wasn't smiling.

Lin pointed at him. "Arben?" she said and smiled.

He nodded.

"Me, Lin," she said and pointed at herself one more time then smiled again. "You, Arben." Point. "Me, Lin."

At least he could speak, he had a name, and she didn't have to vision-shift, although she tried. Nothing, not even a glimmer. It was the same problem with language. Whatever he spoke it wasn't Chinese or English.

Okay. Now what? Lin sat on a large rock and gestured

for him to sit on the one he'd hidden behind. The hunter didn't move. He stayed behind the boulder, his body stiff and tense, spear clutched in one hand, club in the other. His eyes never left Lin, his distrust obvious. Lin didn't know what to do now so she unclipped her bumbag and put it next to her on the rock.

Lin saw Arben's body stiffen and his eyes widen. His mouth fell open. *What's wrong with him now?* They'd finally got past 'Hello' and he still looked worried. *Well, he can sit there. I need a drink, I'm thirsty.*

Lin opened her bumbag and took out the anodised water bottle. Arben drew back, ready to run. His eyes followed Lin like a frog stares at a snake. Lin unscrewed the silver lid and poured water into it with a flourish. Arben looked on open-mouthed as she tipped it back and drank. Then he licked his lips. She poured a small amount into the lid and offered it to him. He shrugged, his faced screwed in a shape that could have been a question.

Lin splashed the water into her cupped hand and drank noisily, obviously. She held out the bottle and signalled him to cup his hand like hers. He mimicked her tentatively and she tipped water into his hand. Most trickled through his fingers but he sniffed his hand and licked his fingers. *Probably to make sure it's water.* Lin took a sip from the lid, refilled it and offered him the bottle cup again. He put it to his lips hesitantly, tilted it, spilled most of it down his chest but got some into his mouth. She poured him some more, which he drank readily. His body lost its tension. Lin thought she glimpsed a smile.

Okay, if water worked then maybe she should bring out the big guns... Wang Mei's dumplings! She had some left. They'd worked with BiZi, why not with this near-naked brute? Sharing food was a sign of friendship and trust; it worked with Little Quilt, maybe it'd help this stranger drop his guard and say something.

Lin reached into her bumbag and took out the food box. Arben followed every movement. The dumplings smelled fine even though they were made a few days ago and had survived possible centuries in a spacepod. Lin took a bite and made loud lip-smacking noises before offering the rest of the dumpling to Arben. She motioned for him to put it in his mouth. He told her 'no' by holding up his hand. It seemed whatever she ate was not for him. So, Lin ate it, noisily.

Lin proffered Arben another morsel. He was wary, but hungry. She could hear his belly gurgling like a waterfall. He studied the dumpling, then licked his lips. Lin knew it smelled good.

With slow deliberation the young hunter plucked the savoury ball from Lin's hand, looked at it, sniffed at it, put the food into his mouth and bit down. His face lightened. Lin smiled; Wang Mei's specialties had won another convert. Lin offered Arben another and watched his response.

*   *   *

Arben had never tasted such food. He rolled it around his mouth with relish. What was it? His people's food was picked off a shrub, dug up, speared or clubbed, maybe skinned and washed, sometimes eaten raw, but often just thrown onto an open fire. Food like the creature had given him was not something he could explain. This creature was amazing. Scary, foreign and not-to-be-trusted... but amazing.

*　　*　　*

Lin relaxed a little and sighed. All morning one of her sneakers had bothered her. The sockette had slipped around her heel and wedged under her instep. It pressed like a pebble. Taking her shoes off in public was not something Lin did as a rule. But rules here seemed different. This place was so not normal. A spacepod brought her here, oversized animals mutely spoke, almost naked people ran around chasing giant kangaroos, large beasts dropped out of trees to kill you while even bigger ones snuggled up to keep you warm. This was so her home town. Not! Removing a shoe seemed neither ill-mannered nor boorish; everything considered, it was rather normal. Besides, her foot bothered her, and she needed to pull up the sock. This brave hunter-type would have to put up with it. It didn't look as though he suffered much from this sort of problem, barefoot as he was. Lin took off her shoe.

Arben was fascinated, and frightened.

*　*　*

Arben watched the strange creature, his eyes narrowed. This was another of those things that amazed and scared him; the screaming creature broke off its foot! He couldn't take his eyes off the alien. First it had come shrieking into the valley and wrecked his hunt. Then it took off part of its body where it stored food and drink and offered him some. Now the stranger had taken off its foot. Was it going to eat that?

The hunter's confusion heightened as Lin sat on the rock and massaged her instep. That's a foot. The blue-and-white striped thing was a cover. And he did that. He rubbed his feet when they got sore. What's more, the creature had toes, five of them, just like his only smaller. He could also see an ankle, slender and bony, hidden under the outer skin. It was attached to a leg just like his. The creature's whole body, except for the arms and face were covered with an outer layer that could be removed. Like the cloaks his people wore in winter. If that was so, then this thing might be human... sort of. But different. And possibly a woman as it had breasts. Now he needed to know where she was from and how many more of her there were. Enemies and threats were ever-present to Arben and his people. Strangers were welcome; you just didn't want them to kill you.

Lin put her sneaker back on and retied it under Arben's gaze. She then removed the small bottle of hand wash from her bumbag and cleansed her hands thoroughly. That done, and with her feet comfortable, Lin turned to face her two-legged problem. He did seem a bit more relaxed after eating her mum's dumplings, but who could say? *What do I do now?*

She was pondering just that when the young hunter chose to speak. It was unintelligible to Lin, the wonder being he'd chosen to speak at all. And she'd take it over the silent treatment anytime. Lin shook her head and shrugged a 'me-no-understand' gesture. Arben took up the challenge of signing using his arms, hands, face, feet and jutting chin. Lin got the idea that he was asking where she'd come from, and she waved at the sky.

Again, using fists, fingers and multiplier motions Arben asked how many of her there were. Lin was cautious about this for she sensed its deeper meaning. She was only going to be here until tomorrow morning so... *Hell, it doesn't really matter.* She pointed at herself and held up her index finger. Just me.

*　*　*

Arben was confused. He didn't know what to do. He'd never seen anything like this creature sitting before him pointing at its chest and mumbling. It was so different.

He'd take it to meet his clan elders. They could question it further. Their wisdom and experience were far greater than his. It was just a short walk to his home camp but how could he convince the creature to go with him?

Arben did his best to show he wanted Lin to meet his people. He made walking motions, number signs, talking gestures, smiles, and symbols that meant women and children. He also indicated he would bring her back here. To do this, a straight, long twig was broken off the kangaroos' shade tree and put in the ground. Using its shadow line and projected arc he showed that it wouldn't take long.

*   *   *

Lin watched Arben as he showed her how long it would take to get to his home; perhaps about three hours. But now she was suspicious. This whole place was strange and dangerous, and she was being asked to take a stroll to a place she didn't know in a country she'd be easily lost in with a man carrying more weapons than clothes. *That makes real sense, right?* What did she know about this barbarian, really? Not much. He seemed harmless enough. But she'd thought trees were harmless until BeBe showed her otherwise. While Arben had not harmed her, his attitude to animals was cruel. Maybe she could talk to him about that.

For Lin was lonely, in need of company. A walk would be good and so might meeting other people. She'd go with him. She'd gone with BeBe and that had worked out... sort of. *Ah well, in for a penny, in for a pound. Again.* How bad could meeting a few strangers be? It might be exciting. Granma would've said, 'Go for it!' Her mother would've reached for a broom.

Using the sun as a guide, Lin indicated with a sweep of her arm to the horizon and a firm point to her chest and the ground that he would return her here by sunset.

Arben nodded. He couldn't see how his family could deal further with the creature anyway. As long as there was only one of them it couldn't be a real threat. And weird though it looked, the creature seemed incapable of real harm. Except for the screaming. His family could meet it, make their judgment and he would bring it back here. The young hunter made a gesture suggesting they move.

Lin made sure her shoes were tied, combed her hair and checked her mobile – it still wasn't working – retrieved her crushable hat from her bumbag and put it on.

This time, Arben watched and smiled, almost relaxed. He was right, the creature wore odd coverings all over. That funny thing on its head was really strange.

13

SAY HELLO TO THE FAMILY

The young hunter beckoned to Lin then strode towards the valley's edge. After a pause, she followed. Lin didn't like traipsing along behind nearly-naked male forms, fat bummed or slender. But if she had a choice, she preferred the latter to BeBe's monstrous rump. That was like walking behind an elephant and about as dangerous if it decided to back up, sit, or shit. Arben was different; he had a neat rear and fit, strong legs. He really was a good-looking young man. She liked walking along behind, so to speak. It was a shame about his gross hunting habits.

When they made it out of the valley the country presented as always, flat and monotonous, the grass tufted and short with patches of bare earth sticking up like so many shaved scalps. Occasional tree clumps presented but Arben detoured around them. Lin thought she knew why. The sun was high, and their short shadows fell behind them. Lin reasoned that if they were in Australia then they were heading north. Arben fell into a steady stride and Lin's shorter legs struggled to keep pace. But like the trip to see a panda with her father many years ago, she wasn't about to complain or quit.

She thought fondly of her dad as the walk lapsed into routine. She wondered what he'd think if he knew his daughter was eons away walking behind a near-naked warrior, admiring the view in a weird and desolate world. He'd be happy to know she was safe. He'd not approve of the near-naked company. Not a bit. Fathers were like that. Lin smiled to herself. *And I love him for it... and miss him.*

I want to go home.

After about a half hour, the country gradually sloped upwards, enough to have Lin puffing. When they reached the crest, Arben paused. Lin caught up and stood by him. The country fell away before them revealing a wide lake in the middle of a circular basin. A ragged ridgeline curved away in both directions. Lin looked over a dip so round it looked as though an asteroid must have hit the area a long time ago. It felt like she was standing on the lip of a giant saucer.

Elevated country and perhaps the dark line of a forest fringed the horizon to the north. Reeds and rushes fringed the still, shallow lake; larger trees choked with scrub surrounded it. Waterfowl bobbed through the reeds; large white birds floated on the water like specks of cotton on a smooth, green blanket. Lin saw no signs of life – no village, huts or people – but her guide kept heading in the same direction. Was that the smell of smoke? Maybe, but she couldn't see anything.

There was no track that Lin could make out. This was so not Shanghai with its laneways, paths, streets, and about a billion, busy drivers. It was quiet too, something Shanghai rarely was. Arben picked his way through the scrub, and Lin had no choice but to follow. After a further 150 metres of sweaty struggle, when Lin thought they must have been getting close to the water, the hunter paused and motioned her to stop. They were in a small clearing beside a tall tree. He signalled he was going to his camp and would come back for her. Or that's what Lin thought. It didn't matter, for he was gone, quietly and quickly. One second he was signalling, the next he'd melded into the olive-green scrub like an actor slipping into the wings.

A fortress of foliage surrounded Lin. What was he up to? *Why's he dumped me here?* Maybe they were close to his camp. Perhaps he wanted to tell his people first, warn them about her. *Oooh, get ready for the scary monster! That's me.* Lin grinned at the thought. But otherwise, why would he dump her here and signal for her to stay? Stay, just like you order a dog. She really would have to talk to him about boy-girl respect stuff. But just how was she going to do that? They'd only got as far as point, grunt, and 'Me Lin, You Arben'. Besides, he was a brute, and she didn't think 'gender relations' would translate well.

Lin found nothing threatening in Arben's actions. Just condescension. And it rankled, but she had to stay put. There was no way she was walking on into that heavy scrub. She'd be lost. They'd walked from the crater rim through connected grass patches among the trees. In places grass and undergrowth had been crushed as if by feet. Whether the feet were attached to four legs or two, friend or foe, Lin couldn't tell. And she wasn't about to risk finding out by walking away. She'd stay where he'd left her, and wait.

The big tree looked inviting. She checked its branches to make sure nothing large and lethal was about to drop on her. There wasn't so Lin sat at the base, her back propped against the trunk. After a while the scrub returned to normal. Up until now Lin had thought the undergrowth uninviting and uninteresting. Yet here there was a treasure trove of birds, mostly small, some little and drab, others tiny but colourful and with narrow, upright tails almost as long again as their owners.

While she stayed still and silent the little birds flittered through the scrub, using their tails as rudders to dodge and weave past and through the leaves and branches. There were birds with flashes of red, some with breasts of iridescent blue. A few had melodious whistles, others just twittered. One, a little larger than most with a black back and tail and white breast, flew into the clearing. It chittered loudly when it saw Lin, its tail twitching agitatedly. The little bird didn't seem happy to see her, but Lin was rapt. She could have sat there longer but Arben returned, his face morose.

He looked even edgier than the bird. Maybe it was her. They were a grumpy lot; BeBe's glum and the humans unhappy, the one she'd met at least. Arben motioned her to stand, and she did. Then turning abruptly on his heel, he walked away. Again. Lin took a deep breath and bit back a cross word. This turning and following stuff pissed her off. Who did he think she was? His slave? But she followed, what choice did she have?

The scrub pulled at her clothing as they wended their way down. By the time they'd gone ten metres Lin was breathing heavily through her nose. Her hands were clenched, and her eyes bored in on the bare back in front of her as they made their way through the dense bush.

Lin had worked up a head of steam about this high-handed gender treatment. *Who does he think he is?* She was about to tap Arben on the shoulder and tell him to take his family visit and stick it. He could take his sexist ways as well. She could make her own way back to BeBe and the gang. Thank you. At least they'd showed kindness and care… and they were animals.

Lin thought she could return safely as she'd noted landmarks when she wasn't appreciating Arben's tight bum. And she knew to keep away from trees. But when she lifted her head after ducking a low-hung branch, she found herself in a clearing by the water's edge.

Hey. A campsite. More people. Lin's irritation ebbed as her curiosity surged. Her breathing eased, and her eyes widened as she took in the scene, a grassed space about 30 metres wide edging a narrow, sandy shore fringed with reeds and rushes. No houses or huts were visible, just three lean-tos, one-sided tents of bark propped against branches.

A bark raft lay pulled up by the water's edge. Some woven grass and hide bags lay on the grass along with tools and weapons like Arben carried. Some of the tools looked like they could've been used for digging, others for fishing. In the middle of the camp a fire smouldered. A block of wood charcoal pushed a tiny bluish flame into the air; a partially burnt tree limb stuck out ready to be shoved back to start the blaze anew. Lin took it all in.

The campsite looked like it held a few more people than the two nearly-naked, older men Lin could see standing by the water's edge. Her appearance didn't help the men's outlook; she could see that. They stood tense, maybe even fearful, their stiff stances suggesting they shared Arben's alarm at her appearance. She'd never had this effect on men before. *More's the pity. It feels good.*

Lin thought the males looked alike, the older ones sharing Arben's dark hair and facial features, even his bright, even teeth. They all carried chest scars. Maybe they were 'rellies'. The men were a handsome lot. Even the older pair had a carriage and bearing that would have been dignified had they not been so nervous.

Arben walked with Lin towards the men, pointed to her by way of introduction and said, "MeLin."

Whaat? Lin's jaw dropped, and her eyes widened. *I am so not MeLin!* Her face reddened while hot protest bubbled in her chest. Anger about Arben's gender gaffes hadn't long subsided and it was ready to flare again. She took a breath then let it out slowly and bit her tongue. Why bother? That's what Arben heard. Any other time it'd be funny. If she ever got the chance, she'd explain it to him. It *was* funny. He could be YouArben and she, MeLin.

Right now, though, things weren't funny. She didn't speak their language and they didn't speak hers. The atmosphere was strained; lips were tight, and shoulders tensed on both sides. It'd take more energy than Lin had to tell these people that she was only Lin. Now wasn't the time. Tomorrow she was heading home, being MeLin for a day wasn't going to hurt. Besides, she didn't understand their names either.

The three men finally gathered a joint confidence that Arben alone didn't possess. Soon they were peering closely at her, talking animatedly and pointing. They seemed very interested in her clothes and hair. Their interest was thorough, intrusive, and much too up-close and personal for Lin. She fidgeted under the barrage of close inquiry.

One of the older men reached out to touch Lin's forehead near her eyes. In indignant response she reached out and touched the scar on his chest. He looked down, surprised, and she did what her father used to do. She flicked her finger up to his nose.

"Gotcha!"

He jumped back, eyebrows raised, his face showing surprise, maybe even anger. He glared at her. Lin smiled, and chuckled. That did it. He threw back his head and laughed. They all laughed. The tension lifted, and they chuckled longer than they would have in sheer relief. That trick of her dad's must be really old, but it worked. Dad jokes forever.

The laughter acted as a signal. Other people emerged from the scrub; men, women, and children, gaping and gasping, their hands reaching to touch Lin. She stayed close to Arben for protection. He was the only one she knew, and that hadn't been for long. *And I'm not too happy with him either.* But he stood by her, put his hand lightly on her shoulder and said something to his family. The pointing and prodding stopped, and they withdrew to stare and chatter. *That was nice of him.* Where had these people come from? They must've been hiding in the bush to make sure she wasn't a threat. The laughter said she was okay.

There was a frail, much older man, an adolescent boy, four women, and a bunch of children, the kids hiding shyly behind the legs of their mothers. *That's what Little Quilt does.* But these kids were even cuter than he was. They didn't share as much as one piece of real clothing between them though. Okay, it was hot, and clothes weren't really necessary, but they must have winter. How did they keep warm then?

When the elders left to talk things over, Lin sat by the lake. Arben joined her, his face a cloud of confusion and questions. The women and children continued to point and stare, but from a distance. Lin sensed Arben wanted to talk but talking was hard. Waving hands, pointing, grunting and smiling could only go so far. But they were about the same age and Lin wanted to know more about this well-built stranger too. There was a poise, a 'cool' about him that appealed to her. She was beginning to like him despite the initial shock of their meeting. Something light and joyous had fluttered in her breast when he'd touched her shoulder.

While she sat out of the afternoon sun another young hunter walked into the camp carrying weapons, and the results of a hunt. He went into flight or fight response when he saw Lin. She was unperturbed. *Yeah, yeah. Another man scared of me. Whatever. Get over it.*

Arben said something to the newcomer and he relaxed. Almost. He also dropped what he was carrying, a small, stiff, and bulky animal.

The creature looked like Little Quilt... dead.

Nooo! Gall rose in Lin's throat, her chest heaved, and tears rimmed her eyes. It couldn't be Little Quilt, could it? Not Ida's offspring, the little guy that helped keep her warm overnight? How could people kill such a harmless creature?

Lin hurried over to the dead animal and bent to look at it. Its killer backed off, his eyes wide. She stood up and glared at him; he shrank back further. Now was not the time to attack him for this murder; her relationship with these people was fragile. But she would've challenged him if she could. She wanted to say, 'Monster! How could you do such a thing?' But did she know it was really Little Quilt? She didn't. And what did she know about these people and their needs? Nothing. What if they hunted BeBe's kind in order to survive? Anguish pierced Lin's heart. Confusion clouded her mind.

Arben touched the animal with his toe and said, "Darrabin."

So that's what they were. Lin pointed at the corpse, swept her arms in a broad move to encompass the width of BeBe's big bum and asked, "Darrabin?" Then bent and indicated the small creature. "Darrabin?"

He nodded; "Darrabin."

Big and small they were all darrabin, but this one was dead, and it looked like Little Quilt. Lin was incensed and sorrowful, but silent.

Arben signed that they'd cook it on the fire and made loud, lip-smacking noises like Lin used to encourage him to eat the dumpling. This was obviously choice food, given Arben's response. He looked at the hunter who'd made the kill and said something. It was meaningless to Lin, probably a chat about where he'd killed the animal. They talked briefly and Arben nodded.

Lin could see the family were hunter-gatherers. The bags strewn around, the tools and weapons lying about suggested they lived by their wits and skill. Lin could see no signs of crops, fruit trees, or animal tending. These people must collect or kill what they need and darrabin were on the menu.

Little Quilt's possible death overwhelmed Lin. She couldn't get the image of the small, stiff cadaver out of her mind. He'd been so alive, so funny and had helped keep her warm. Her foodbox still held berries for him. Ida's loss would add pain to the sad store of memory for whatever of their kind came after... *if* they came after.

The next half-hour passed in sad distraction for Lin. She talked and signed to the adults, played peek-a-boo with the little ones who scuttled behind their mothers' legs screaming in fright, most of it fake, some of it real. But her heart wasn't in it. It was with Little Quilt and his larger kin. Lin's pain and anger about the dead darrabin were not pretence. Volcanoes, hunters, fire and drought threatened the animals. Something had to be done if they were to survive. And what of Arben's folk? Animals died so they might live. How would they survive? She had a lot to think about.

Lin signalled a reminder to Arben that she had to return to where they met. He nodded. But her hosts weren't about to let her go without honouring the occasion. Arben mimed later that they would talk about this day forever. Nothing this exciting had happened since his uncle – Lin thought he meant an uncle – had fallen into a river while collecting honey and a small crocodile bit him on the bum. This meeting had to be respected.

The older of the two men – possibly Arben's father – presented Lin with a cloak. These people didn't wear much of anything so how come they had a cloak? And what a garment it was! Made from the skins of many small animals sewn together to form a ground-length robe. The outside was warm fur, the skin side had a pattern of attractive drawings Lin couldn't interpret. The cloak was topped with a small hood that one of the women, struck with a fit of giggles, gestured was for Lin's baby when she had one. Then it was Lin's turn to giggle. Whatever gave them that idea? They signed that she should carry the babe so it looked over her shoulder. *Yeah, that'd work back home.* Lin smiled.

Though the cloak was finely made, Lin thought first to refuse it. It must have taken weeks to put together. Arben's people had amazing skills for the small toolkit she could see. It was just a shame that so many critters had to die. Lin didn't want it, but it'd be impolite to refuse. And the elders were insistent. She swallowed her misgivings, smiled her gratitude and bundled the cloak up with a long leather lash they gave her. Maybe she could dump it when they were out of sight. They really were a kindly people but what could she do with a fur coat in this heat?

Arben seemed pleased with himself, and her. He was smiling at last.

14

THE DECISION

The return walk didn't seem as long. Lin balanced the rolled-up cloak on her shoulders to get it through the scrub. On the plain, as she walked beside Arben, the cloak rode easily on top of her bumbag. The gift wasn't the problem; her heart was. It hurt. Lin couldn't explain why she felt so stressed about the death of small animals, the little darrabin and others whose lives had been taken to make the cloak. It happened all the time. Millions of pigs, chickens and cows died every day to feed the people of China. But baby animals were adorable, and Little Quilt was a cutey.

On the other hand, the darrabin were a cumbersome species, smelly, not overly bright despite the vision-shifting, and certainly not pretty. Far from it. They lacked the piebald patchwork of the panda, the human-like charm of the orangutan, the majestic grace of the tiger.

As megafauna went, they missed on the charisma. Yet Lin knew they were not harmful to anything but trees, shrubs and grass. And there were never-ending supplies of those. Besides, the bulky beasts had a plodding charm that came with their innocence. She knew they'd evolved to fill a niche and were part of the food chain for others. Perhaps it was their helplessness against multiple threats that opened her heart. They were here, alive, expectant for their existence, and helpless. They were vulnerable against the onset of hunters as competent as Arben's kin. Lin sighed deeply, and her face sagged in sorrow.

Well into their journey back to the water spring, Arben abruptly changed direction, beckoned Lin to follow and walked quickly towards a thick spinney of trees. This was unusual, he was going towards trees! There had to be a reason.

Lin went along with it; but she was uneasy. Her eyes narrowed, and her senses sharpened as she reluctantly followed the young hunter. She thought she could trust him, but what did she really know about Arben and his people? Maybe they were into rape and murder. Besides, she was still touchy about his habit of ordering women around. When they arrived at the trees, Lin searched his face, looking for a motive, ready to defend herself in case he turned on her. All she saw was tension. The young hunter wasn't giving a reason for the detour, but he looked serious, even grim.

The clump of trees was dense, about ten metres across and choked with scrub. Arben chose a well-concealed spot. *What's he up to?* Lin's chest tightened, and she watched him closely, ready to fight or flee. He motioned her to untie the robe she carried and put it on. *What the hell for? It's hot.*

Lin raised an eyebrow, drew a finger across her brow and blew to indicate heat. It was far too hot for a cloak even in this shaded glade. He frowned and made an insistent gesture that she put the cloak on. Now. With a sigh, she did. *It was his country and he's familiar with it. Besides, putting on clothes suggested he didn't have ideas about ripping hers off. But who'd want a cloak in this heat?* Her companion wasn't letting on. After she wrapped herself in the garment, Arben signalled for her to sit and cautioned her to make no movement or sound. He squatted close by. Obviously, they were hiding, but from what? This wasn't like him, the little she knew of him anyway. He seemed worried and, for a change, it wasn't about her.

Several minutes of silent, edgy waiting and watching lapsed before Arben put a finger to his lips and motioned Lin to be still. Seconds went by; not a sound disturbed the spinney. Lin looked at Arben, her eyebrows raised. He frowned and shook his head.

Just then two men strode by close to where they hid, weapons clutched in their hands. Lin went rigid. The intruders were silent, walked swiftly and ignored the clump of trees where the pair sat concealed. Lin could just make out their bodies through the scrub. They were too distant and Lin too hidden to make out details, but they seemed shorter than Arben, and stockier. Their hair was tight and curly, their faces broader and flatter than those of the family she'd just met.

At a point almost past the copse, one of the strangers touched the other's arm and whispered. The new arrivals stopped, turned, and stared intently at where the pair hid. Lin saw Arben's body tighten and his fist clench around the club. She froze. *Have they seen us?* The men separated two steps apart, raised their spears and moved stealthily towards the grove, peering intently. Lin just knew they were looking at her. She held her breath as sweat oozed from her forehead and trickled into her eyes. She couldn't lift a hand to wipe it away. Arben's toes curved into the earth. He moved his club hand slightly to give it freedom. The intruders took another step, and another. Lin couldn't control her trembling. The sweat ran in a rivulet down her chest. Arben waited, his back against a dense shrub, poised to attack or defend.

A bird flapped away, its wings clattering loudly.

The strangers halted.

The panicked bird flew towards the two men then swung away to land behind them. The strangers followed its flight, then looked at each other. One muttered something, the other shrugged. Both lowered their spears, turned in the direction they'd been heading and kept walking.

Arben breathed out, looked at Lin, shook his head and raised his hand furtively as if to say, 'quiet'. Lin didn't have to be told twice. She exhaled slowly, suddenly aware she'd been holding her breath a long time.

Her body trembled. That was scary. *They* were scary. The strangers had a hard and hostile look; something about their stern faces and strong, stocky bodies frightened Lin. They looked menacing. She didn't want to talk to them, but she wondered why Arben hadn't chosen to say hello. Why did they have to hide? The young pair remained hidden and silent. Finally, at a point that saw the newcomers well clear of the spinney and heading for the horizon, Arben spoke quietly.

"Bandarken," he muttered, his face grave, even scared.

"Bandarken," he repeated and made a strangling gesture at his throat.

Lin learned nothing more about the strangers other than that they were Bandarken, and dangerous. Lin hadn't seen the men until they were right on top of them. This surprised her. Her eyes were good but Arben must've seen them from a kilometre away. He had amazing eyesight. Lin was impressed with his alertness and skill. And he'd taken care of her. He was an unusual man.

Arben explained why she needed to wear the cloak. He indicated by holding his nose and pointing at her that her scent was strong, and any smart hunter could pick up such a smell, even at a distance. The other point was less obvious and harder to signal. He pointed towards her clothes and waved his hand towards the blue of the sky. He flicked his hand to his eyes then back to her. It was an easy colour to see. Okay. She got the point. The cloak had hidden the colour of her clothes and disguised her scent.

So, he had a good sense of smell, too. Lin was not happy

with this. Most people liked the clothes and perfume she wore; especially boys. But Arben was definitely not like the boys she knew. This was a different world with different values. Perhaps she'd forget the gender business for the moment. Humbled by a different perspective of her place in this world, Lin bundled up the cloak and settled it over her bumbag as they resumed their trip back to the valley of the darrabin.

It wasn't far from the spinney to where they'd first met, where she'd charged at Arben to defend the little kangaroo. They'd covered the last kilometres quickly. The darrabin should be on the valley floor around the next bend. Or maybe they'd be up on the plateau looking for food. She didn't want Arben to see the darrabin; he had a club and a spear and maybe his family was still hungry. She couldn't be sure. It was time to thank him though. He'd given her the most exciting afternoon of her life.

✼   ✼   ✼

For his part, Arben had no idea what this strange creature would do in this valley alone. He asked her in sign language where she was going, and Lin waved towards the sun as if to say she was going there.

Arben looked at Lin and thought... she might be from the sun. She was that different from anyone he'd ever met or heard about. But he worried for her safety. She was a visitor and his people – the Pelluken – welcomed strangers and cared for them. Whereas the Bandarken disliked everybody, and this area was contested territory. If they should come upon MeLin he couldn't be sure what they'd do. He hoped she returned home soon and stayed out of their way

Where they stood now was a place the darrabin often occupied, but while they were big and ugly, they were harmless and wouldn't hurt her. Dropcats lurked too but she would be okay if bushier trees were avoided, and she seemed to know that.

The presence of Bandarken alarmed Arben. This was not their usual range; their home territory spread towards the sunset. If they were expanding or changing, then everyone was in danger, including MeLin. He would have to tell his family, and soon. The Bandarken occupied this land long before his people arrived. They repelled visitors and met attempts at friendship with violence. He worried for his family, yes, and as he looked at MeLin, he worried for her too.

*   *   *

Lin caught Arben's gaze. If she was emotionally strained over Little Quilt, she wasn't prepared for her feelings about parting from this good-looking, young man with the quiet, competent manner and quizzical smile. Barbarian he might be, but he was no knuckle-dragger. He may not be the boy she thought she'd meet, but gee, he was cute. Arben aroused feelings in her that hadn't been stirred this way before. She smiled to herself remembering how she'd walked behind his near-naked body a while. And she couldn't forget the gentle shiver of excitement when he'd put his hand on her shoulder back at the camp.

As nice as Arben was to be around, she didn't know him. Departure was near, and Lin was grateful it was taking place before these mounting sensations got the better of her. As it was, she just wanted to kiss him lightly on the cheek. So she did.

He reared back as though he'd been struck.

Arben was as startled as the elder had been when she tipped his nose with that old trick of her dad's. Maybe they didn't kiss here. *Naah, they must.* She'd just surprised him. But his response to her was just as unpredictable. When he saw this was another of those very different things she did he reached out, took her by her shoulders, drew her gently towards him and put his nose close to her nose and cheek. She didn't resist, and they stayed close for long seconds... a pretty Chinese girl and a handsome hunter-gatherer.

There was no space between them as they stood close, bodies touching gently. Lin shivered with the intimacy. She felt Arben do the same. Lin wanted more, but there was no time. They'd found something together, and now they had to part. Finally, Arben drew back, his face soft and sorry. He said something to her, smiled ruefully and held up his hand in farewell. She held up her hand then turned away before he could see the regret in her eyes. When she did look back he was gone, his lissom frame vaulting up the valley wall.

The darrabin were beyond the bend in the valley as Lin had hoped. BeBe was there, large and impressive, and so was Ida... but no Little Quilt. Lin looked around, hoping to spot the stocky infant. They did look much the same and perhaps the dead darrabin at Arben's camp had belonged to another group. Little Quilt wasn't anywhere to be seen. Arben's clan brother must've killed him.

Lin's heart fell, tightness choked her chest. Tears welled. This was not how it should be. Lin needed to share her sorrow with Ida and slowly walked towards the mother darrabin, wondering what if anything she could vision-shift that would make any difference to her grief. She hadn't moved more than a few paces when the missing delinquent trotted out from behind a bush where he'd been having a piss. He ambled back to twist around Ida's stocky legs. Strange little creature he might be – affable, odd and not-too-bright – but here he was, unkempt, unhurt, and very much alive

Lin sobbed with sorrow and joy. The afternoon's emotion found release in the survival of a baby quadruped. She cried loudly; no point holding back in this lonely, desolate world. There was no-one here to listen or care now that her one human contact was gone.

When her sobs subsided to sniffles, Lin blew her nose and took to wondering why she worried so about these frail and vulnerable creatures. The irony that such sturdy beasts could be considered frail and vulnerable was not lost on her. Maybe that was the hassle at the heart of it. Such heavy-duty giants were never going to survive the onset of volcanoes, humans, drought and fire. Maybe they'd adapt to one or two, but not all four at once. They weren't flexible enough.

Extinction was the only end.

It was happening everywhere. Danger threatened life forms from so many sides. Yet people were rallying to help. Someone had to help the darrabin, otherwise it'd be all over for them. *And that someone's gonna have to be me.* There was nobody else. She'd take these creatures to the North Forest, wherever it was. It might only delay their end but, as a member of a species responsible for so many animal extinctions, Lin thought she owed it to them. She could spare whatever days it took. Her parents would understand. They knew her love of animals, and they'd forgive her. She'd tell BeBe her decision now.

BeBe retained an impressive cool upon receiving the news. No jumping up and down, no high fives nor spraying champagne. The first two he couldn't do, something about being supersized with four large legs fixing him stiffly to the ground; the third he'd no idea about. Maybe he'd take a drink from the muddied pond at the head of the ravine.

His response was the quiet, stolid approach he'd always shown; maybe his eye twitched exuberantly. Lin couldn't tell with twitches. BeBe dropped his head. She nodded back. He'd always known that a saviour would lead them to safety in the North Forest; it had been promised. If this slight, strange creature in front of him was the one to take on this task, then so be it. He'd known it from the moment the visitor exited the new sun and was content in his gruff, sombre way that she now knew it too.

BeBe's first job was to gather the members of his clan and any other creatures that wanted to go north. His little pointy-eared buddy would be one. The vision-shifting would do its work and animals would gather to leave upon the dawn. They had no houses to tidy, no services to shut down. They didn't have to pack, they had nothing to take, just the legs, feathers and fur they stood up in. Passports and tickets weren't needed. Food and water would be wherever they could find it. There was no need to wait.

The group would assemble in the valley when the first rays of the sun streaked the eastern horizon, and they'd be on their way. As for Lin, she knew which way was north. *Well sort of, it's thataway.* She swung her arm ninety degrees to the right of the setting sun. She'd wait for the morning and more inspiration. Granma always said good things came to us after a night's rest.

This night Lin stayed warm. The cloak made the difference. Worn inside out with the fur against her skin, Lin tossed and turned worrying about the next day, but she was never cold. There were no flashing images to Ida and Little Quilt to keep out the chill. The cloak was magic and did a complete job of keeping her warm. A comfy Lin thanked the small creatures sacrificed for her comfort and tried to telepath her gratitude to Arben's family for the treasured gift of warmth. She was going to hold onto the cloak whatever happened. It would not be tossed aside; it was a boon in this strange place... and a personal link to Arben.

Lin thought of him often during the night; another gift in this weird world. Her first response to him as brute had morphed into an appreciation of his skills, warmth and generosity. *And he's good-looking.* She pictured his smooth, lithe frame and serious face with the quirky smile resting in one of the bark shelters. She smiled in memory of the troubles she'd caused him and reflected on how people come to us, we know them so briefly and then they're gone. Maybe one day that'd change for her; she had time. She hoped it was with someone as competent and cute as Arben.

Okay, maybe with more clothes and fewer weapons.

15

'MARSUPIALS MARCH'

Lin Beibei, unassuming accounting student, daughter of Lin Xia, mining engineer, and Wang Mei, civilian broom handler, spent a cold night in a warm cloak on a rock ledge in the pre-historic past. She certainly wasn't in Shanghai any more. Peculiar dreams had disturbed her sleep. Curious sensations – images of Arben, his touch, his family, the Bandarken, and Little Quilt, dead and alive – wove a flimsy tapestry of the day just gone. The dream didn't last. With the sun's first rays, the reverie melted like hailstones in the rain.

Suddenly Lin recalled where she was, sat upright on her rock bed, and bumped her head.

"Oww! That hurt!"

She rolled off her perch and stood, holding her forehead. The breath caught in her throat and her face stilled at what the morning had wrought.

Company.

Lots of it.

All staring at her, waiting, and ready to roll.

As she'd gone to sleep, Lin had thought maybe there'd be fifteen to twenty in her travelling troupe. There'd be BeBe and her little buddy, BiZi, and their clans, no more, not a huge group, just big enough to be a challenge. This was so not the case. Vision-shifting had worked; the news had got around and a crowd had gathered in the valley overnight.

A huge crew of animals shuffled about in front of Lin, excited and edgy, like iPhone shoppers queuing for a new model. She was now the designated driver for some two hundred feral creatures of assorted shapes, sizes, and attitude. They stood, sat, or perched in home groups, ruffling their feathers, scratching their hides, shuffling nervously, glaring suspiciously, all watching, all waiting for the saviour to lead them to the promised land.

The saviour was not happy. *What have I done?* Suddenly, the size of the task Lin had set herself hit home. Her head dropped and her shoulders slumped. *Am I crazy?* Sympathy for the darrabin was one thing; leading a massive mob of weird animals to a place she didn't know was another. What did she know about this country, this time, and these creatures? Nothing. She didn't know where the North Forest was. Or if it existed. This was a bad joke. *And, Granma, if these are the good things I get after a night's sleep, then I've slept too long.*

Lin stood on a rock abutment facing a massed mob

of fur, feet, and feathers. With her head bowed, eyes closed and knuckle to her teeth, Lin fought back tears as she battled her doubts. This was so not her. She was not leadership material. *I can't do it. I want out.*

She lifted her head, opened her eyes and looked for an escape. BeBe stood in front of her, Ida and Little Quilt by his side, staring, waiting, their faces a blend of hope and promise. Visions of a small, dead darrabin and scenes of fiery carnage flashed through Lin's mind as she took in this family tableau. *Noo! I can't let them down. I'm all they've got.* But if she hadn't told BeBe she'd do this, she'd quit now. But she couldn't. These animals had to be cared for.

Gotta do it.

C'mon, girl. Pull yourself together!

Lin sucked a deep breath, shook her shoulders, nodded to BeBe and strode to the front of the herd before her backbone shrunk to sardine size. Perhaps they wouldn't know how stupid she felt if she looked to be in charge.

What next? *Maybe I can count them?*

Numbers and lists were Lin's thing; they calmed her, gave her a sense of control. She needed to know how many critters there were; that way if she lost any, she'd know. Lin commenced a count.

It was hopeless. A large part of the party was white birds and none of them would sit still long enough for Lin to get their number. And they all looked alike. Lin thought it might be simpler to survey a shoal of salmon! Maybe she could sort them into home groups.

Some of the creatures Lin knew. The darrabin and giant kangaroos were there, so was BiZi, his ears swivelling and nose twitching in the front row. Well, she thought it was him. He jumped to one side as Lin watched, avoiding the stamping feet of his bigger neighbours.

If he doesn't watch himself, he'll be rural roadkill before we start.

She had to get him some help. There was more than one of him, though. A number of identikit critters ranged alongside the one she thought was BiZi. Some were smaller, but they looked similar. This was going to be a problem. They were like Europeans... they all looked alike.

There were creatures Lin had never seen. A new crew of animals stared at her. Lin looked, blinked, and adjusted her head to another odd reality. The newcomers had BeBe's general body shape but were smaller, even uglier. *Wait up. Uglier is unlikely. BeBe is gross!* The new lot had heads like hippos but with floppy trunks like elephants, only smaller. They were big but not as big as BeBe. He was a four-wheel-drive to their city-sedan. They certainly weren't charming, but they didn't look savage. The alpha male, a particularly battle-scarred brute, stood at the front of the group and stared aggressively. Lin gave him the name Yingjun, Chinese for 'handsome'. His pals were the Snouts.

If Yingjun and the Snouts didn't look overly fierce then there were creatures that did. In particular, four oversized birds about two metres tall. These weren't flighted creatures. They looked like giant, long-legged ducks but without the floppy feet. The fearsome four stared at Lin with a ferocity a duck could never manage; it was as if their eyes bored holes through her. What should she call them?

Bigbirds, of course; that's what you'll be.

The fearsome creatures accepted their new name with an unblinking intensity that made Lin shiver.

The other birds – white, pigeon-toed and with hooked black beaks – were raven-sized with curved yellow crests that spread like a hand fan when they were excited, which was most of the time. The worst thing about them though was their screech... an ear-piercing squawk that left scratches in Lin's brain. These were possibly the birds she'd seen when she'd walked onto the plateau near the disc. So, why were they on this trek? They could fly anywhere. As it turned out the flock was gregarious. The birds were bossy, loud, and liked to stick together. When one decided to come along, they all came. Just like gatecrashers at a party, only noisier.

Koalas were perched in trees in numbers that suggested they were in for the ride. They were twice the size of the modern Australian icon, so how come she hadn't noticed them before? Lin knew koalas to be nocturnal tree-climbers; not daylight trekkers. So how were they going to get to the North Forest? There was no other way but walking. She hadn't seen a bus, although BeBe was big enough. Hopping from tree to tree wasn't on. It'd be up to them to keep up. If they wanted to come, they'd have to make the same speed as everything else.

The oddest animal in Lin's custody turned out to be a prickly customer, an animal the size of a sheep but stubby-legged and stoutly clawed. It had a thin, pointed snout and black eyes protruding from a narrow head at one end of a body-barrel of spines. It was covered from nose to tail with thorns. She hoped these guys were as odd as she was going to get. There were six in her custody, their beady eyes peering at her from just above ground level. She had no idea what they were except they looked like oversized porcupines. Arben would have had a name for them. She didn't. Lin just called them Spike and the Gang.

Lin thought to arrange the creatures into marching formation for the long haul ahead. She had to get them into groups. But how? Where was the famous general Yue Fei when she needed him? If she could channel him, he'd tell her how to organise this lot. But he lived in the Song dynasty which, if she was right about the present time, was a long way in the future. Normally, he'd have been a long time in the past. *Whatever; he's not here. I'll have to be General Lin this morning.*

The speed they travelled was going to depend on the slowest walker. Right now, that'd probably be the koalas although she didn't know how fast Spike and the gang could cover ground.

Bigbirds looked capable of speed with those long, strong legs. And Lin knew how fast a kangaroo could hop, but she wasn't sure how long they could keep it up. BiZi and his clan had short legs; they were a problem. Maybe some riding help could be offered. Lin presented an idea to

BeBe when she was sure it was him she was 'talking' to and not mentally babbling to the first three identical darrabin she tried vision-shifting on. Somehow, he seemed better at it than his buddies. She asked if it were possible for him to carry other creatures on his back. BeBe considered this odd but he didn't think about it long. He would do it if Lin said so; she was taking them to the North Forest after all.

When the solution finally presented, Lin could have kicked herself for not seeing it sooner. The animals staring at her were mainly marsupials, animals with pouches. That's what made them marsupials; from the smallest to the largest, they all had pouches. Even the darrabin had them, although theirs opened backwards. Probably a good way to keep the dirt out. Marsupials were the movers and carriers of the mammal set. The large kangaroos had pouches the size of a backpack. Maybe the kangaroos that didn't have young could carry the small folk like BiZi in a frontpack, more or less. She'd check it out.

Lin could vision-shift with BeBe; Yingjun; the two lead kangaroos including DaJiao (Bigfoot), and to a lesser extent the koalas and Spike. Birds were a problem. Bigbirds and the white birds she couldn't 'talk' with at all, although BeBe could in a limited fashion. So that's how it worked. She vision-shifted with BeBe, DaJiao, Yingjun and BiZi; they communicated with the others.

After some baffling brainwork with BeBe, Lin sorted a plan. DaJiao agreed that the female kangaroos in his group, those with small young, could carry BiZi and his family alongside their usual family members in a traveling twin-pack. The leader of a band of smaller kangaroos also agreed; carrying BiZi's band was okay with him. One of them could fit into a pouch alongside the usual occupant. They were in there already; BiZi loved it. He'd always wanted to ride like this, warm and safe in a fur-lined pocket. It was just like life as a pup. Lin thought maybe the koalas could straddle the backs of the darrabin as long as they didn't dig their claws in. That should work, in theory. It might be harder in practice. She'd 'talk' it over with BeBe. Spike was a problem. For the time being he and the gang would have to walk. They weren't at risk from anything much as they were well-defended, but they might be slow.

The eastern sky creased gold and pink as the cavalcade readied for its journey to the North Forest. The centre of the valley flooded with early light; it was also awash with grunts, coughs, squeaks, squawks and screeches. The groups shoved and shouldered, bumped and bustled, finding a place but far from politely. Snarling, kicking, growling, hissing and biting seemed the way to deal with intrusion on your space.

Lin was appalled. *This'll be interesting. They'll kick and butt each other all the way to the North Forest.* Who's going to keep them apart? Not her. Get between two ornery darrabin and she'd be squished flatter than a wonton wrapper. It'd have to be BeBe. He was bigger. Only Spike and the gang stood quiet in the middle of the melee. The restless cohorts shuffled about them like coyotes dodging cactus.

Through BeBe, Lin waved two bigbirds to their places as outriders on either side at the front. They were tall, had good eyes and could run and kick if necessary. Lin hoped that wouldn't be necessary. They were insurance. And out in front, they wouldn't be staring at her. Those birds had eyes like zombies and thighs like sumo wrestlers. They were scary. The other two bigbirds took up the same task at the rear.

The two male kangaroos found their places on opposite sides of the front line; their females behind them... the heads of the BiZi clan sticking out of their pouches like big-eared headlights. The darrabin were in the middle; BeBe's group towards the front, the other male and his clan towards the rear. Separating the two darrabin groups were Spike and the gang, the koalas and Yingjun and the snouts. The white birds squawked in the trees. Lin 'told' them through BeBe to look for accessible water and trees and lead them in that direction. Lin hoped this would work. Keeping these critters together was like clutching an armful of eels.

Lin's one purpose was to have these animals live a little longer, a wish built more on hope than certainty. It seemed okay so far. She'd done her best and was ready to roll. The cloak hung down her back supported by a loop around her shoulders and balanced on her bumbag. It was comfortable, and necessary. The water bottle was full. She was wearing the same outfit she wore when she started this adventure, along with her crushable hat. She felt less like a legendary leader and more like a tourist in Tiananmen Square; all she needed was a camera, but her phone wasn't working.

Lin took her place upfront as head shepherd of an odd flock, BeBe by her side. As main marshal she thought to say something memorable to get them moving. 'Wagons Roo-ooll', came to mind. Among her dad's DVD collection was an ancient John Wayne movie about wagon trains in the American West. That's what Wayne said at the start of an expedition, waving his arm forward and spurring his horse. Her dad admired John Wayne. Lin didn't know why, and he couldn't explain. Wayne was an actor playing an invented character riding a rented horse in a fictional film. He wasn't real. But this was. Lin was a college student who didn't know what she was doing or where she was going. There was no horse to ride, and BeBe didn't look equine material.

"Marsupials, march," Lin mumbled, and with a wave of her arm as a tribute to old movies and her dad, led the herd out on an uncertain trek to an unknown destination.

The mob rolled away like an ancient caravan on the Silk Route. The tight lines of Lin's legion lasted one minute, just the time it took for a darrabin to decide he couldn't go another step without tasting the leaves of a small shrub. He stopped to graze. The following animals crushed to a halt behind his broad backside, trampling over each other like pedestrians on a blocked escalator. The teeming animals somehow managed to avoid the needle-like points of Spike and the gang. The spiny creatures stayed quiet in the centre of the milling melee. Others ringed about them like revellers stepping round a drunken derelict on a city street.

Lin heard rather than saw the confusion.

"C'mon guys, we've got to get further than this. We're not even out of the valley."

She vision-shifted BeBe to get his wayward mate on the move and keep him that way. He did, and the group moved on, if not quite as organised as before.

The crested white birds returned together. One of them flew down to land on BeBe's back while the others squawked to the ground. One stayed in the tree; Lin had noted that one of them was always on watch while the others did stuff. They were rarely quiet though; their rasping screeches an annoying constant, like out-of-synch elevator music, but louder. So much louder.

After the informant flew back to the flock, BeBe turned his slow-moving body slightly right and continued plodding. Every animal simultaneously changed direction. Lin went with them.

This ability to move in unison impressed Lin. When she 'talked' with BeBe later he showed her that the birds had spotted water and trees, more towards the rising sun. He didn't show how far this would be or how they all made the move together. They just did. There was so much she had to learn about these creatures but half-an-hour in and the plan was working. Maybe three hours was all they could walk in a morning, followed by a snooze in the shade. The midday sun was too hot to continue the trek. Another long walk in the late afternoon would see them up to feeding time, and sleep.

As she walked, Lin watched the bigbirds she'd chosen

for point duty. She couldn't tell them apart. A whiteboard marker would have been handy; she could've written numbers on their legs. Next time.

The majestic birds never deviated from their task, even through the darrabin-diner debacle. They were an extraordinary sight; tall, stately creatures moving with impressive dignity, upper bodies still, large legs pulling up at the knees to plant their heavy feet forward. The birds' heads swung like gun turrets, scanning the horizon as they walked. They looked like giraffe-sized wading birds high-stepping through a swamp.

Lin didn't know anything about these fantastic creatures. They never made it to the 21st century or their photos would've been on the 'net with a Twittertag #reallybigbirds. What a loss! They looked super-scary, but she thought she could rely on them. It was silly, she knew, but bigbirds' presence, their size and strength carried a sense of security the other animals didn't. They were formidable creatures whose penetrating stare would scare even Nian, the New Year monster.

As they walked through the morning, a hillock eased over the horizon. Lin saw it coming. *Now that's different.* She hadn't seen many hills at all. Not even a bump. The plain they crossed was grass-covered and level but with an uneven surface. Now and then a shallow gully sliced across the flatness. They'd arrive without warning and when they did Lin had to walk one way or another to find the lowest point to get the herd across. There was no water in these gullies. None. Lin wasn't impressed.

The hillock grew larger as the herd plodded on. Lin made it her mid-morning target. She'd get there with this motley mob, stand on top of it, take a break and see what lay ahead.

Maybe she'd see the North Forest.

16

AWAY FROM THE HILL

Lin Beibei, one-time accounting student and now head wildlife wrangler, found herself standing, then sitting on a small hillock in an alien world, leading a mob of animals she didn't know on a quest to a place she wasn't sure existed. Putting it that way was really comforting. *Not.* But she'd got them this far without losing any. That had to count for something. Still, doubt hung around her like a fog and worry shook her shoulders as she remembered her home, her parents, her friends and the studies she should be doing.

She turned to look at BeBe, Ida and Little Quilt. The trio stared back at her. Lin saw hope in their freaky faces. Her shoulders lifted, and a smile flickered across her face only to disappear like a snuffed-out candle. Doubt and indecision gnawed at her self-belief. Lin shook her head. *Stop it! I can do this; I can get them there. We're going on!*

Lists gave Lin confidence, so she ticked off what she'd done so far.

Okay, they'd assembled at dawn. With help from BeBe and BiZi she'd sorted them into groups, organised some pouch-sharing, got directions from the birds and headed north. *I think.* She'd got them to this hillock; no fights, no losses, no drama. And they were okay so far, although she couldn't see anything like a forest ahead. It could be a long journey. Time to get going again.

Lin waved at BeBe and he signalled the herd to get moving. She waved at bigbirds and they nodded in unison. Lin was amazed and amused. *How do they do that?* The four giant birds made ready at the corners of the cavalcade as the animals jostled into home groups. The mob rumbled and grumbled into action, following their two-legged leader on a trek to the maybe-mythical North Forest.

It was almost noon when BeBe signalled a stop could be near. The white birds had told him, and Lin agreed. This much walking was not BeBe's thing; he was weary and in need of rest. So were his kin. The larger animals were munching meanderers more than tireless trekkers. A stop would be good.

Next to a waterhole some way ahead stood a small woodlot. Birds and koalas could rest in the trees, the others could graze or lie in the shade. BeBe, at Lin's request, asked the white birds to survey the trees for dropcats and assess the water supply. The last thing she wanted was to draw these creatures under the ripping claws and jaws of an apex predator. The white birds took off to scout the woodland and returned a few minutes later still chattering, still squawking, still busy. They could see nothing in the trees, one of them reported to BeBe, and the water looked good.

Like rental ponies returning to stable, the parade moved quickly to drop in contentment in the shade. Lin let her bundles fall to the ground, retrieved her water bottle, took a sip and sat with her back against a tree trunk. It was so good to get off her feet.

Within seconds Lin's odd entourage foraged for food. She watched as they scattered to their favoured places and began to graze. Could there have been a weirder, wackier group in animal history? Probably not, well not since Noah's Ark, the boat The Bible talked about. If Noah had gathered animal pairs onto an ark, though, it was probably into the future from where she was now. Just how did he cope with all that cooped-up, pooped-up livestock? Who cleaned up after them? What did they eat? How did he keep them from eating each other? She'd have to talk to someone who knew about it when she got home. Maybe she could write the book.

Soon it was time to move on again. But there was trouble at koala camp. The tree dwellers were drowsy, unwilling to go on. This was nap time and they were grumpy. Daytime never saw them at their sweetest, and more walking was about to shift grumpy to surly. Lin knew koalas weren't walkers; they were climbers, scratchers and sitters, nocturnal ones at that. The only walking they did was from one tree to another. And then only if they couldn't get across any other way. If forced to the ground, they clambered awkwardly on all fours. The distance they'd covered this day was more than most had walked in their lifetimes. If they were to walk on, then it'd be at night when they were awake. Had they been able to stamp a foot while sitting jammed in a tree fork they would have done so. As it was, they scratched branches and coughed agitatedly. They were adamant; they weren't putting another paw forward. No way.

Time for Plan B. They couldn't walk at night. It'd be too dangerous. And Lin couldn't abandon them. They were with her on this trip, and she liked them. She had to find another way. So, what was Plan B? Lin racked her brain but the only thing she came up with was something she'd thought of earlier... get them onto the backs of the darrabin. The idea sounded okay; the darrabin were big enough to carry just about anything short of a blue whale, and she didn't have any of those. The problem would be organising it. It'd be tricky but worth a try.

With his approval, and forewarning, Lin stood behind Max – short for Maximum – the alpha male koala, reached round his stubby frame, grasped him by his forearms, squeezed them against his body and lifted. No go; Max was far too heavy. Lin was strong, but she might as well have tried to pick up his tree. And Max was okay with the idea and almost obliging for a slow-moving, cranky critter. The others would never be so helpful; they were wild animals and wary of humans, even those with honest intentions. They weren't about to have Lin pick them up and put them on a darrabin even if she could.

Lin tried another approach. This time she got one darrabin onto its haunches and had Max get onto its back. The darrabin grunted in pain as Max used his claws to climb up; they sunk in deeper as the darrabin stood up. Max's claws were long and pointed; they could cut through the thick hides of darrabin. That wasn't going to work.

So much for Plan B. What was Plan C?

Lin vision-shifted with BeBe and Max. *Get your buddies into a tree, Max. That one.* She pointed at a tree with a long, strong, horizontal branch about three metres from the ground. The darrabin were to walk under the branch and the koalas could drop onto them one at a time. *And gently, Max,* Lin emphasised. *Gently. Easy with the claws. Drop carefully onto the darrabin.* Once aboard they could hang on, firmly but lightly, as they did when they were cubs.

The darrabin were totally unenthused with this but BeBe volunteered them. He was to do it too, so it must be okay. Plan C worked. Lin was impressed. The koalas dropped on like jockeys mounting horses at the Hong Kong races. Only one of them fell off and had to get back up the tree to reload. A baby, she took to the experience like a kid going up and down a playground slide. She fell off more than once just for the fun of it, an unlikely koala trait. If this country had dropcats, it now had dropbears. Lin hoped they'd be dropping off to sleep, clinging snoozily to their hairy hosts as they lumbered on. After a short break, the mounted cavalry was ready to ride.

The darrabin were slow walkers; Lin reckoned a hot Friday after lunch in Mr Wu's maths class was hyper-lively by comparison. But Spike and his pals were even slower, and more ponderous. Their bodies were strong with powerful legs and clawed feet that ripped through wood and earth. But when they walked their front feet turned in making their shoulders swing, their bodies swaying side-to-side like three-masted galleons in a rolling sea. Just not as fast.

Lin didn't doubt their heart and commitment; it was their speed that had her worried. They dawdled. They'd be like the tortoise in the tortoise and hare myth; they'd get there, but late... very late. Tough and strong. Sure! But walk long distances? Definitely not. They were a worry. Like the koalas, they weren't built for long-distance hiking. She'd have to have a Plan B for them soon.

Where was the North Forest? To the north. *Yeah, sure, but how far? And will I know it when I see it?* Probably not. That was Lin's next problem as the herd trudged on. North's where the forest was, and she hoped they were heading that way. She was supposed to know; that was part of her great-saviour job description. It was nice of BeBe and BiZi to think she could lead them along the high road to a haven. But a routemap would have been helpful. Maybe the white birds could flap around and find forests to the north. Then there'd be something to aim at. Otherwise, this colourful cavalcade risked becoming an unruly roadshow. BeBe could seek help from the birds at the next stop.

And the next stop wasn't far. The herd bivouacked by a bunch of waterholes fringed with tall grass and scrubby trees. The white birds scattered over the grassland like cotton buds on carpet. Crests raised, eyes flashing, mouths agape, they squawked raucous claims at each other over insults real or imagined. They were noisy.

At some point the waterholes had been bigger. Over the seasons they'd shrunk to muddy pools connected by sluggish rills of murky water. Those animals that needed water drank noisily and gustily, their huge feet trampling the edges of the pools, spreading the muddiness further out. Yingjun and the snouts wallowed in it, frolicking about like pigs in slop.

Lin looked on. "I'm not drinking from that. Uuergh!"

There was still water left in her bottle. It'd do. It'd have to. Maybe they'd find a clearer stream tonight. It'd be nice to get clean water and maybe a pond deep enough for a bath, even rinse her clothes. She needed it; her jeans and t-shirt needed it. She could shelter in her cloak while the clothes dried on a bush. It all depended on whether the birds could find such a place.

The birds? The waterholes were suddenly silent. At first, deep in thought, Lin hadn't noticed the quiet. But when she did, it was almost tomblike, akin to walking into an exam room mid-test. The birds' crests were down, their cackles quelled. The herd had stilled. Drinking stopped, chewing paused, grumbling quit; the travellers stood poised like actors waiting for a cue. The world around the waterholes lay eerie and expectant.

Lin remembered the previous tremor. *Not again?*

Suddenly, somewhere, something shifted under her feet. Upwellings of molten magma rumbled through subterranean caverns. The animals stood trembling and terrified as the earth shuddered. The shaking stopped long enough for a collective gasp of breath from the herd, then started again. Lungs hurt, hearts pounded, and voices stilled. The quake was over in seconds, but it took time for the fearful animals to settle. Lin looked around, found BeBe's terror-filled eyes and communicated they might move on. He dropped his head in agreement, turned to the north and recommenced his slow plod. The others fell into place.

As fear of the tremor ebbed, Lin's thoughts turned to Arben as they'd done often since their parting. She had known boys at school and college, some better than others. Yet she'd never met a man who stirred her in quite the way the young hunter did. *Yeah, I'm a long way from home and maybe I'm lonely. And, okay, he's the only human I've had anything to do with for a few days, and he was different.* There was more to it than that, though. And it wasn't just his neat, tight bum, nice as it was. She wondered if hers looked as attractive to the creatures walking behind her?

Lin glanced over her shoulder into the glum face of a plodding darrabin, a furry-eared sidekick asleep on its shoulders. Lin sniffed, miffed. That said it all; they so weren't pawing the earth in primitive passion over her shapely bum in tight jeans. *Too bad, they don't know what they're missing.* Maybe it was something to do with

Arben's hunter role; the Me Lin-You Tarzan, routine. A primal excitement had edged their meeting. His touch on her shoulder, their brief embrace when they'd parted stayed in her psyche, smouldering like the embers of his family's fire. And it wouldn't have taken much to kick it into a roaring blaze.

Lin contented herself with reminiscences as she shepherded her wobbly flock towards wherever the North Forest might be.

17

MONKEY AND
THE DRAGON

Lin didn't see it coming. Towards evening, with her body bent and eyes smudged with sweat, the little leader wasn't looking for drop-offs. Most of the walk had been over flat grassland, but, after cresting a slight incline, she almost fell into a shallow dale much like where she'd met Ida and Little Quilt. But this time there were more trees flanking a clean, clear stream in a verdant valley. The bigbirds looked at her; they'd come to the edge, and paused. Lin stared back at them and wagged a finger in mock rebuke.

"No fair, you guys. You're taller than me and you saw it coming. Let me know next time. Squawk or something."

Bigbirds looked at Lin then each other, and said nothing.

A long day had passed at the head of her rumbling

roadshow. Driving the herd was hot, dirty work. Lin was worn out and weary. She needed water, food, rest, and a bath. A clammy t-shirt stuck to her chest, denim clung to her legs and sweat trickled down her face and back. Lin paused to suck in a breath while she tugged the t-shirt off her chest with two fingers and flapped in air. It worked for all of a second. She pulled off her crumpled hat, slapped at the flies and wiped the sweat from her brow. The flies were back before she'd donned her hat again.

The herd rumbled to a halt behind her. BeBe lumbered in at the head of the darrabin, the koalas sitting like furry jockeys on large woolly steeds. Lin knew it was BeBe without turning her head. Lin's nose wrinkled; she shook her head and made a face. *He's so rank. He stinks like rotting garbage wrapped in manure.*

The kangaroos hopped in next, their pointy-nosed free-riders jutting like headlights. The snouts ambled in after them. Finally, the other two bigbirds ushered in Spike and the gang, whose short legs and leisurely walking pace guaranteed they'd bring up the rear. Nobody wanted to risk one of those quills in their own rear, so they let them arrive last. A squall of white birds flapped in and settled on the grass. They were all here. All of them had got through the day.

Lin had kept them together.

That felt good. *I can do this, okay?*

The herd snuffled and snorted, nostrils twitching at the smell of water. Like her, they wanted food, water, and rest. And they wanted them *now*. The animals stood poised on the valley's edge like a lost tribe looking over its homeland. Lin held them back. It didn't look like home to her. The valley didn't feel right. Lin gazed over the terrain, wary and suspicious. There was something wrong with this place. She didn't know what, but she didn't like it. The valley looked too pretty, green and serene, the peace so prevalent as to be ominous. Lin had been in this land long enough to know things weren't always as they seemed.

BeBe stared out over the hollow, his head swinging slowly. The big beast's ears flicked, and his nostrils twitched. Lin looked at him; he was watchful as well. And he knew this country. If he was worried, then something was amiss. Right? But what? The giant darrabin and petite human exchanged glances. BeBe continued swinging his head – listening, looking, sniffing – scouring the scenery for anything odd. Lin didn't know what to look for as the whole country was odd to her, and she could see nothing different. But the bad feeling festered.

The rowdy, white watchmen were sent to check. The trekkers waited, hungry, restless, and thirsty. Those with four feet shuffled them, those with feathers fluffed them, those with pointy ears twitched them agitatedly and all swivelled their heads impatiently awaiting the white birds' return. Eventually the flock flapped in, quiet and subdued. A couple landed on BeBe's broad back and made their message known. He sent images to Lin.

The birds had flown to trees each way along the river and couldn't see anything wrong; they couldn't see much movement at all, and that puzzled them. But their senses were as sharp as their squawks were loud, and Lin welcomed their silence. They were never quiet for long and if they couldn't find anything wrong then there was nothing to stop the herd from eating and drinking.

She looked at BeBe; he dropped his head. Lin took that for a 'yes', skipped over the valley's edge and scooted to one side. Seconds later an avalanche of fur, feathers and feet rolled over the valley's lip and bumped and bustled to the bottom where it trundled towards the water like kids to a candy counter. Little Quilt slid the whole way on his bum, front feet and rounded rump taking the shocks. If he could have squealed with joy, he would have. After the rush, bigbirds, the koalas, and Spike and his buddies found their way down slowly, their very long or very short legs not right for downhill dashes. Picking her way demurely, Lin felt more like a teacher in charge of naughty schoolkids than a leader on a long march.

By the time she made it to the stream the drinking was nearly done. Lin watched them finish. The darrabin waded into the stream up to their bellies and guzzled litres of liquid, raising their huge heads from time to time while water sloshed from their sloppy chops. The smaller creatures went at it tails up, heads down, daintier, but just as desperate. Bigbirds thrust their beaks into the river, lifted their heads and let the water flow slowly down their long throats. It was graceful and effective, but slow. White birds did the same. The snouts went at it differently. They waded into the stream and held their mouths under water while their high, wide nostrils stayed above it. It was fast and efficient. Not for the first time Lin thought BeBe was like a rhino whereas the snouts were hippos.

What the herd drank from, they dumped in. Large pads of fresh droppings steamed downstream like circular tugboats.

"Eeeuw, you guys, that's gross," Lin complained to the heedless herd.

"Didn't your mothers tell you not to piss in the sink – let alone poop in the bath? Obviously not," she finished, as another brown barrage hit the water and steamed away.

The herd's hygiene-happy leader walked upstream to seek clean water in a shallow rill. Lin washed her hands, splashed water on her face and refilled her bottle. On her way back to the herd she picked berries from shrubs that stood next to each other by the valley's edge. Lucky she wasn't a big eater; there was barely enough to stop her belly rumbling. This place didn't provide easily-gettable food. There was nothing like her mum's dumplings about. Arben would know where to find stuff, but he wasn't here. *And that's a shame 'cos he was nice. Don't even think about it; he's gone, and you've got work to do.* With dinner done, it was time to rest.

Lin was on her way to a possible campsite when she saw the hubbub before she heard it. Downstream by a wide pool a number of kangaroos jostled about, their movements edgy and agitated. What were they up to? *We're done for the day, guys. Give it a rest, please.* A tired Lin couldn't see what bothered them; their jumpy bodies blocked her view. But she was curious, and a crowd had gathered. Like a shopper drawn to a bargain, Lin went looking for action.

The kangaroos' shuffling movements drew some of them aside and Lin saw what disturbed them.

"Oh my God," she rasped, half aloud, a queasy feeling spreading in her gut.

Lin stepped back, hand to throat, heart drumming, eyes wide, and ready to run. Then she froze.

"Oh my God. No!"

An enormous snake lay coiled in the water in front of her, its long body wound around a small kangaroo. As the herd had spread along the waterhole the serpent had reared from the reeds, seized the young animal by the foreleg, dragged it into the stream and wrapped it in suffocating coils. It happened in seconds. Most of the kangaroos bolted in terror. A few remained, restless, fidgety and frightened. But not one would enter the water to help their struggling kin.

Lin shuddered.

If she'd thought the black snake was big, this creature made it look like an earthworm. It was massive, slick and sinuous with a body as round as a small tree. The serpent's head, small for its body, squared near the eyes then tapered to a long, rounded snout packed with fangs, raked back and sharp. Yellow-grey scales with a repetitive black pattern like clubs on a playing card ran its length. Lin's frantic brain thought *Anaconda*, from an old DVD. But this wasn't Brazil, and this wasn't a movie.

This was a massive python, real and deadly.

The victim, coils wrapped around its chest and forepaws, was struggling desperately... kicking, thrusting and splashing wildly. The young kangaroo fought doggedly but the serpent's size and strength made the end inevitable. The snake had seized the kangaroo with its teeth, but they weren't the killer weapon. Lin could see that, and it horrified her.

Every time the kangaroo breathed out the python squeezed tighter, not letting the trapped animal expand its chest to pull in air. Lin knew it was a matter of time, and not much at that. The victim – head thrown back, ears flattened, mouth open, eyes bulging – wheezed painfully, straining for oxygen it couldn't suck in. The little creature's movements were becoming less frantic and more pitiful as Lin watched. It was losing the battle for air... and was about to die.

Lin's head screamed, 'Go!'; her heart said, 'Stay'. The last place she wanted to be was up close with a lethal serpent crushing a kangaroo. She turned to run, then stopped. Bile swept into her throat, but even with her belly churning Lin couldn't break clear. Flight had become freeze. She stood petrified, staring at the kangaroo's death throes while her mind whirled in confusion. Her job was to get the herd to the North Forest. Something had to be done, and fast. She was the leader. It was up to her. If the kangaroo was lost, the quest was lost. How could she hold them together if she couldn't protect one little one? Lin shook off her inertia, swallowed her fear, cleared her throat, spat into the grass and looked for a weapon.

Fallen branches littered the bank. Lin dropped her bumbag and cloak, picked up a bough, shouldered a kangaroo aside, swung the bough high over her head and smashed it down behind the serpent's head. Lin winced as she hammered the snake with everything she had. The blow jolted her arms and jarred her body. But if it hurt her it barely bothered the python. The lethal creature just swung its head to stare down the threat. Lin shrunk back, petrified by the monstrous serpent that glared at her over a short stretch of riverbank, its eyes black and hooded, jaws gaping, fangs dripping water and blood.

The brute'll kill me. It'll crush the kangaroo then kill me. The flash of fear stirred something visceral in Lin, something primitive and primal like never before. Rage flamed in her gut, the lust for vengeance surged through her blood. Her head cleared, her eyes narrowed as her jaw clenched and her fists gripped tightly around the bough; Lin was in the fight now.

Cold fury replaced fear.

The herd was her tribe, her family; she was their leader, protector and 'mother'. This creature could destroy them, and her quest. *Not while I'm in charge.*

The world shrunk to Lin and the murderous serpent. Everything else blurred into nothingness. The snake started this fight, but she'd finish it. Lin hefted the bough, holding it two-handed over her head like a spear. The python hadn't let go its grip on the kangaroo, but it reared its head, hissing hostility, and struck at Lin. Screaming with rage and defiance, she drove the bough at the serpent.

The shaft drove into the snake's throat and the creature reared away in pain and shock. With the weight of her forward thrust Lin stumbled into the stream falling hard on the bough. The python's head went under water and Lin rammed home her advantage. She jammed the bough down and leant on it with all her weight. The branch wedged in the python's throat and its head caught under a sunken log. It couldn't pull free. Lin kept pushing.

Struggling to get loose as water entered its lungs, the reptile released the kangaroo, which scrambled to the bank. Lin couldn't let go; she had to hang on or it would kill her. The serpent writhed and thrashed like an insane slinky. Waves and troughs surged across the pool. Water flayed the reeds and rushes. Muddy breakers crashed against the pool's edges and splashed over the bank to run back in seething whorls. The stench of rotting mud caught in Lin's nostrils. The remaining animals bolted in terror. The massive python waged a fight for life, its coils twisting, flashing and flailing until they reflexively wound around the one thing that threatened it... Lin Beibei.

The snake's body whipped around Lin then clamped, the coils tightening like wire around a bale. The python squeezed harder, ever harder, jamming Lin's ribs against her spine, squashing her breasts, stifling her lungs. She shrieked with pain. *But I can't drop the bough, it's my only hope.* Crushed by the coils and knee-deep in water, Lin kept driving the serpent's head into the mud as the snake wound ever tighter around her body.

"Got to hold on."

As her chest cramped and her breathing laboured, Lin wheezed noisily, each breath harder to drag in than the last. Drenched with water, struggling for air, every muscle and bone strained, Lin fought for life... the serpent's or hers.

"Die, you evil bastard. Die!", she gasped.

The battle took its toll. Lin's strength was fading. But with her energy ebbing and oblivious of everything but survival, she kept forcing the python's head into the muck. A black mist descended on her brain as her oxygen was lost. She would die in the river, alone.

"No! No, you won't kill me, you bastard! Die! Die!"

Lin wheezed as she sagged forward clinging to the bough, the weight of her exhausted body the only thing between her and death. She dropped to her knees, the heavy body of the snake dragging her down. The water rose to her waist, her chest. Lin's hands slid down the bough as her grasp weakened. Her head fell forward.

Release.

The pressure left her chest.

Lin staggered to her feet, sucking air in short, shuddering sobs, her lungs greedy for oxygen. Mired in the mud and still leaning on the bough, the warrior woman felt the coils loosen. Finally, they flopped limp and inert as the serpent succumbed to the water and the weight of the woman who'd driven it down to death. The snake's lifeless form slowly unwound, the current dragging it from around Lin's legs. The body stretched out downstream waving slowly like a tethered streamer, its head impaled at Lin's feet and the long shape and pale underbelly glistening in the ebbing ripples and slanted rays of the late-afternoon sun.

The battle was over.

Lin dropped the branch, collapsed onto the bank and hauled her body out of the water.

"Yesss," she sobbed. "Yes."

Hands clenched and face down on the sodden bank she struggled for breath, her wet body racked with shudders she couldn't control.

"Beat you, you bastard," she hissed.

It took time, but the warmth of the sun and the soft comfort of the thick grass eventually brought her around. The shaking eased, and her pent-up muscles relaxed.

Lin pushed onto her elbows and looked around. It was late afternoon and the sun was descending behind layered cloud. A gentle breeze flitted through the trees. A cascade of tiny, white moths fluttered and fell over the far side of the drifting stream. A scatter of small birds flew in to feed off waterside shrubs, their light, bright chirping the only sound. The valley was calm, pleasant and peaceful.

No creatures clustered around. Nobody was watching. There was no 'family' gathering. The herd was somewhere else. The darrabin and kangaroos were grazing along the valley wall, the white birds clustered downstream. Bigbirds strolled alongside the river while the snouts waded upstream through a shallow pool. The waterhole had returned to calm. The valley had resumed its placid, pristine state. The only evidence of the fight was a dead snake, the turbid water and a young kangaroo gently licking its forepaw.

Lin struggled to take this in. She'd risked her life to save that little hopper, went to war with the largest snake she'd ever seen, and no-one wanted to know. No-one was there to applaud her courage, rejoice in the victory, hold her hand, wipe her brow, offer her a medal, give her a kiss... anything. What's more, no-one seemed at all interested. *What's wrong with this lot?* Lin looked at DaJiao cropping a nearby tree branch as if nothing had happened.

"Hey you, you oversized, leaf-munching lunch-bucket. It was your offspring I went to battle over. I saved him! Where were you? You'd think you'd wanna shake paws or something."

DaJiao glanced at Lin, looked back at the branch, and munched another mouthful.

Understanding came slowly to Lin; this was life for DaJiao and the herd. A kangaroo could've been killed; so what? Another would take its place. It hadn't died so life went on as usual. A near-death was nothing. No such thoughts entered the large leaf-eater's brain as Lin watched him chomping on the tree; his grey matter wasn't that big or active. If he could've spoken DaJiao might have said, 'Whatever, thanks, but get over it', or the kangaroo equivalent. This was raw life in a harsh world. Even now, somewhere in the valley an offspring of the dead serpent would look to expand its territory and find a mate.

Lin's one offer of solace and support came from BiZi. The little creature had been in a gully when the battle began and had stayed there, timid and terrified, until the fight was finished. With the hubbub over he hopped over to sit by Lin as she recovered at the water's edge. She reached down distractedly and scratched behind his big ears as the tiny creature rubbed tentatively against her wet legs.

"Thank you, BiZi. I should've known you'd care."

It was the first close contact between Lin and the little visitor to her room. BiZi didn't know what this ordeal had taken from Lin, but he sensed its importance. For her part, Lin was comforted by his company. She spoke knowing he wouldn't understand.

"I'm not sure why you and BeBe brought me here, my little friend. But I could have died, and nobody would've known. But I didn't, and you're here and we'll go on and find this forest for you."

Finally, Lin got to her feet, unsteady and bewildered. She found her damp and dirty hat, jammed it on her wet head, retrieved her bumbag and cloak and bent down to pat BiZi. He looked up at her, rubbed against her legs then moved away to return to his kind.

The stream was still muddy. At the far end of the pool where the river broke into a shallow run, the body of the snake lay washed up crossways, cast upon rocks and debris left from a previous high water. The serpent's length spanned the width of the stream, congealed blood trailing from its slack jaws, long body bowing downstream where the water pressure was strongest. The current rippled over its lifeless form. The bough Lin had used to deadly effect bobbed in the water, nudging the dead serpent as if trying to prod it awake.

Just seeing it again made Lin's shoulders tremble and her gut cramp. Tears came, and she turned away. *That could have been me.* This time the snake lost; the serpent would feed the carrion creatures. Monkey slew the Dragon, but she mightn't be so lucky next time.

Lin had no idea how she'd summoned the strength to kill such a serpent. Her feelings swirled in confusion. The rage that possessed her, the fury that stormed out of her psyche to kill the creature was an unknown. *Was that really me? I've never felt such rage before. Ever.*

It might all have ended very differently. Lin looked again at the massive serpent lying lifeless across the pool and shuddered.

18

ONCE BITTEN

The battle over, Lin sat back against a tree, the late afternoon sun warming her body as it soothed her spirit. Nothing in Lin's life had prepared her for the callous savagery of a cruel serpent in an uncaring country. She never wanted to see a snake again. Never. Ever. *What a brute!* She could've died, and her parents would've known nothing. Lin's mind drifted to her parents; her mother busy at home, her dad away working somewhere. Lin had never been away from her parents for long and she worried about them. What must they be thinking with her gone?

And what of Song? What would her buddy make of this weird world? Maybe it'd be strange enough to stop her talking. Not likely. Lin smiled as the thought. More likely pandas'll eat porridge and tigers vote vegan. She'd want to hear about this snake, though. It'd freak her out. She hated snakes as much as Lin. *I'll text her...*

Lin laughed.

"Yeah, right, and after that I'll go to the stall behind that tree and buy a bowl of noodles, chicken and chilli. I wish."

Gotta stop talking to nobody. So not a good sign.

With her reverie shattered, and back in this weird world, Lin thought about what to do before the sun set – what she said she'd do if she found clean water – wash. All she had were the clothes she was wearing and from hat to sneakers, they were wet, slimy and filthy. *I've gotta wash everything.* But not in this part of the stream. She wasn't going near that pond again. Not ever.

She'd find a snake-less place. The stream must have spots where the water was shallow, and you could see things before they leapt up to bite you. While Lin thought the snake was probably a one-of-a-kind, apex predator, she couldn't be sure. Most likely it had killed everything in the area, which was why the white birds saw so little life. *BeBe and I were right to be suspicious of this place. Granma always told me to trust my instincts.*

Lin walked upstream to where the darrabin were grazing and watched the animals foraging. It was quiet, peaceful, almost farm-like, so different to the thrashing violence of minutes earlier. Snakes aside, this was a green and pleasant valley, a sweet spot to spend the night and wash her clothes. A wide, flat run sheltered by tall trees looked a possibility. She saw no lurking monster as she patrolled the streamside grasses, checking closely. *No more snakes, please.*

Lin took off her clothes and entered the water. It

was unlikely there were prying eyes, so she wasn't embarrassed. The darrabin didn't care what she looked like, naked or clothed, and while Spike might be horny he was no threat to her... unless she mistook him for a chair. Lin walked out a few metres. The water flowed cool, but the stones were slippery. More than once she slipped and pinwheeled her arms for balance. Lin put the hand wash in an indent on a rock; it'd do for soap as long she used just a little. When she'd finished washing her clothes – even her sneakers and hat – Lin stepped carefully to the bank and draped them over two shrubs at the water's edge. The breeze that moved the leaves would dry them quickly. Now for a bath.

Lin eased her body into the water and luxuriated in the soft and sensual flow. It was so good, the water cooling and cleansing, caressing her body and restoring her spirit. The memory of the serpent drifted away, and her muscles relaxed. She wiggled her bum down the stream, found a comfortable sandy niche behind a rock and leaned back, her arms trailing. The water flowed around the stone, running over her shoulders and between her breasts before trickling back into the stream. It was pure magic and Lin revelled in the feeling. It seemed years since she'd enjoyed a bath so much. She wished she could lie there forever.

Something bit her toe.

"Shit! Snake!"

Lin snapped her foot back and leapt upright, arms waving, water cascading off her body like a surfacing mermaid. She peered at her toe, and then the water. It was hard to see anything with the light playing over the dappled surface of the stream. If it was a bite then it hadn't been savage, more a nip. *I'm still on edge.* But something had bitten her. She was sure. Or did it? Maybe it was her imagination. Tension could play tricks, and the snake had yet to slip completely from memory.

Lin waited and watched until her panic eased then lowered herself down again. She watched closely. Was that a movement by her submerged hand? Cautious but curious, she kept still. It was hard to be sure if anything lurked in the shadows near her fingers. She withdrew her hand and a small creature flipped away. A crayfish! That's what had nipped her.

"A crayfish! Hey, you can eat those."

Catching and cooking a cray was a good idea. It'd make a nice change to berries. But she'd have to be quick because the sun was setting. A cooking fire was possible as she had Grampa's lighter. There were two dumplings left, one would do as bait. She'd been saving it for BiZi, but her needs were greater right now. And what the little critter didn't know wouldn't hurt him.

Lin got out of the stream, dressed in her dry briefs and bra and got ready for crayfish catching.

A fishing line was something else she hadn't put into her bumbag. And a net. The list of 'next time' objects was getting longer and the bumbag might morph into a backpack. But her shoelaces were long and thin – about a metre in length – and slipped easily from her still-damp sneakers. Lin tied them together to get one long line. A dumpling was bait; it was compact and cold.

Lin pushed an aiglet through the dumpling and tied a small knot on the end of the shoelace so the savoury bait wouldn't fall off. She moved upstream until a likely crayfish hole appeared. A sturdy, broad shrub on the bank looked big enough to hide behind.

Lin lay on a patch of grass behind the shrub with the hide cloak for protection. She eased the line out on the end of a stick and lowered the bait gently into the water. Ever-so-carefully she then took up the slack. The young hunter held her breath, but not for long. The ruse worked. The shoelace line edged slowly away. Lin couldn't see anything in the water, but the line was moving. She had something! Lin slowed the line and eased it back and up. Within seconds two large, blue-black claws emerged through the water hanging onto the dumpling. Behind the claws, she could see a small head and feelers at the front of a body about 15 cm long.

"Thank you, Mum," Lin giggled.

"The locals love your dumplings. You should start a shop."

Now that she'd caught something, though, how could she land it without losing the little critter? A net was on the 'next-time' list too, but Lin figured if she slipped her other hand into the water and slid it under the creature, she could toss it onto the bank. The crayfish might be too busy with its dumpling dinner to notice.

Her face hidden by a clump of riverside rushes and, holding the line as lightly as she could, Lin drew the creature towards her. It edged slowly to the surface of the pool, large claws hanging onto what it thought was a meal. Lin looked at it the same way.

"Hello dinner," she whispered.

When the cray neared the surface, Lin slid her hand slowly under the crab-like creature, paused, then flipped it out of the water. The small crustacean flew through the air like a tossed pancake and landed on a grass knoll where it snapped to attention, formidable claws raised and ready to attack. Lin was wet but well pleased. She had to stop the little critter getting back to the water though. It was heading there faster than BeBe could walk. The critter was small but quick, and the claws looked sharp.

A swift clout behind the head with a thick stick dispatched it. She wished the snake had been that easy. Lin caught two more crayfish the same way. She missed a few too before she had enough for a meal. All in all, a good haul.

With her garments dry and laces back in her shoes, Lin dressed. Going naked was easier than she'd thought. It surprised her how quickly she was adapting to this strange place. Fighting awesome snakes, saving kangaroos, surviving earthquakes, catching a meal, strolling around naked, 'talking' with a gargantuan grass-eater... all in a day's work for your average accountancy student. *Yeah, right! Maybe that Me Jane, You Tarzan routine is working.* But where was her Tarzan when she could use the company? The object of this musing was far away. More's the pity; she'd have liked to have him around. He might've been impressed by her crayfish hunting. He probably had a name for the critters.

Lin was weary; it'd been a long day. It was time to eat and rest. The herd was gathering in their preferred places; the koalas up trees, the kangaroos beneath them. The darrabin spread out in a broader section of the valley floor as did the snouts. Spike and BiZi's clans chose a small valley running off the main one. It would be their night-hunting territory. Bigbirds occupied a spot under a tree by the water's edge not far from Lin. The white birds flew to trees within a couple of hundred metres of where the snake had struck. That was the closest any of them got to that place.

The hunter-turned-chef moved away from the herd to cook her crayfish. Lin worried even a small blaze might disturb the animals given their tough times with fire. She chose skewer sticks from green saplings and gathered twigs, branches, and dry grass. The country wasn't short of stuff that burned.

Lin dug Grampa's lighter out of her bumbag and put the flame to her stack of kindling. Smoke billowed. The herd would see it, and so might anything else around. Darrabin and kangaroos raised their heads, nostrils twitching, but showed no panic. The blaze was small and barely visible although the plume of smoke rose readily. The skewered crayfish cooked quickly. Lin pulled the now-red creatures apart and ate the tail and claw flesh greedily, burning her fingers and tongue in the process. She used two stones to crack the tough shells. The flesh tasted of stream water but to Lin they were perfect. And she'd caught them herself. One of the tails she held back to use as further bait should she find another fishing hole.

Lin didn't know how she could live here without a hide cloak; it was so handy against the cold, the damp, and the mosquitoes. With the garment pulled tight around her body she stood on a large rock to watch the sun sink, its last rays layering the clouds into downy coverlets of orange, red and gold.

As twilight gathered Lin prepared her bed under a small tree. A pall of loneliness fell upon her but not as heavily as the mosquitoes that descended as the sun set, homing on her flesh like a miniature bomber fleet, their bites fierce and itchy. Lin hid herself within the cloak, the hood wrapped around her head to guard her face and eyes. Protected from the insects but not the loneliness, Lin thought again about the day. It had been one hell of a fight with the snake. She was lucky to have survived. She wondered anew why all the animals, except BiZi, had shown no interest in her after she'd gone into battle for them.

With her one human contact gone, Lin felt alone and alien. This world was different, and she didn't understand it. She'd taken on the task to help the animals find the North Forest after they'd wangled a plan to bring her here. It'd help save the lives of their kind. Yet the near-death of a kin member barely raised an eyebrow or twitched an ear, and *her* near-death was a non-event. What if she'd died here? What then? What would've happened to the herd? How would her parents and friends cope when she never returned, never knowing what happened to her? And what of her death? Her body would be rotting in the pool as the snake is now. Or maybe she'd be food in that monster's guts. *Nooo. What a thought.*

Lying alone under a tree, covered by the cloak, Lin's shoulders trembled. This strange time and place, meeting and losing Arben, the struggle with the serpent, the task she'd set herself... all the shocks of her strange journey sought release. In a strange world, surrounded by the weirdest of creatures, beset by mosquitoes, bereft of friends, family and all the things that made her who she was, Lin shook uncontrollably. She couldn't stop.

When at last her body drifted into slumbering stillness, two bigbirds left their places under a tree and sat either side of Lin, one facing forward, the other back. With legs tucked under their upright bodies, huge bony knees jutting forward and their heads held rock-steady, they looked like feathered sphinxes guarding a resting pharaoh. They held those positions all night. In the hour before dawn they moved away only to keep a protective eye on the still-snoozing North Forest Queen.

19

ENTER THE DROPCAT

Lin grunted awake in the pre-dawn light, her body hurting as if she'd run a marathon. Walking darrabin and fighting pythons had come at a painful cost. Ugly memories of yesterday's battle crowded her mind. *No wonder I'm stiff and sore.* A stretch would help. Lin eased her arms over her head and gently straightened her legs. The cloak fluffed up like a pastry case.

"Unnh," she mumbled.

"That's better. Not as sore as before."

She breathed in and out, her muscles less angry and resentful. The ease was short-lived. Lin tensed, the skin on her neck tingling. Something was out there watching her. She knew it.

Lin lifted her head, raised a corner of the cloak and peeped out. Eyes were everywhere, hundreds of them and all staring. Lin exhaled and relaxed. The herd stood around – watching and waiting – ready to roll. They'd not washed; they weren't much into hygiene, just an occasional dust bath to keep fleas away. But they'd foraged for food, drunk from the stream and done whatever pre-walk prep they needed before Lin opened her eyes. What was it with these creatures and morning? Hadn't they heard of a sleep-in?

The herd mightn't need a wash, but Lin did. She unfolded from her cloak, hurried to the stream and splashed her face and hands, flinching at the shock of the cold and the memory of the menace within. *No snakes today. Please.* The air smelled of fresh and damp, of new grass, and old mud. The bird calls were striking, the sky full of song and movement as coloured flyers flashed and cried in the morning bright.

Lin reached for her makeup, hesitated, then picked up the comb and pulled it through her hair. Wash finished, she snatched a bite from her food container, swigged from her water bottle, refilled it, tied on her bumbag and cloak, nodded to BeBe, scratched Little Quilt and took her place at the head of the motley mix of marsupials. The herd continued north, a still-sleepy, stiff and sore commander-in-chief in the lead.

As the day plodded on Lin sensed the animals becoming uneasy. They walked as usual, bumped, snapped and snarled as usual, but something wasn't right. The herd's collective condition was edging into Lin's awareness, and they weren't happy. Maybe the serpent stuck in their minds. Perhaps they were weary of the walking. Lin wasn't sure, but like surface eddies signalled what happened deep in a stream, so the twitches and quivers of the animals hinted at their unsettled state. They were edgy.

BeBe sensed the tension too and sent the white birds to check it out. Lin thought that BeBe sent the birds on long flights to weary them so that when they returned they'd be too pooped to party, too weak to squeak. Like parents running two-year-olds around to wear them out, it seemed a forlorn hope. The white birds were forever noisy and busy. Three of them returned in a rush to perch on BeBe's broad back. Three? Lin reckoned this must be important.

The white birds waddled crab-like over BeBe's huge hide – yellow crests raised, heads bobbing – before scuttling up to squawk at his head. Lin made her way over to the bulky herbivore who stood as glum as ever, white birds dotting his back like coconut shards on chocolate cake. What he pictured was not good; there was a dropcat following them over the grassland. All the birds had spotted the creature and relayed the news to BeBe in a flood of frantic vision.

Panicked images flickered among the now-nervous herd. Fur, feathers and fear stirred at the approach of a deadly predator. Lin worried along with the animals. How big was it? How long would it take to catch them? What could they do?

BeBe had answers to most images, except the last. He didn't know what to do, like he didn't know why the dropcat had broken a lifetime of instinct to stalk them over open plains. Hunger was Lin's guess. Maybe moving the herd had taken its food supply and it needed to keep in touch.

None of the animals would confront a dropcat. Except for Spike none of them had any defensive talent, and all he and the gang could do was bury themselves. Useful for them, but it wouldn't stop the dropcat, which'd just take down something else.

An instant pile of smelly dung signalled BeBe's fear and confusion. Lin was just as fearful, if less expressive. Her breath went ragged and her gut rumbled but she held the contents down. Memories of the snake were with her still. She didn't want to confront another lethal creature, particularly a dropcat. Not now. She'd been lucky yesterday but wasn't sure her luck would hold against a fast, four-legged assassin. She could lose the herd. Maybe they could leave it behind if they walked faster.

That was the plan, such as it was. Stay ahead of the dropcat. Maybe it'd get bored, find something else, drop away and stop pursuing them. BeBe agreed. The herd members were urged onto their feet, rumbling and grumbling, but eager to distance themselves from the predator. They trudged through the early afternoon boosted by fear that took them through the heat. The darrabin jiggled as they jogged, the koalas hanging tight like anxious passengers on a bumpy plane ride. The kangaroos were okay, the snouts kept pace. Bigbirds treated it as a gentle warm-up. Spike and the gang were the problem, their legs as small as their hearts were big. They waddled willingly but, in the end, it was futile. The herd was held back by the slowest, and the dropcat was not letting up.

Lin had to do something. *It's gonna be up to me.* The group would scatter and at least one would die if the dropcat attacked. The herd would be lost and the trek over. The dropcat had to be dealt with. The only way Lin thought to do that was head on – tooth to tooth, claw to claw – and that'd take planning. It certainly wasn't going to happen in a valley full of trees, shrubs and water that'd split up her forces. Battling the dropcat meant a group effort. Lin thought General Yue Fei would be impressed. She'd make a plan while on the move; keeping distance between the herd and the dropcat for as long as she could before she had to face the marauder.

The herd moved north as fast as it could. Lin devised plan after plan on the way. Maybe the darrabin could sit on it or squash it, maybe they could have it drop into a pit, maybe it could be lured into water and drowned, maybe... maybe. Lin took on and tossed idea after idea; this one too simple, that one too crazy. Another simply crazy. And so it went, her worry and frustration building such that when two smooth knolls loomed out of the plain, she grasped at an idea hatching in the back of her brain.

They weren't big hillocks, maybe five metres high at the crest and fifty to sixty metres across; nondescript, grassy bumps like the one she'd arrived at on the first morning. But you couldn't see the second one until you'd got around the first. When they reached the second knoll Lin's plan had gelled. *It's crazy but it just might work. Time to find out.*

Lin asked BeBe to get the big boys and bigbirds together for a war council. He did so. A few white birds attended, perching on his back, eyes bright and crests spread. A war council wasn't something the herd could get its head around, but it sounded impressive to Lin. And she was the one who needed confidence-building. The animals were brave in their own way; she didn't doubt that. But they were a scatty lot and she feared panic would catapult them away like loose balls in a rustic slot machine. The white birds were sent to locate the dropcat and report back.

Lin had just enough time to reveal her plan before the white birds returned; the predator was close and gaining. She sensed the animals' reluctance; the plan was borderline bonkers to her. But it'd have to work; it was all she had. She'd get them through this, she hoped, but they'd do it as a group. They'd have to trust her and do what they were told.

Together. Together. Together, and only together are we stronger than a dropcat. This was her message. The herd got the hint. This was their leader and she'd see them through. If she could subdue a snake, then she could defeat a dropcat. Maybe. Lin wished she felt as positive. But BiZi was her biggest fan. Bigbirds were confident too; the warrior birds recognised the fighting heart of this featherless foreigner

The dropcat was closing on the first mound. *Okay guys, time to move. BeBe, get every animal in the troupe onto this little hill. Now!* The herd was not enthusiastic. They'd rather have been anywhere but on an open rise with a vicious enemy skulking towards them. But they did it. Spike's gang squatted in the middle like a crown of thorns. Around them ranged the koalas and BiZi's clan. The smaller animals, including the bigger babies like Little Quilt, were all on the top of the hill. Around them spread the kangaroos, all but DaJiao and his alpha buddy. Finally, the snouts and darrabin were circled around the inner group, heads in, bums out. The larger creatures stood flank-to-flank, shoulder-to-shoulder, jostling and shivering in a tight circle around the top of the knoll. Circling the wagons, darrabin style.

BeBe, you and the other big boys are not to let the group break up. You must not let the group scatter. Keep them tight and together. Lin stressed this until her brain ached. *You're the leaders. The animals inside and forming the wall are in your care. If you want to get to the North Forest, then hold them together.* The larger animals were not to break the circle wall until BiZi told BeBe it was okay. If any darrabin felt legs walking over their back, they were to ignore them. It wouldn't be the dropcat. *Keep them in a close circle, BeBe – a tight, bunched band.* That would be their survival.

"God, I hope so," Lin whispered to herself.

Lin's head hurt. Vision-shifting was tough, but she had to be clear. BeBe signalled they'd do it. That was enough for Lin. She trusted him. She had to.

The alpha kangaroos and bigbirds were to work with her as a group, close to the trembling rears of the circled darrabin and snouts. The little general gave them their final instructions. She'd watched kangaroos fight and knew what they could do; the same with the bigbirds. They had huge legs and could kick like kangaroos.

BiZi would help; he had an uncanny sense about what creatures would do, which way they would leap and when. The little critter was already on a bigbird's back, hanging onto its neck, watching and waiting. They were ready. Sort of. Lin crossed the fingers on both hands for luck.

"Get ready guys! 'Cos it's coming."

The dropcat skulked around the first hill and stopped, dropped, and watched. It was not an open-plains predator. Ambush was its style, the cover of trees and rocks better than attacking creatures on an open plain. Animals massed on a hilltop were unknown but so was the small, blue-clad creature hopping over their backs. The fearless creature stared at Lin, its eyes level and steady. She returned its gaze. Lin hadn't been this close to the killer carnivore before and, from a distance, she couldn't see what the fuss was about; it was nowhere near as big as a darrabin, not even as large as a leopard.

The marauder was the size of a large dog, but stronger and built differently. The creature's killing power lay in its shape and strength; a deep chest, powerful shoulders and legs tipped with massive claws. A sheathed talon on a front paw slid out like a cutthroat razor to gut victims in a stroke. Fangs, claws and jaws were its weapons, backed by formidable strength and smarts. The jaws were vicelike, strong enough to take down and hold larger prey.

The creature prowled and growled around the nervous herd. A wall of darrabin and snout rears, a forest of shivering legs and wobbly bums was all it could see. Behind those were legs and more legs, above them the heads of the taller kangaroos. There wasn't a break in the grey-brown wall of tree-trunk legs holding up fleshy rears, the tails twitching and dung piling. A small blue-brown creature stalked the bum battlements in her robe like Empress Zhangsun walking the castle walls.

Lin tracked the dropcat around the circle, skipping over the backs of the in-turned animals, her eyes fixed on the killer. The herd members flinched as she hopped across them but held position. *Keep it up BeBe,* Lin vision-shifted. *Keep it up. Keep them together.* The kangaroos and the large birds followed too, moving with Lin but shuffling along outside the circled herd with the stalking killer six metres down the slope. They had their tasks. *Do not challenge the dropcat, just keep between it and the herd wall. I'll deal with it,* Lin had vision-shifted. *You do what you have to when the chance comes.* Every time the dropcat paused they stopped and faced it, the two kangaroos a pace or two apart, bigbirds watching, two either side of the kangaroos. If the dropcat increased speed, so did they. If it slowed, they did likewise.

Lin knew the dropcat wouldn't attack the group. It didn't work like that. BeBe had shown her. It needed to isolate a victim; charging a mob was a way to break it up so the killer could take out one animal, preferably one smaller or weaker. Lin's wall of darrabin and snouts was a clever tactic; the in-facing animals couldn't see the marauder, weren't so frightened, and the wall wouldn't break if BeBe and the big boys did their job. The larger creatures in front of the wall were a foil waiting for their opportunity. No kangaroo or bigbird would charge a dropcat. That would be fatal, and these creatures weren't about to put their lives on the line. They'd much prefer to be anywhere but on this hill. But they were here, they were persisting and the little general was still in charge.

The dropcat had to be brought closer. Following Lin's plan, they were to wait. BiZi sensed the dropcat was about to feint and signalled his small troupe not to panic. The dropcat charged, snarling up the hill. The group shivered but stayed solid. The predator fell back, confused. Lin screeched insults from her bum-high battle station.

The blue-clad creature and her mob of marsupials unsettled the dropcat. But it knew a thing or two about hunting. It threw more feints, scaring the kangaroos and the large birds. They looked ready to panic and so fall victim to his teeth and claws, but something was holding them in check.

Patience and time were on the dropcat's side; they always were. They were not on Lin's. Maybe her nerves were getting the better of her. For while it didn't look scary at a distance, up close the creature was a powerfully built beast with the most alarming set of teeth, and jaws. Lin was fearful. The herd's getting edgier and she didn't know how long it would stay together. The tension grew.

Lin didn't have the dropcat's patience. *I've gotta do something.* Daring all, Lin jumped in front of the kangaroos, picked up a stick and, screaming loudly, ran at the dropcat then dashed back to safety. The stalking beast stopped, watched, then continued to prowl and growl. Something more was needed. She'd have to stir the creature further.

Hurling more abuse, Lin lunged at the skulking menace, which instantly dropped onto its haunches. The warrior woman realised her error; it was going to be tight to get back to the herd before the dropcat could take her down.

The dropcat bounded forward... and sprang.

Lin threw herself between the kangaroos just as the marauder leapt. The Queen of the North Forest flew with no regal dignity through a gap between her subjects and rolled under the magnificent rump of another. As the dropcat flew by, the kangaroos propped on their tails and delivered two powerful, double-legged kicks as only they could. It was their main, their only means of attack. And they pulled it off. One set of flying feet struck the airborne dropcat under the chin, the other pounded the beast under its shoulder. Both prodigious punts heaved the lunging dropcat upwards and backwards, howling in rage and pain.

The creature flew through the air, twisting agilely to drop on four paws facing downhill, hurt and pissed off but not out of action. Facing away, it missed seeing bigbirds deliver four of the most brutally effective kicks Lin had ever seen. The dropcat didn't see them, it felt them; one blow split its lip and maybe a tooth, another crushed its groin and two more crashed into its chest, enough to break a rib. The animal roared in rage and pain. That was it.

Panic.

The circle broke.

The herd bolted.

Animals dashed every which way in a rolling thunder of shapes, sizes, legs, feet and dust. The injured dropcat fell under the blundering footpads of galloping darrabin that barely noticed their feared enemy and cared not. The predator was kicked, tossed and twisted in the dirt.

It was too much for the dropcat. The wounded creature took off howling towards the first hill, limped around its edge and hobbled back the way it had come. The panicked flight of the massed animals was not part of the plan. But it worked. The dropcat had been vanquished.

Lin missed most of the melee. Crouched under BeBe's abundant bum, she stayed safe because he stayed put. Under the shadow of that massive rear she was okay... provided she evaded dung deliveries. Lin took in the plan's aftermath while her heart thumped, sweat rolled down her chest and her body shook with the release of tension. The dropcat was gone – maybe not forgotten – but gone.

"You did it," she yelled. "You got rid of the dropcat. Great work, guys!"

Not that any of you can hear me. Or understand. But everything had worked out, if not quite as she'd planned.

Lin breathed heavily, her heart pounding and her

face taut with strain. The pressure of these conflicts was getting to her. *Can I go on like this?* If the trek was going to have life or death battles every day it'd likely be the end of her. Seriously. It so wasn't her to be weeping, screaming and swearing. Mum and Dad wouldn't be impressed. But they weren't here; she was, and it was a different world. Different situations called for different approaches, her father said; she wasn't sure her mother would agree with any of this.

Lin's doubts returned and redoubled. The trek was crazy. *She* was crazy. There were shocks at every turn. What was going to happen next, and would she survive it? With the herd disappearing in every direction, Lin took a deep breath and reached for an answer. It came from an unexpected source.

For shambling out of the maelstrom of madness, the whirlpool of dust, dung and grass that swirled around her like a desert storm rocked the familiar figures of Spike and the gang. They were nonchalantly manoeuvring their ponderous bodies around piles of steaming dung, heedless of what had just taken place. In snaking file, they walked their measured gait, bodies swaying like an armada in an ocean swell. On the way past, Spike stopped and looked at Lin over his pointed snout as if to say, 'Where is everybody? What's the fuss? We're off to dinner.'

That is so cool. Lin smiled. No land could be better off without creatures such as Spike and his pals. She knew she'd do what she could. *Get 'em, girl.* She stood and patted BeBe's flank.

The little general leaned on her lieutenant's ample shoulder, her arm draped up and over his neck. BeBe adjusted his stance but his face never changed. It rarely did, neither did his smell, but that was a part of him Lin was coming to accept. Did it make him any less worthy or dependable? Hell, no. It was a part of who he was, and it certainly wasn't the important part. Besides, she was getting used to it. After all this sweaty effort maybe she smelled too. *Who cares?*

Lin put those thoughts aside. Where were the herd members and the dropcat now? All the alpha males would be gathering their scattered clans and bringing them back to the valley, or so BeBe indicated. That was his task too. He'd also sent white birds off to locate the predator.

One of them finally discovered the killer carnivore lying on a low branch of a scrubby tree back down the river. The beast had returned to the haunts it knew to roost and recuperate. Blood congealed under its jaw and it moved unsteadily, when it moved at all. The dropcat wasn't out of the picture; it would recover, but it seemed unlikely the predator would risk another confrontation. That was good news; there was more.

One of the white birds, more adventurous than his buddies, had flown well to the north and told of a long range of hills and trees on the far horizon. The white bird had flown to a greater height than it had ever been in the search for the dropcat and thus beheld things it had never seen. One was a dense, dark-green forest, another a low pointed hill away towards the setting sun that was breathing smoke. The bird didn't know what to make of either.

Lin hoped the daring bird might have just found the North Forest.

20

WALKING WITH
GRANMA

Two days had passed since the herd defeated the dropcat
and nothing harsh had happened, no marauder attack, no
predator ambush. Lin welcomed the peace.

"No more snakes, no more dropcats, please. The calm
is sooo good," Lin said to the bigbird on her left, her face
relaxed and body loose.

Bigbird looked at her but said nothing.

The herd no longer bunched up. The animals spread
out, each group to its own pace confident they'd catch up
if needed and just as sure they wouldn't lose sight of the
others on this uncluttered plain.

Walking without worry in the warmth of the day
brought a smile to Lin's face. This was better. She hummed
as she strode out, sometimes moving forward to walk

beside bigbirds, her shorter legs pumping to keep pace. Other times she dropped back to saunter alongside the stumpy-legged Spike. Occasionally she'd plod beside a trudging BeBe. One time he pictured the North Forest and its compelling saviour figure. Lin glimpsed a dark-green forest cut by streams and with ample, grassy plains. Fresh water flowed, food grew, shelter abounded and, as far as she could tell, no humans. *Except me.*

"But we've got a long way to go, BeBe. And who knows what might happen," Lin muttered to herself.

For two days Lin had fought off killers; for the last two she'd walked. Dealing with monsters was action-packed and exciting, but right now she preferred walking, and peace. She didn't want to put her life on the line again today, tomorrow, or anytime soon. The last two days had been uneventful and welcome; they'd given her the chance to breathe, take stock and have her heart beat normally. The break had let her absorb things, reflect, and think on her special role in all this. Lin got high on the thrill of the unknown but today she was relishing the comfort of the quiet and honouring the ordinary.

They camped that night by the same small river that meandered through the plains. Bigbirds attracted her to a bushy tree about four metres high growing in bright sunlight by the valley rim. It stood with a larger companion like a contented couple in a park. The smaller tree had slender, spiky leaves with small, cherry-like fruit. Bigbirds liked the fruit. Lin thought it couldn't be harmful because they were scoffing serious numbers. Long necks extended they reached into the tree to gently, almost elegantly, pluck berries from the branches.

It was these delicate eaters that delivered decidedly non-delicate blows to the dropcat. That time they'd seen off a savage predator. This time they were getting blood-red stains on their feathered necks. Lin chuckled.

"That's so not a good look, guys."

The colour reminded her of the snake, the violence and the blood. The smile left her face and her shoulders shook with the memory. *Hey, get over it, girl; you're here to eat.*

Lin liked the berries. *Mum would make a great sauce out of 'em.* But she was at a height disadvantage as she couldn't reach the higher fruit. While the berries lower down were fleshy and cherry-like, they just weren't as sweet. Still, she picked and ate as many as she could, ducking among the sturdy, feathered legs, reaching into the centre of the tree to get what she needed.

Bigbirds weren't bothered; they abided her company and she liked theirs. Lin knew these wild creatures were distrustful of difference and suspicious of strangers. She didn't touch them although occasionally their bodies collided in the pursuit of a choice morsel.

"Move your bum, bigbird," Lin said, when they'd bumped more than once.

"The berries aren't all yours."

Bigbird stopped, stepped back and looked at her, its intense black eyes checking her out, looking for danger. Reassured when nothing further happened, bigbird resumed feeding. Lin did likewise.

Dinner done, it was time for a wash, and fill her water bottle. The trial of a long day's walk behind them, the herd got ready to rest. Their leader did the same. There wasn't much else to do; there was no-one to talk to. Lin wrapped herself in the cloak and lay down. Night came swiftly. The valley lapsed into quiet, or whatever quiet could be expected from a herd of large mammals shuffling and snuffling, farting and pooping in the gloom.

A night bird flew silently into the tree above her head to perch. The bird's melancholy cry sounded to a weary Lin like 'More Pork, More Pork'. An apt call for a meat-eater. Pity she hadn't seen a pig. *Some of Mum's pork dumplings would be great.* Her eyelids drooped. Tomorrow she'd like to be awake before the herd was up and ready.

Lin slept.

Two bigbirds maintained a silent vigil by her side until just before dawn.

* * *

The rising sun streaked the sky with a palette of dusty red and pink as it had every morning since she'd arrived. The birds celebrated with an enthusiasm that suggested they'd never seen anything like it, ever. Their songs and calls rang through the valley and out over the plain, echoing in Lin's wakening mind like a bell calling her to class. She opened her eyes and stretched. A lizard slid off the cloak and scurried into the grass. A tiny bird zig-zagged swiftly through the tight branches of the tree overhead. Every day was another step on a long learning curve. And with this morning, like all before, Lin didn't know whether it would reveal some monstrous horror or slide her back into the old world she knew.

Lin was certain she'd gone back in time but to when and to where, she couldn't be certain. It looked like Australia; there were koalas and kangaroos after all. Yet there were monstrous creatures that didn't feature on QANTAS calendars, cuddled by tourists and fed hay by visitors. A dropcat could take your arm off that way. Modern Australia, no; ancient Australia, possibly.

Granma's image came unbidden to Lin as she walked; a tender feeling warmed her heart as the old woman's face blossomed in her thoughts. It was always like that with Granma. She said she'd be with Lin, and she was. Always. Granma had passed away nearly eight years ago, when Lin was ten. *Omigod, today must be near the anniversary. Maybe that's why she's with me now.* It'd been a sad day, one that Lin could never forget. One thing she knew for certain: Granma loved her and she adored her granma

It was as if they'd shared a soul, tied by some mystic knot that could never be undone. Lin's feelings for her granma grew stronger, not weaker, as time went by. Differences in age, life, or death were of no matter. Lin and her granma were yin and yang, sound and silence, light and dark, where one was the other abided.

'Wherever you are, Beibei, I will be there too', Granma had said, and Lin knew that to be true. She sensed her presence every day, every time she saw that red vase.

God, she hoped it was still where she'd left it. *I should've brought it with me.*

Granma's love expressed itself in a togetherness beyond words. Lin believed in her granma like she believed in her own heartbeat. They'd done everything together; gone fishing, made clothes, laughed, sang, watched TV, shared stories, grew vegetables, kept chickens, visited the market and bought food. Then they came home and cooked together. All the while they talked, and Meng Wu told her tales; Lin knew the life and times of her grandmother's China as well as she did her own.

Meng Wu lived through the turmoil and trouble that ended with Mao Tsedung's revolution and the beginning of modern China. Meng's mother had been born before the end of China's old period and was one of the last women to have her feet bound. As a baby her feet were wrapped tightly in cloth to keep them from growing. As she got older her feet were kept so cramped that as an adult she could hardly walk.

"Why would people do that?" an incredulous Lin Beibei asked.

"To make women more feminine, and desirable to men," Meng Wu replied.

"That's crazy," Lin said.

"It sounds like that now, Beibei, but those were different times. Women were possessions more than people. I don't want you to be like that."

Her grandmother then went on to repeat words Lin heard more than once.

"My mother's feet were bound, Beibei, and my generation had bound minds. Your life and world will be unchained. But you'll have to take risks, grab your chances and make the most of them."

Lin never knew what her granma meant by this. She'd just raised her eyebrows, murmured, "Yes, Granma," and thought this must be what LOLs said. The last time she'd heard it, Meng Wu was dying.

Granma had been sick and confined to bed a few days when her dad hugged Lin gently and said, "Granma will be leaving us soon, Baby."

"What? Why? Where's she going?"

"She's dying. Her time with us is nearly over. She will soon go to join her ancestors. Best to say your goodbyes today."

Lin sat by Granma's bed for long hours, not wanting to leave her. Their hearts joined; they talked and cried as they had through their years together. As her body weakened, Meng Wu asked Lin to fetch the small, red vase that stood on her dresser. Lin handed it to her.

Meng Wu clasped the vase and her granddaughter's hands in both of hers, looked at her steadily, and murmured, "This is yours now, my sweet child. It belonged to my mother. She gave it to me; and now I'm handing it on to you. You are a darling girl, Beibei; brave, forthright, pretty and smart. You will be a lovely woman. Remember me and remember this. Be like this red vase; be beautiful, useful, strong and clear, but don't ever be afraid to break. Promise me?"

"Yes, Granma, I promise."

The ten-year-old Lin had no idea what these words meant either.

"Good, then I can go now, my precious one. Hearken to your heart and pursue what you believe, always. Follow your dreams. Know that I love you and will be with you wherever your journey takes you. Wherever this vase is, I will be there with you. This red vase is you and me, together forever, Beibei. Don't lose it."

"It will be with me always, Granma. I promise. Please don't leave me."

Meng Wu sighed, and closed her eyes. She reached out to her son and placed her other hand over Lin's hands holding the vase. Tears streaked Lin's cheeks as she laid her head on her grandmother's once-strong body and listened to life depart the now-frail figure of the woman she loved beyond all else.

"She's gone now, Baby," her father had said gently as he put his hand on her shoulder then held her close. "She so loved you."

Lin clutched the red vase and swore a silent vow to Granma's memory that it would be with her always. *I won't be parted from it, Granma, ever.*

* * *

Late morning and the plain dipped to reveal a hollow about 300 metres wide. The river had coursed through it once and eroded a cliff on one side. A deep overhang sat like a curved fireplace facing the morning sun. A black-water pond fringed with weed lay in front of the hollow; a scattering of trees dotted the quiet, secluded basin. Lin signalled BeBe and DaJiao and the herd rumbled to a halt. It was time for a rest and this place was as good as any.

Lin walked to the hollowed-out space to rest out of the sun. She ducked under the overhang, squatted on the gravel floor and looked up. She was not the first person attracted to the cool of this natural vault. Above and around her, covering the walls and ceiling like a paleolithic picture show, were colourful paintings daubed in strokes of brown, black, white and red. Etched outlines of fingers and palms took up one part, a laying-on of hands as if to bless the sheltered niche. Lin thought the paintings were like the pop posters she had on her wall at home. No guitars though. *I've gotta take those posters down when I get home.*

The other daubed pictures were of hunters, big-breasted women, kangaroos, darrabin, a dropcat, bigbirds, a doglike creature and something Lin didn't recognise. It looked like a large lizard. There was also a pointed hill with smoke billowing from its top. The snake could not be seen; the closest the paintings came was the lizard-like creature. *Was it Arben's people who'd painted all these images? They were good. Other people lived in this world, though. Maybe it was the Bandarken.* Arben would know. Lin sat awhile admiring the art but, gallery excursion over, she was soon on her feet again and heading north.

A heat haze shimmered low on the horizon separating

the distant trees from the ground, making them float like island outcrops in a silver sea. The animals walked a few hours in the morning and did it again in the afternoon to keep out of the worst of the sun. Lin relied on her hat. If the forested area was where the white birds thought it was, there'd be two or more days of this before they got there.

Then I can go home.

The afternoon was humdrum. The herd kept together except that Spike and his mates fell back as the hours went by. Their strong legs were too short for speed. Despite their will, their waddle wasn't fast enough. Lin thought of ways she could help. Putting them on darrabin wouldn't work; their claws were too long and sharp. They'd draw blood. Besides, the koalas had that gig. Maybe a travois might be possible; like the sleds North American Indians dragged behind horses.

Lin had seen them in old photos on the internet. They were long poles yoked around an animal's shoulders and neck that were then dragged along behind loaded with stuff. No wheels though. Lin was not into reinventing the wheel. Or inventing it. Whatever! If wooden slats were fixed over the trailing section of the poles, she could sit Spike or one of the gang on them. It'd have to be sturdy to be pulled by a darrabin, but it could work. Lin could see no ropes or the right trees for poles. But she'd keep it in mind.

There was little to do when the herd stopped, and the sun sank. Lin spread out her cloak, sat in the middle of it and watched the animals forage. The kangaroos grazed on trees or grass, the koalas ate leaves, the darrabin supported their bulk with any vegetable matter they could find. BeBe ate grasses, small shrubs, roots and leaves. Lin laughed as she watched, her affection growing daily for the giant creature. He was the garbage disposal of the marsupial set. But it kept him going. He needed it; he'd set quite a pace today for a darrabin. Hardly sprinting, more the pace of a trotting tortoise, but it was super speedy for the big guy. Usain Bolt he wasn't.

The herd was eager to get to the North Forest. So was Lin; the sooner they got there, the happier she'd be. Then she could go home. Home? Why hadn't she thought of this before? After they'd arrived, and she'd settled the herd, how was she going to find the disc? Directions weren't her strength; how would she find her way back? Maybe one of the herd could take her or point her in the right direction. Probably one of the bigbirds. Lin pondered this problem as the day came to an end.

The weary wanderer slipped her bumbag to the front, wrapped herself in the cloak and settled into the valley's quiet. Lin's body relaxed but her mind buzzed. How she'd find the disc and the vase again bothered her. But she'd find it, and she'd get home. *I can't stay here forever.* Her thoughts drifted to Arben, to her family, and then to Song Qili. *What's my BFF doing while I'm in this otherworld? Will I ever talk to her about it? Or, is this a dream and I'll wake up and lead a normal life?* A normal future for Song meant a husband, career, one child and an apartment in Shanghai. *It's what Mum and Dad want for me too.* Lin just wasn't sure it was what she wanted any more.

21

ROUGHED-UP
AND RESCUED

Rough hands ripped Lin from her reverie. Snatched from the ground she was held hard within the cloak and jolted away. Frozen with fright she could do nothing at first. Then, when her panic eased, Lin struggled and screamed against whatever had captured her.

"Stop this! Put me down! What are you doing? Let me go!"

Lin didn't know who or what had seized her. Probably men, as an animal killed then carried. But who were they and why had they kidnapped her?

The cloak wrapped Lin's body like a straitjacket and she was sweat-damp in seconds. She arched her body and drove her legs up and back. This slowed the kidnappers and they grunted at her frantic efforts to escape. She butted one abductor with her head. The cloak flapped loose and she saw his features; a broad, flat face with short hair, tightly curled, thick eyebrows arched over a wide nose. It could be a Bandarken; the men she and Arben had hidden from in the trees. Her captor appeared naked, but all Lin could see was his upper body. He shifted his grip, stuffed the cloak tight around her head, and kept moving.

The kidnappers went on, bumping Lin over the terrain. They were tough, muscular men and covered the ground at a steady pace even burdened with a struggling body. Finally, Lin heard grunted words. The men stopped, dropped her to the ground and unravelled the cloak abruptly. Lin rolled out and leapt up raging at her captors. If she was going to die or be raped then they'd know about it, maybe even regret it.

They were shorter than Arben but strongly framed and, from what Lin could make out in the moonlight, just wearing loin straps. The trio seemed stunned by her appearance; one more painfully so as Lin swung a fist into the side of his head. Her attacker swore and clutched his face. The other two crashed her to the ground. One jerked her upright, held her upper body tight and swung her off the ground. She kicked his mate in the thigh while aiming for his groin and swung her other foot back to crack the shin of the man who held her. He let her go, cursing. As she got to her feet the third man stepped up and swung a fist at her head. The blow jolted her body, split her ear against her skull and dropped Lin to her knees, stunned and bloodied. The men jammed her back into the cloak and continued running.

Within minutes the kidnappers dropped her again. The fall took Lin's breath, and jolted her shoulder. Her captors didn't come near this time; they let her crawl out of the cloak onto her hands and knees. Lin was exhausted, hurt and confused. *C'mon, girl, get up and face them. Let them know it'll cost them to hurt you.* She struggled to her feet and faced the men, her hands clenched and face tight, a trickle of blood oozing down her neck. The four stood in moonlit, treeless grassland, Lin in the middle, the men at points about three metres distant – close enough to catch her if she ran. The kidnappers stood tense and wary; whether it was her appearance or her attitude, Lin couldn't tell.

"You bastards will pay for this," she muttered.

"You bastards will pay sometime, somehow."

They didn't understand, and the threat sounded hollow. *What can I do? I'm alone, there's three of them, and the herd can't help.* The moon was high and flooded the plain with wan light. The four stood shadowed by cool moonglow, baleful players on a vast and grassy stage.

For a moment it was like a set piece in a Beijing opera, all stares and fixed positions but no high-pitched voices or clanging gongs. Just hostile, malevolent stares. Lin could see the men's silhouettes, not their faces. They were fearful; it showed in their stances. She pivoted slowly and looked at them one by one as if to memorise their features for an unlikely police line-up. Each one looked away as her gaze fell on him.

Finally, one of them gestured in the direction he wanted her to move. Lin hesitated but could see no point resisting. The plain was empty and wide, and she had no idea where she was or which direction they'd taken her. It was night, and this place was dangerous enough without these thugs. If they left her here, she'd be on her own and lost. She'd go along with it. She had to. Lin tied her cloak, swung it over her shoulder and followed the leader. The others fell in behind.

They walked for what Lin guessed was another hour over much the same flat country. The walking was easy, cushioned by a thick, grassy bed and lit by the moon. Lin thought about running but knew it would be useless. They'd catch her again. But where were they taking her?

Another shallow dale with another stream dropped away in front of them. In the middle, close to a bend in the river, Lin could just make out a smoky fire and a small camp. *That'll be where we're going. Doesn't look like many people. What do they want of me?*

The first of her captors entered the valley down a grassy track. Lin followed, the other two at her back. It was a steep path and her knees jolted as she strove to stay upright. The track widened when it hit the valley floor. Her kidnappers clustered around as they brought her towards the fire. Other people waited as Lin and her abductors made their way into the smoky firelight.

There were men and only men, a few young, mostly older, maybe eight in all. A gnarled, hobbled man appeared very old. There were no women. This was like meeting Arben's clan. No-one was sure of strangers. The women and children were probably hiding in the scrub. Lin had nothing to lose so she walked up to the man who appeared to be the chief.

"You can let me go, now. And take me back to where you found me."

It was a bold show and might have sounded convincing... in China. Here, he understood none of it and would have none of it. His response was equally baffling. She had no idea of what he said. A standoff took place. Lin didn't know what to do; her captors didn't know what to make of her. Lin reckoned her appearance in the dark might have been as scary as theirs was to her.

Lin looked coolly at the leader. It was a sham; she was terrified. Alien people had captured her, and she didn't know why. But they hadn't brought her here for the sheer pleasure of it. *Shit, maybe that is the reason.* The headman reached out to touch her shoulder or breast and she slapped his arm away with an upswung forearm.

"Don't touch me, you bastard," she said hoarsely.

"I'll die before I let you touch me."

He doesn't know what I've said. What happens now? The headman didn't respond in anger. He withdrew his hand, signalled to the others and turned away. The three men ushered Lin towards a lean-to that stood away from the main camp, indicated this was where she was to sleep and returned the cloak and hat she'd dropped as she confronted the leader. Lin watched the clan scatter to their sleeping places and leave her alone. She found a makeshift club among the wood litter, placed it under the lean-to for protection and sat down, watchful, her hand on the club.

The lean-to was bark and wood propped against a slender stripped branch a couple of metres long held up at either end by two sticks a metre tall. On one side, the half-tent was open to the elements. It wouldn't keep the wind out; it might help against the rain. Not that there'd been any. She wasn't likely to get wet. Dew, maybe. The cloak would help, of course. Thank God, she still had it.

Lin didn't know what to make of what had happened. She was scared. Her hands trembled, and her breath came unevenly. Why had they brought her here? The men were probably Bandarken. And Arben said they were dangerous. She grimaced when she thought of the strangling gesture he'd made when he said their name. They'd been rough with her. Lin touched her ear and winced.

She dug a tissue from her bumbag, wet it with spit and cleaned the dried blood from her ear and neck as best she could. It didn't feel too bad; she'd check it in the mirror in the morning.

Lin was worried for herself, but she was more concerned for the herd, which would wake to find her gone. What would they do then? Go on without her? She didn't know. She could try to escape as no-one seemed to be watching. But her captors knew she had no idea where she was and nowhere to go. Her kidnappers weren't bothered about her running away. They'd track her down and bring her back.

Sleep for now if she could. Granma was right, she hoped. Sleep might bring answers. Tomorrow could give her a chance to escape and look for the herd. Lin wrapped herself in the cloak and lay down, her head on the bumbag, her watchful eyes staring at the campfire and the men around it.

What did they want of her?

Strange sounds and night noise came to Lin as she lay tense and frightened under the bark slab. Probably only the women and children coming back was her first thought. But the darkness was never still. While daylight brought forth animals to live and die in the light; shadow creatures entered the void as the sun descended. While they weren't always seen, they were seldom silent. The night sounds carried clearly... grunts, coughs, squeaks, squawks, scolds and growls. Lin, a day person, heard the unseeable sounds as threat and menace. Darkness increased the fear. Noise took on fearsome form; rustles became Bandarken, grunts turned into dropcats. The silence screamed snake. Her fingers felt for the cold comfort of the club.

The night was chill. Lin shivered, drew the cloak more tightly around her body and crossed her arms for warmth and protection. Lying under the moon and stars with none of the comforts of home, surrounded by sound and movement she didn't understand with people she feared in a place she didn't know, sleep finally came.

Something woke her. What was that? Lin lifted her head and peered into the darkness while her fingers found the club. Everything seemed as it was when she rolled into the cloak. But she'd heard something. The valley was still, the moon silhouetted through the trees above her lean-to. The smell of smoke hung in the cold air; dampness lay like a blanket over the valley floor. Lin's breath condensed in front of her face.

I heard something. I know it. The laboured breathing of a sleeping clan member rippled through the camp. That wasn't it; she'd heard something different. An animal squealed in the scrub, a creature splashed in the stream. A night predator flew swiftly and silently into a tree. The hairs on her neck lifted as leaves rustled with the passage of something unknown. Lin's hand grasped the club. Something scratched the bark at the back of the lean-to; the wood frame trembled slightly.

There was something there.

Lin stared at the bark slab. Nothing moved. She slid the club away from her body, ready to swing. *If one of those thugs wants to get at me, he'll find I'm no pushover.* The scratching happened again. Something *was* behind the bark. Lin eased her upper body out of the hide-coat and prepared to fight. The snoring stopped. The valley paused, hushed and waiting, the silence as ominous as the dark. Lin strove to see or hear something, anything. She edged up on one forearm, club clutched in the other hand. Could she hear someone breathing, maybe a heartbeat? Could it be a dropcat, a snake... a Bandarken? Lin's body held rigid, her senses alert, ready to react.

Nothing.

She must have been mistaken and got ready to lie

down again.

Then came a whisper.

"MeLin?"

Lin's tension drained like a punctured tyre. Only one person in this world or any other knew her as MeLin.

Arben.

She whispered his name, and Arben's face – serious but barely visible – appeared around the edge of the lean-to, finger to his lips. "Ssshh". He crooked his finger to mean she should follow him. Without question or noise, Lin rolled quietly out of the cloak, gathered it, stood, grabbed her hat and bumbag then moved away behind the swiftly-moving form of her would-be rescuer.

Arben strode up the same path Lin had followed into the valley; she followed as quickly as she could. Halfway up the slope Lin caught up to the young Pelluken warrior and touched his shoulder. He stopped and shook his head, put a finger to his lips again and went on. Lin kept up as they made it out of the valley and onto the plain. No cries betrayed their escape. At the top of the ascent Arben turned to her and again made the sign for silence. They trotted alongside the valley some twenty metres or so back from its edge.

After about ten minutes, Arben pointed to the valley and they descended to the valley floor. There was no path. The pair scrambled and slid down the hillside until they reached the river. Arben walked into the shallow-flowing stream and turned in the direction of the flow. Lin followed; nothing was said.

The pair walked down the middle of the current, stepping carefully as the rocks were slippery and uneven. Lin knew it would take but one misstep for her to twist an ankle, slow their escape and cast them into the clutches of the Bandarken. The pale moonlight reflected off the river's surface and spread silver ripples around them as they threaded their way along the stream. But the water was cold. The chill numbed Lin's feet and she was relieved when Arben moved out of the water and up a wide valley leading away from the river basin. He kept to the valley wall, staying in the grassed area and avoiding the damp middle section. When they reached the plateau, Arben headed for a small clump of trees and picked up the spears he'd left there.

Lin caught up. Arben's face in the early light looked pleased and relieved to see her. For her part, she was overjoyed. Her heart filled with happiness like a kid at the Mooncake Festival. Still, she said nothing for he looked anxious. But he didn't like the Bandarken one bit. Maybe they were still too close, and they needed to keep moving.

Lin was right, as Arben told her much later when she could speak something of his language. He knew the warriors would search for her when they found the empty lean-to, and that'd happen soon enough, first light at the latest. The Bandarken would know she had help and they'd be incensed that a stranger had invaded their land. They would follow. Their tracking skills were exceptional and were the reason Arben had detoured so much and kept away from places where they might leave footprints.

Their walk down the river would delay the Bandarken, but not for long. They'd find the tracks again. Knowing a stranger was involved would galvanise their anger. They were a relentless, hostile people with no respect for strangers.

The Bandarken had maintained a bitter feud with the Pelluken, Arben's people, since the young hunter's ancestors had arrived in this wide-open land many generations before. They were different. The Bandarken resented their presence, despite the country's capacity to sustain them all. Whenever they met, violence happened. Arben's life would be at risk if they caught him and right now he and Lin were in hostile territory.

Lin's happiness shone in her face. *It's so good to see him. And he's risked himself to rescue me.* Her heart swelled, and a smile reflected her joy in the early dawn. She was relieved to be out of that camp and away from her kidnappers. Lin wanted to talk. There were so many things she needed to know. But right now, she couldn't ask. A touch on Arben's shoulder was all she could manage as they walked away. Lin signalled to her rescuer that she wanted to return to the darrabin. He seemed to understand, hesitated as if to speak, then nodded and changed direction as they walked.

The sun had risen since they'd left the camp; the herd would be standing around, restless, waiting for her to show. BeBe would have his usual glum expression, DaJiao would be eating and BiZi would be trying to keep an eye on everything. Spike would be with the gang, Yingjun with the snouts, and the koalas would be where they usually were... up a tree.

The return to the herd was difficult. Arben wanted to keep going but Lin was tiring as she hadn't eaten. She made her hunger known to her companion. Arben understood but didn't want to stop for fear the Bandarken would overtake them. He detoured towards a cluster of low-growing shrubs. Tiny white seed-pods grew around the edges of the leaf clusters. Arben signalled that they could eat them.

It was hard work to get a handful, but the seeds tasted fine, firm to the bite; a bit like wheatgrass. After eating, the pair hurried on. Lin could see they were heading towards trees on a distant rise. When they reached them, Arben lowered his weapons and clambered up a trunk to stand on the first branch, three or four metres off the ground. Lin was impressed at his climbing speed and agility, his fingers and toes finding grips and holds she couldn't see. To get down, he simply swung from the branch and dropped lightly to a crouching position on the ground then bounced up.

Lin marvelled at his lithe physique and supple strength. She was getting accustomed to his near nudity and it did nothing to hinder her appreciation of his firm, fit body.

Arben was encouraged by what he'd seen; the Bandarken were not behind them, yet. They had time. Not much though, as the trackers would be following. It was a matter of hours before they were seen and hotly pursued. How MeLin and he would deal with the pursuers, Arben had no idea. Rescue had been the plan. After that, he didn't have one.

But Lin did.

It took about two hours to return to the herd. When they got within sight of the mob, Lin stepped in front of Arben, put her hand on his chest and brought him to a halt. Even at a distance she could see the animals milling around, nervous and confused. They didn't know Arben, but they'd picked up his scent, and were fearful. She was going to have to explain who he was to BeBe and he'd relay it to the herd.

First, she signed this to Arben and pointed to a place where he could hide for a while. He didn't understand but did as he was asked. There was so much to be done and Lin had to keep moving. The herd had to get to the North Forest, and safety.

BeBe exhibited his usual enthusiasm, dipped his head and looked morose. Ida and Little Quilt stood at a distance and likewise bobbed. Lin saw that the littlest darrabin was growing fast. He was bigger than he was yesterday. *He's gonna be bigger than his dad.* BiZi registered excitement at Lin's arrival and ran to wind around her legs. Bigbirds formed what seemed like an honour guard of apology for allowing her to be kidnapped. It would not happen again, they implied.

BeBe took in Lin's vision-shifted explanation reluctantly. He'd seen people like Arben slaughter his clan; he didn't like them, and he never would. Lin 'told' him she needed Arben to walk her back to the sun she'd come through to help them, and he understood. He 'replied' that it was Lin's job to protect the herd from Arben; she agreed. It was BeBe's job to explain to the herd why this hated alien was here, and he began the task as Lin returned to her bewildered companion. Lin reckoned BeBe had the tougher job.

*   *   *

For his part, Arben was baffled by MeLin's connection to four-legged foodstuff. He couldn't figure out why she was putting her life on the line for creatures you could kill and eat. They were walking fodder and none too bright. Arben's clan had relationships with animals and birds that went beyond predator and prey. There were spiritual connections that bound them to each other, but it didn't stop the creatures being hunted. Why was she doing this?

Arben had been watching MeLin for some time. The smoke from her crayfish cooking fire had attracted him as it had the Bandarken. Smoke indicated many things, cooking was just one, although an important one. He'd come to see who or what had created the fire. He was surprised and pleased that it was MeLin; he thought she'd gone home. Travelling in Bandarken territory meant Arben kept his presence concealed. It was a lucky thing, for he noticed the Bandarken spying on MeLin without them seeing him. After that he made doubly sure he kept hidden. They were harsh and unpredictable men.

Arben came upon the dead python in the stream and could only think MeLin had killed it. It wouldn't have been any of her travelling companions. They'd have fled in terror. The snake was a top-line predator and he was amazed MeLin had fought it and lived. He'd also been looking on from a distance when she'd led the herd into battle with the dropcat. He'd seen the connection she had with the group.

Arben had been close by when MeLin was kidnapped. He'd bided his time for a rescue. His tracking skills were almost equal to theirs, but he couldn't see to track at night. He thought they'd return to their home camp and he'd guessed where that'd be. He was watching from a safe distance when Lin was brought to the camp and the elders questioned her. The young hunter hid until the pre-dawn darkness before he tried a rescue attempt. It was going okay so far, so why was she dealing with these nomadic nobodies?

*　　*　　*

Lin sighed. How could she explain to Arben that she'd come through a spacepipe from the future? And that upon arrival she'd met a group of local livestock who thought she was a super saviour, or something. It was her job to save them – take them to a forest – although she'd no idea where it was. *Yeah, sure.* What's more, she could 'talk' to them using some weird telepathy while she couldn't share a word with him in his own language!

It was crazy, and Lin knew it. Still, she tried to have Arben understand. When she thought he wouldn't harm the animals, she drew him to the herd. They didn't welcome him. But he was with their leader so bigbirds didn't break his leg, DaJiao refrained from putting in the boot, and BeBe held back the urge to knock the visitor down and stomp him flat. Yingjun ignored the interloper, Spike and the gang didn't care, and the koalas stayed up the trees. *A promising start.*

Arben stood with his mouth open and eyebrows moulded in arches of surprise as BiZi and the crew loaded themselves into kangaroo pouches and koalas dropped onto darrabin. Lin looked at him and smiled. His eyebrows would make a good Macca's model, they were that high and bent.

Lin gave Arben an encouraging smile when bigbirds took their places as outriders and the herd moved out. Lin and Arben were at the front. He was there, first, because he was with Lin and, secondly, because BeBe needed to keep an eye on him. The morning trek was the easiest of the day. The animals were rested and ready; they could walk easily if slowly. Lin and Arben had a chance to talk. It was good to have company, and such attractive company at that.

Walking through wilderness at the head of mega-marsupials on a mission made Lin feel like she was the first woman on earth. And Arben the first man. That thought had so many pleasant idylls and off-shoots that she let it take over and got lost in the daydream.

22

BACK WITH THE HERD

Lin wanted to talk with Arben. But not in Chinese. Better to know what he called things. She began by pointing to BeBe and saying, "Darrabin." She then pointed to the others with a questioning look, "And... ?"

BiZi and the crew were murrabin, Spike was a koorabin, the koalas and kangaroos were close to those names, and the white birds were kokatu. Yingjun and the snouts were tulangi. The bigbirds were yarravan. Lin practiced the names until she got them right.

Lin described her battle with the serpent to Arben by pointing at the little kangaroo, picking up a stick, gesticulating wildly and vividly, her face flushed with the memory. Arben's eyes widened and his eyebrows rose to pinnacle position as he murmured the name, "Durakkan."

No Pelluken ever went near it, so scary was the serpent. Lin had fought one and lived. For her part Lin didn't know whether seeing one, fighting it, or surviving surprised Arben the most.

The terrain roughened as they walked through the

morning; the surface pitted, grass clumped underfoot, and the soil got soggier. Rivulets cut through the sod. At times the animals picked their way around, mostly they splashed through mud up to their hocks. The damp didn't bother them. Lin tried to keep her sneakers clean, but it was hopeless. Walking through mud was like peeling beetroot, you were going to get stained.

She hoped the wet meant they might be nearing the stream's headwaters. Maybe it began in the North Forest. She could make out a heavy blue-green line on the horizon. A forest *was* getting closer. They should make it by tomorrow. *Let's hope it's the North Forest*. It'd have to do; the herd wouldn't know anyway. She'd just tell them it was and then her job was done.

"Yess," she whispered and clenched her fists. "Yes!"

She pointed the would-be forest out to Arben, and he gave it a name she couldn't grasp. She'd get BeBe to have the kokatu check it out.

Spike and the gang were falling behind. The country wasn't easy walking for stumpy pincushions. Lin told Arben about her plan to have them dragged on a travois, not that he understood the word. He didn't comprehend her signs either, so she waited until their mid-day stop and drew a diagram with a twig in the soil. She left off the wheels. Lin knew the sci-fi caveats about time travel; she couldn't bring in something that won't be around for thousands of years. She wasn't supposed to be interfering to save these creatures either, but she couldn't help it. Granma said to follow what she believed. She couldn't let them perish if she had a chance to save them.

Arben contemplated her drawing, chin in hand. He scratched his head, walked around the copse awhile then cut down two saplings. Clambering up another tree he brought down lengths of flexible vine. Together he and Lin measured up a darrabin and assembled a travois around it, long poles angling along both flanks, a harness connecting them over the shoulders, cross-branches providing a platform at the rear. BeBe took on the job of test pilot. The poles were a bit short, but his rear was bigger than most darrabin. A slightly smaller animal might be better. Maybe this was a job for Yingjun and the snouts. Lin vision-shifted to BeBe that the darrabin were too big and wide, would he seek help from the tulangi? He would. Yingjun volunteered himself.

Lin got one of Spike's buddies to test the contraption and Yingjun dragged him around for practice. The rider fell off the first time, but he'd got on crossways. The forward force jerked the bristly jockey off and he'd rolled onto his back. A few frantic leg-waving seconds passed before he got reorganised, feet down, spines up. When Spike's buddy crawled on the second time he crouched the way Yingjun was pulling, and that worked. It'd be okay for a while, Lin reckoned; but she wasn't sure for how long. And it could only pull one, maybe two at a time unless they built a second, or third travois. And right now, they didn't have the material, or the time. One would do.

*　　*　　*

Arben knew even a blind Bandarken could follow travois tracks across this muddy country. Yet the way MeLin worked with these banal beasts impressed him. They possessed a togetherness, a special bond. He knew they were traveling somewhere together, but why? There was an affinity he couldn't grasp. The animals, large and small, respected their leader. He could tell from the way they looked at her when she wasn't watching. Another part of it was in their contact; it looked as though they spoke to each other, silently. Lin would stand by one of the darrabin for a while and then it'd wander off and do something as if following orders. Or she would. The Pelluken knew the animals by their habits. They had to; they survived by the knowledge. Yet they had no bond with the creatures as MeLin had. She was together with them like family, a little mother with a brood of massive children.

Arben noticed some of the animals were very special to Lin. She would put her arm around the largest of the darrabin, the one she called BeBe, and lean against him. One of the little ones would come up to her almost begging to be scratched. Arben had never seen this before. Darrabin fled in terror from his people. The murrabin she called BiZi, huddled around her legs like an infant around its mother and she'd reach down and stroke behind its big ears.

These creatures treasured Lin in an extraordinary way that Arben could not understand. The birds were in it too. The kokatu were like winged messengers, the yarravan were different again. They hung around Lin at a distance, watchful and wary. Every time Arben went near her they closed around like a ring of sentries, their stance attack-ready. They didn't trust him; he knew that. Arben was cautious of the birds. He'd been on the end of a kick once when his family had tried to bring one down. The blow nearly broke his leg and the swelling took a long time to subside.

*　　*　　*

Lin, for her part, was impressed with Arben's skills. He had comfort factor built-in and she felt grounded when he was around. He did things surely and swiftly; nothing fazed him except, maybe, the Bandarken. And now she knew why. He wasn't like the young men she'd met in China, obsessed with computer games, iPads, money and mobile phones.

Arben had none of those. He carried all he owned: spears, club, a hand axe, and a belt around his waist. There was also a stick with a small hook on the end, but she didn't know what it was. If he had a cloak like hers, or anything else at all, it was back at his family camp. He travelled light. If he lacked for anything, he didn't show it. Arben made do. He lived life in the now. Lin didn't know if he even thought about a future or whether such an idea meant anything. He also stirred her physically and emotionally in ways she wasn't used to. She did like him even though he'd come across like a barbarian at the start. He was cute and bright. They were good feelings and warmed her body and soul. She and Arben had the makings of a team.

The mid-day heat built quickly. Lin was used to the 'furnaces of China', big cities where the summer temperature soared into the 40s and the humidity climbed with it. Here, the heat baked dry and intense and her hat did little to stop the harsh rays. The early to mid-afternoon sun pressed like a hot pillow on her face and the dry heat choked her breath. Water became precious. Lin tried to get to waterholes first so she could drink before the herd walked in them, or did whatever else they needed to do. That way she kept hydrated. The herd gathered for their afternoon journey early, keen to reach the sanctuary they sought. Lin and Arben took their places up front, the other animals in their usual spots, the kokatu off to check what lay ahead.

Spike gave one of his two younger pals first ride on the travois. Yingjun had ceded the job of pulling it to one of his younger males. Arben had managed the travois re-assembly and reloading. They were waiting and ready to roll.

About to step out on the afternoon's trekking, Lin paused. She felt that peculiar silence, and hesitated. The air charged with static; an ominous hush fell over the herd. She looked at Arben. He returned her gaze and raised an eyebrow for he, too, sensed the strangeness.

Lin turned to look over the animals. They were still, nervous and expectant. There was no sound, no movement until just the faintest of rumbles deep beneath the earth rattled their composure. It was nowhere near as severe as previous tremors, but it was sinister and scary. The seismic spasm was over in seconds. When the shuddering stopped, the herd breathed a collective sigh of relief, shook their bodies and shuffled their feet in fright.

Nervousness sped them through the afternoon.

23

BATTLE THE BANDARKEN

Three kokatu scrabbled over BeBe's broad back, their yellow crests spread and claws scratching his hairy hide while they squawked at his head. It happened an hour before the evening halt. The day had been uneventful since the tremor, but Lin sensed it was about to change. She joined BeBe and he shared vividly that seven fully-armed Bandarken warriors had moved to a place between them and the North Forest. The huge beast's eyes twitched along with his nose; his ears spun like tops. His dung output could have filled a wheelbarrow. BeBe distrusted humans. He was afraid. So was Lin. But what to do? She pursed her lips as her eyebrows creased.

Lin reckoned the Bandarken had guessed where the the herd was heading and moved to cut them off. Why? Perhaps they thought the darrabin would be lost to them, maybe they wanted to get her back and deal with Arben.

Whatever, the armed warriors and the herd were aiming for the same place, but from different directions. The kokatu guessed they would reach the edge of the North Forest at much the same time.

Lin sketched this scenario to Arben using a mud map and miming, something she was getting good at. She flashed her fingers for seven, pointed at his weapons, said 'Bandarken' and pointed ahead. His eyebrows rose, his mouth dropped open and he shook his head vigorously.

Arben sought to avoid a clash at any cost. There were too many of them and they were formidable. It could be dangerous, even fatal. Lin was drawn to ducking out, but in the end, she had to get the herd to the North Forest. She said she would and if that meant a battle with the Bandarken, then so be it. Whether it was now or later, it had to happen. Might as well get it over with.

The big question was how. Lin knew that directly confronting seven armed warriors was not an option for two people and an easily-spooked herd. The animals were terrified of humans; they certainly wouldn't want to fight them. That wasn't on. Too many of their kin had died under the bloody spears, clubs and axes of Bandarken and Pelluken alike.

The weapons made the difference, Lin knew that without them her species was as vulnerable as any other. People were not as strong as darrabin, as fast as kangaroos or as powerful as bigbirds. And they couldn't fly. The Bandarken were cunning and smart though, and armed. How to put all this together and get the herd safely past the Bandarken and to the North Forest? *It's my gig now. What would Yue Fei do?*

Lin worried as they walked. The first thing a general would do was locate the enemy, assess its strengths and weaknesses and work out what they were capable of. Then a leader would assess her own strengths and weakness and figure out a plan. Okay, so where will the Bandarken camp tonight? The kokatu could find out; Arben might find more if he could scout about later. Lin had BeBe tell the kokatu to find the warrior's camp and let him know where it was. A couple of kokatu flying overhead would neither alert nor alarm the Bandarken. Kokatu were everywhere and at any time. It'd be unusual if they weren't around, squawking and scolding. When Lin found the Bandarken, the next question was what did they do when the sun went down?

Arben knew the Bandarken would make camp before sunset. That's what his people did. He signed to Lin that the men would make a fire, eat, talk and work on their weapons before resting. One of them, however, would always be up and awake. Every so often another would take over without being asked. It just happened. A bit like the kokatu; they all took turns at being sentry. In the faint, grey light before dawn, the men would be up and active.

Lin didn't have much time to arrange her furred and feathered forces.

The plan, as she later conveyed to Arben and BeBe, meant moving the herd at night. This was received with no enthusiasm. None whatsoever. BeBe was reluctant and Lin understood why. Darrabin were not nocturnal; they stayed together between dusk and dawn. Predators patrolled the night and darrabin sought the security of numbers during the hours of darkness. Some of the other animals weren't night critters either. The koalas were fine after dark. Having them walk all day had been a big problem and they'd spent most of their travel time snoozing on darrabin backs. That had worked so far. But Lin knew having Max and the koalas as lively night jockeys would be a big help. BiZi and the crew were night prowlers and they would do what they could, especially BiZi. Kangaroos could see well enough after the sun went down.

Lin didn't want to give out all her plans in case the herd got edgy. She could rely on BeBe, BiZi, and the big boys; these were determined creatures if unused to dealing with difference. Novelty freaked them out. That's why a night march didn't excite them. They didn't do that, but they would for Lin. She'd have to handle it carefully, though, otherwise the others could panic as they had at the dropcat finale. She'd dripfeed the details. Otherwise chaos could reign. *There'll only be one leader – me – and I'll stand or fall by the plan.*

Lin knew failure could mean death for some of those in her care – maybe even her own – but she accepted that to see the job through. She didn't know where she was getting all these military manners from; there were no soldiering skills in her family. It was as if she was channelling Hua Mulan, the woman who took her father's place in the army and served without anyone knowing she was female.

For his part, Arben was gobsmacked. This different woman with the odd garb and strange manner was doing all the thinking and planning. What's more all the animals – large and small alike – accepted it. She was their warrior chief. Lin delegated; the herd did it. He'd never known this with animals; it was unheard of among his people. Pelluken women did the gathering, cooking, child bearing, child raising, and nursing; men did the fighting, protecting, tool-making and hunting. Everybody passed on their culture to their children. It was neither good nor bad; it was just the way it'd always been.

Lin issued her orders through BeBe and the plan got underway. If the herd had known of the general's uncertainty they mightn't have been so keen. But, she'd dispatched a giant snake, seen off a dropcat, and returned from the Bandarken; she would prevail. Lin just wished she felt as confident.

The kokatu returned with news; the Bandarken had struck camp in a forested glade ahead. Lin guessed from the time the kokatu took that it might be an hour or so. Arben should be able to jog-walk that quickly. She asked him through sign language to find the camp, stay hidden and safe, come back and tell her as much about it as he could. It was important she knew about their weapons, how many they had and where they kept them when they slept.

Wait until dark, she told him. If he needed to take someone with night eyes, BiZi would go with him. The little murrabin could vision-shift with Lin but couldn't get to the Bandarken camp as quickly. His legs were too short. Arben felt he was being upstaged by a food item but agreed. He worked out a sling using his belt to carry the small creature. He and BiZi would leave well after dark when the Bandarken camp would be settled and the animals that emerged after dark had returned to their roosts.

BiZi wasn't fond of this co-travelling idea. Nobody was happy about Arben, but he would go along with it because it was the wish of the Queen of the North Forest. BiZi would do anything for her.

Before Arben left, though, he and Lin had to eat. The young hunter got sticks and branches together with some dried grass. Lin knew his purpose. It was almost dark enough to light a fire without it being seen by the Bandarken. Arben signed to Lin that he'd be gone a short time and would bring back food.

She smiled, nodded 'yes', and relaxed back against a tree to finalise the plan. It was nice to have this young man gather food because she had other things to worry about. Keeping the herd together and alive was the priority. She didn't want to make the warriors pay despite what she'd said on the grassy plain when they'd kidnapped her. She disliked them but had no wish to hurt them. That wasn't her way.

The North Forest lay ahead, and it wasn't far. The Bandarken stood between the herd and their journey's end. Lin had to get the mob past the warriors and safe. Then her work was done. After that she could go home and see her mum and dad, wash her clothes, catch up on homework, and have a long chat with Song on the bus. *This story'll freak her out. Would she believe it?* Lin smiled, and returned to planning.

By the time Arben returned with a leaf wrapped around things to eat, Lin had the plan fully-formed. She got out Grampa's lighter and put the flame to the grass and watched it flare. She couldn't help notice Arben's response; his face lit up in astonishment and his eyebrows arched, a look he wore often when he was with her. In the short time he was gone Arben had picked up two large, white grubs, four eggs and a handful of small berries. Lin recoiled. Grubs?! Where did he think she was from, Guangdong? They eat anything there.

*   *   *

Arben shook his head. How did she do that? How did she make fire from a coloured stick? He'd been with MeLin long enough to know how different she was and not be struck dumb by everything. She was different, and he went along with it. But fire from a coloured stick? That was special even for her. But now they had a fire going, it was time to put food on it and that was something he could do.

The white grubs were the larvae of moths. They had to be dug out of the ground or pulled out from under bark. It was usually women's work, but all children learned the skills. Arben was now familiar with the idea that women could do men's work and vice versa, even if he wasn't sure he agreed.

MeLin didn't look enthusiastic about grubs so he'd have to show her, because he knew they tasted fine. They weren't a food staple, but they were common enough. The eggs he tossed into the ashes to cook and roasted the grubs on twigs in the embers. When they were done he popped one into his mouth, bit into it and retained a small bit for her to try. Brave as she might be, MeLin was wary of food that had recently wriggled. But Arben smacked his lips to suggest it was tasty.

"Good, good," he said in simple Pelluken, and nodded encouragingly.

Despite her unease, MeLin opened her mouth, and wrinkled her nose as Arben popped a small morsel onto her tongue. She bit into it. Surprise! It was okay; a bit like chicken.

"Good, good," MeLin mimicked his words.

She eagerly shared the other one and would have eaten more but there weren't any. You couldn't buy them by the kilo at the local supermarket.

*　　*　　*

They sat a while after eating, watching the fire burn down. Arben made sure it never died. There were always coals ready to stoke. He taught her more of his language. Lin could get her head and mouth around some words, even short sentences. She understood more of what he said because she was good at languages. Plurals meant you said the word twice.

"Kokatu, kokatu," she said, and he laughed.

There were so many of them that once was probably enough. She'd never seen one squawking to itself. Learning a language was fun and she already had Chinese, Cantonese, and English. If she had more time with him, it might be possible to have a useful conversation. At least a little better than Me Lin, You Arben. Eventually their talk lapsed into quiet as they thought of the night to come, its challenges... and risks.

The plan meant moving a reluctant herd a couple of hours before dawn. Lin knew it would be a tough call; harder than getting her father out of bed on a weekend. And without a mobile phone, working out the hours would be tricky. She followed the trajectory of the moon and thought she could work the departure hour out with the moon's position and her own sense of time passing. It was time to get the plan in action.

"I want to know everything about the Bandarken; where they are, the number of men, their weapons, anything that will help us defeat them."

Lin asked this of Arben through rough Pelluken and

sign language. She even threw some Chinese in, not that he understood.

It was dark enough. Arben and BiZi prepared to leave. Lin put her hand on the young Pelluken's shoulder and told him to be brave... careful and brave. She wanted him back. She also said, "Trust BiZi," but wasn't sure of the words. She'd probably said, 'Don't eat him', or something.

Arben smiled. He knew how much she liked the little critter.

With the warmth of MeLin's smile in his heart and the memory of her light touch on his shoulder Arben got ready to depart. He wouldn't let her down. Clutching his spear and club, and with BiZi in a sling around his chest, he disappeared into the night.

BeBe was worried about the night march. It was hard to tell he was worried; he always looked six-parts glum, three-parts morose and one part just plain ornery. That was his personality formula. He pictured his worries to Lin and she reassured him as best she could. It had to be a night plan. Surprise was all they had going for them, a pre-dawn surprise assault on the Bandarken.

BeBe wasn't to know that yet, no-one was, not even Arben. Lin couldn't share the plan with BeBe. He needed confidence. They all did, otherwise it wouldn't work. For this plan was weirder and wilder than the dropcat war. And that barely made it home. If any of the big and little beasts faltered, one or all of them could die. That meant her and Arben as well.

Arben and BiZi were gone about two hours. Upon

their return they reported to Lin that the Bandarken weren't far.

"How many are there?", she asked.

Kokatu weren't usually big on numbers; anything over me and him (or her) being two was a challenge, and it usually had to be white and fly to be counted. But this time they'd got it right.

There were seven, fully-armed warriors between the herd and the North Forest.

BiZi and Arben had smelt the campfire long before they'd counted the sleeping figures around it. BiZi went in to find out about the weapons. He was light and quiet enough to get in, around, and out without being seen. Besides, his kind was known to the Bandarken and in no way a threat. What he couldn't do was relay information to Arben; he had to wait until he got back to the Queen of the North Forest. The Bandarken kept their spears and clubs next to them as they slept.

Prodded by BeBe and the big boys the herd grumbled into life in the early-morning hours. Lin's only instruction at this time was, *Quiet!* And that was hard to vision-shift. But Lin stressed, *The plan depends on quiet. No noise.* The leaders had to get that across to their troops.

The animals bumped around like drunken sleepwalkers as they sorted their marching order. Some could see well at night, others couldn't. All somehow avoided the massed spines of Spike and the gang. The murrabin and the smaller kangaroos did their best to evade the massive feet of the rallying darrabin. A misstep by any of those heavyweight herbivores and the little crew could've been crushed.

The koalas knew the best branch from which to drop onto darrabin; Max and his team were there and waiting, safely separated from the jostling throng beneath. One by one the darrabin shuffled under the tree and silently took on their lively night-jockeys. Bigbirds gathered, alert and ready. One tulangi was pulling the travois but he couldn't pull it all the way as the noise would be a giveaway. BeBe told Spike to rest his grumpiest companion on the travois for the first half of the walk. The sled would then be dumped.

They set off, BeBe and Lin walking together with Arben who knew the way and was carrying BiZi again. Lin liked the way the pair had a friendship of sorts even though they couldn't communicate directly. Arben had a new respect for his big-eared bodyguard. Bigbirds fell in behind the lead bunch. The rest of the herd strung out in a file behind the feathered fighters. The koalas would head the darrabin in the right direction, the kangaroos could see well enough to cope. They had night-sighted murrabin in their pouches as well. Spike and the gang brought up the rear, following the tulangi with the travois like tired three-year-olds trailing their mum through a market.

BeBe, BiZi and the big boys had stressed to their clans that quiet was essential; even the kokatu, not great night flyers, had been told to cork the squawk. Lin doubted this would happen. *They never shut up.* Still, the herd was hushed as they headed off, a muted excitement shared among them. Something big was about to happen and they were part of it. Lin sensed the pent-up tension. They were like children waiting for the Spring Festival; they didn't know what the night might bring. Lin hoped to keep it that way for as long as she could.

After an hour the tulangi shed the sled, the poles and harness left to rot in the scrub. The herd was closing on the Bandarken camp and Spike and the gang were back to plodding. Silence was crucial now. Lin sought out her massive co-leader; *Tell the spiny critters to make their own speed, BeBe, but be as quiet as they can and catch up quickly when we stop. We can't lose them. They're needed. They've got our only real weapon.*

The leader signalled silence. The key to surprise was that the target didn't know about it. Lin relayed to BeBe that the kokatu were to fly to a tree near the Bandarken camp and, once there, sit, settle, and shut up. Roosting was probably the closest they ever got to shutting the squawk and squabble. Even if the Bandarken did notice they'd probably think it was the usual kokatu cackle and not be alarmed.

The pack plodded silently on their padded feet, or as noiselessly as a herd of one-ton titans could, not as loud as mammoths and certainly quieter than elephants... but not much.

Arben signalled Lin that they were approaching the Bandarken camp. The herd stopped, apprehensive and excited. *No noise now, not a bit,* Lin ordered, *and that means no dung dropping.* If she could plug the plop, she'd have achieved something. Lin then drew her lieutenants together and vision-shifted their final marching instructions through BeBe.

First, she told them they were as brave, strong and fast as humans. They mightn't be as mentally smart, she said to herself, she just hoped she was. *Bandarken strength is in their weapons, but when you face them, as soon you will, they will have no weapons. Things will be equal. Be strong, be calm. They will not stop us getting to the North Forest. We will make it.*

That was the confidence builder; Lin hoped it worked. Now for the plan. DaJiao and Yingjun were to lead the larger marsupials; the darrabin, tulangi and the kangaroos. BeBe, Ida and Little Quilt were to stay with Lin; so were bigbirds. The birds were fine with this; they'd taken it as their special privilege to be the Queen of the North Forest's palace guard. The senior darrabin was not happy as the gargantuan grass-eater wanted to be with his kin. But he knew it had to be; Lin made it known she needed him and Ida. They had special tasks.

Lin had a brief whisper and sign conversation with Arben. She told him BiZi knew what to do. Arben gathered his spears, club and axe and with BiZi and six murrabin in tow took off for special weapons training. Spike and the gang who'd just arrived got their battle briefing, and two of the kokatu flew down for a confab. It was now a matter of waiting until the dark hour before the dawn.

*   *   *

The time had come.

The animals rose from their brief rest, tense and quiet. The smell of dung hit Lin's nostrils.

"Aaargch."

It was like living downwind of a poo pit. The not-to-plop order hadn't worked. All that vegan consumption had to work its way through.

Lin hoped the rest of the plan was better. If it wasn't, they'd all be in the poo.

Lin went to her animal commanders and gave them an encouraging pat, except for Spike. She just bent down and smiled at him. She hoped he saw it because Spike and his buddies were very important to the plan.

The kangaroos, with the darrabin and their koala jockeys alternating, took off in two single files, one in either direction around the sleeping Bandarken. Half the tulangi attached to the rear of each file. They were to trudge a big, hairy noose around the warrior camp.

The plan was away!

BiZi and his pals headed towards the sleeping Bandarken. The murrabin moved quietly and swiftly, blending so well with the scrub that Lin lost sight of them in seconds. Kokatu left their roost and flew silently to a tree over the Bandarken camp. All was in place. Almost. Would this work? Lin mouthed a brief prayer to whatever strange energy had brought her down the spacepipe and placed her among these odd animals. She was worried and fearful, but no-one would have known for she exuded calm and confidence, far more than she felt.

This was make-or-break time.

BiZi's crew approached the sleeping Bandarken with caution. They knew the ferocity, skill, and speed of these people; they knew what'd happen if they made a mistake. One of the men was awake, the other six were sleeping, weapons by their sides. BiZi knew which one was awake; it was a skill of his, a talent evolved through generations of hunting small animals, lizards and bugs. He could tell what was alert and watching, and what was not. With all the temerity and courage he could muster, BiZi made his way towards the sentry. When he got to a distance just outside club length, he stopped and squealed softly. The man's head swung around, and he reached for his club.

BiZi feigned an injury. There was a pigeon that lived near his burrow home that would fake a broken wing to draw predators away from its ground nest. BiZi had fallen for the trick himself when looking for eggs. The bird would splay out a wing and hop pitifully away faking feather damage, drawing the attacker with it. When bird and interloper got far enough from its nest the pigeon would drop the fake pose and fly off.

So BiZi feigned an injury. He mewled pitifully and limped away from the man with the club. The Bandarken followed, thinking that one swift clout and breakfast would be sorted. BiZi kept moving and mewling, drawing the hunter away from the camp.

With the guard decoyed, the other murrabin slipped noiselessly and swiftly into action. Doing as Arben had shown them with his weapons, they began to move the spears, axes and clubs away from the sleeping men. It wasn't easy to move a long spear when you are a third of a metre high. Small front paws made it that much harder. It needed a murrabin at each end to avoid dragging the spear on the ground and alerting the sleeping warriors. But all six had practiced removing Arben's weapons from him while he lay on the ground. They knew what to do.

Three pair of them were doing this while BiZi lead the sentry away, dodging doom from a club swing when he let the warrior get too close. The weapon thudded close to BiZi's ducking body as he scurried away, still limping, still mewling his piteous, wounded cry. One spear couldn't be retrieved; it was lodged under the Bandarken's arm. The murrabin tried to dislodge it but, fearful they'd wake the warrior, they left it and took the club and axe. Arben gathered the retrieved weapons into a pile well away from the camp's edge. He would have broken them but couldn't risk the noise. One spear and the sentry's club were left to the Bandarken.

Five of the murrabin returned to let BeBe and Lin know their job was done; the sixth hopped away to tell BiZi his acting career was over. He was reluctant to stop as he was enjoying himself. Still, he dropped his Oscar-winning limp and scurried into the scrub leaving his confused pursuer to scratch his head, turn and trudge slowly back to the camp.

The returning sentry knew immediately his spear and axe were gone. They were always in the same place and, when he laid his club down, he saw they were missing. So was everyone else's. He roused the camp, kicking and cursing his drowsy companions into action. Bandarken stirred, grumbled and peered sleepily into the gloom. They could see nothing wrong, yet their weapons had disappeared.

This was it; time to capitalise on the confusion. One lone kokatu flew from BeBe's back to a central tree and screeched, loudly. The tree-borne kokatu responded instantly. A riotous uproar of squawking and squalling blasted through the forest camp. The kokatu loved it. Their cries rent the forest, shattering the quiet like thunderclaps. The din was deafening. The white birds bombarded the Bandarken with shrill screeching that made Lin cover her ears. She was impressed. *So far so good. Now for the hard part.*

The squawk was the signal. The kangaroos, snouts, and darrabin with koalas on board turned in and lumbered towards the Bandarken. They moved deliberately – stomping, jumping, growling, thumping – making as much racket as they could. Surprise meant noise and the kokatu excelled, but the herd members weren't far behind. The koalas coughed, darrabin snorted, bellowed and roared, tulangi grunted, kangaroos stamped their huge feet, cracking and snapping twigs and branches. And the kokatu, din masters extraordinaire, continued unabashed, unabated, their screeching louder than a hostile crowd at a basketball game. Other birds, screeching with fright at the sudden noise, contributed to the caterwaul. Small, startled animals scattered in panic and bolted through the camp, adding to the pandemonium. The herd made an awesome, frightening bewildering barrage of sound.

Chaos was complete.

The Bandarken were stunned and confused. Din and movement were everywhere but the warriors couldn't find an enemy, just a screaming, screeching, thumping, bumping barrage of sound. They'd no idea what was happening. The warriors milled around, bewildered, uncertain, falling over each other in the mayhem. Despite this, the men with the club and spear stood ready to attack.

The Bandarken warrior chief finally had his men hunt for their missing weapons. They searched under trees and shrubs, lifted logs and scoured the scrub, cursing the world and their comrades. They finally found the tools wedged under a waving wall of spines. Spike and the gang had dug themselves in and around the spears and clubs. The Bandarken tried to free them but, barehanded, they couldn't get close to the gang's needle-sharp spines. The koorabin burrowed deeper burying the weapons with them. They couldn't be budged. The weapons were lost.

The warriors finally sighted the encircling herd. One shaped to throw their one spear at the advancing animals. He never got the chance. A fury of flapping feathers dropped from the trees; three kokatu wrapped their claws around the spear, three more ripped into the warrior's hair and face. Silly, noisy birds they could be, but they were ferocious, their black hooked beaks, sharp claws, flapping wings and ear-splitting screeches used to terrifying advantage.

The Bandarken let go the spear to protect his head, the kokatu flew with the weapon and dropped it clear of the warriors. It fell with the spearpoint on a rock. A bigbird ran to the dropped weapon, placed its foot on the shaft, broke it in two and tossed the pieces into the hostile, heaving pincushion that was Spike and the gang. They shivered it through to the ground where it was buried.

Another warrior, the sentry, confronted a kangaroo in the circle with the one club left to them; the line didn't flinch even when he raised it to strike. He didn't have time before a bigbird swooped from the side, drove a kick at his leg and dropped the Bandarken screaming to the ground. The club went the same way as the spear, swallowed by the menacing mass of thorns.

At the start of the racket, Lin and Arben leaped on top of BeBe and Ida like mahouts on elephants – this was her special request – and began to gallop forward. Probably more a ponderous trot but it covered the ground quickly as they converged into the large lariat choking the Bandarken. The warriors were jammed into a cluster. The terrified men tried a mass breakout through the encircling herd. They failed and were forced back. Without weapons they were frail creatures, no match for the size and strength of one-tonne, two-metre behemoths, just as Lin had said. With their confidence boosted the kangaroos, darrabin and koalas kept moving forward, grunting, thumping, a stout-hearted noose tightening around the necks of the hapless humans.

The final insult was Lin and Arben astride the

darrabin. To the Bandarken, these beasts were their clan totems ridden by a foreign creature and a despised Pelluken, such a cruel act as they'd never thought to see. The disappointment was devastating. How could the darrabin disrespect the Bandarken in this way? This was total loss of face. When Lin tweaked BeBe's ear and the mountainous marsupial reared onto his back feet, front feet pawing the air, it was so much worse. They were scared witless. They'd never seen the like.

Lin thought BeBe would rear like a fighting stallion. Not quite. He really looked like a stodgy, circus elephant, but he was big, lumbering and effective. Lin clung tight to the hair behind his head when he dropped to his four legs and thundered across the campsite leaving Bandarken bobbing in his wake like a destroyer cutting through kayaks.

Lin would never know the energy and will it took for BeBe to rear his huge body; he would only have done it for her. Yet, he turned at the end of his run and gamely did it again. Other darrabin left the circling wall to punish the Bandarken further. The once aggressive and untouchable warriors were bruised, beaten and demoralised. When one tried to escape the wall, he was felled with a kangaroo kick that reduced him to a writhing wreck of pain.

The darrabin, tulangi and kangaroos maintained the mayhem – grunting, bellowing, stomping – the koala jockeys sitting firm like rough riders at a rodeo. Finally, the Bandarken huddled forlorn, dazed and broken in a group, beaten by a herd of wild animals, wilder birds, and a warrior woman wearing a funny hat.

Lin and Arben stood on the backs of BeBe and Ida and stared at the defeated Bandarken. *I said I'd get you bastards, and I've done that. I've no wish to hurt you further, but I'm not too sure about Arben.* His people had long hated the Bandarken, and maybe it was something he might want to act out. Lin cautioned him for her sake. She had one last plan to protect the North Forest forever.

For the sight of the forest had exhilarated Lin. She hadn't known it was so close until she stood on BeBe to address the beaten warriors. In the early light she could see the forest they'd been searching for. It loomed but a short walk away, the dark, ragged outline of a peak etched against the sunrise sky. Behind the mountain, stretching away on either side spread a range of tree-clad hills and valleys. The North Forest took her breath away. It looked like the end of her journey, and the haven BeBe and BiZi sought for their clans.

From where she stood it appeared inviting and peaceful. It had to stay that way for she had work to do. Lin sought help from Arben with some words she didn't know. Arben was to tell the Bandarken what she said and, when they didn't understand, he would sign to them. It wouldn't be much. Lin knew only little of Arben's language. Lin spoke.

"Bandarken men."

"Bandarken men," echoed Arben.

This'll take longer than I thought. I'd better use more words at a time.

She swung her arm to encompass the range of trees and hills they all could see.

"North Forest is mine," she said.

Then, quickly, before Arben could open his mouth,

"North Forest belong me and the kangaroo, darrabin, koala, tulangi, yarravan, murrabin, koorabin and kokatu," she said, pointing to herself and then each group in turn, using their names.

Arben followed suit, waving his arms, speaking loudly.

"These animals are my heart," Lin said putting her hand to her breast. "North Forest is taboo to Bandarken. Never come here again, never hurt these animals. Or I," she said, rising to her full height on BeBe's back, "The Queen of the North Forest, will ride the giant darrabin and hunt you down."

At that, Lin gave BeBe's ear a tweak and he rumbled and reared, forcing her to hang on while the Bandarken cowered in fear.

Lin saw the circled animals exchanging nervous glances. *What's wrong with them now? I'm doing this for them.*

"Do not come to this land or you will die," she roared at the beaten Bandarken.

At this the earth rumbled and bucked beneath her. The ground shook violently scaring Lin, Arben, Bandarken and the herd alike. Lin recognised it for what it was. *Omigod! Another quake.*

Sapped of strength by previous tremors, a massive tree finally succumbed to its weight and weaknesses. Slowly, awkwardly, the huge trunk shuddered, held, then toppled through the circled wall like a cleaving sword narrowly missing the kangaroos and crashing to the ground near the Bandarken in a rattling scatter of branches and leaves. Dust and dirt blew around them while the once-solid earth continued to tremble. The impact was awesome; the herd froze in fear, the Bandarken shrunk to a tight and terrified mass, the two injured warriors huddled in the middle.

Lin now understood why the animals had looked at each other. They'd sensed the quake before she did. She had to keep control or risk losing everything. It was now or never. She signalled to BeBe, BiZi and DaJiao through the strongest vision-shift: *Keep control, hold the animals here. Do not let them panic and run.* She sprang to the ground and threatened the cowering Bandarken who shrunk further at her approach. Lin held up her arms in a menacing gesture and screamed,

"I did this, I commanded the earth to shake and the tree to fall, and I will destroy you if you ever come near the North Forest again. Now go, and never come back. Go!"

Lin flung out her arm in a gesture of dismissal. A now-confused Arben had only a rough idea of what was happening, but he got the intent and followed up forcibly.

The beaten Bandarken scrambled to their feet and took off in a panic. Two stayed, too injured to move. Lin signalled a couple of bigbirds to chase the escapees and told BeBe to tell the birds not too far. *Just run them out of camp.*

It was a close thing. The Bandarken left running with the birds after them while the rest of the herd struggled for composure. Some broke ranks and scattered but it wasn't seen by the departing men who wanted to escape with their lives. They were not returning. The battle with the Bandarken was over.

Lin beckoned to Arben and the two stood over the injured pair. The abject warriors shook in terror, fearing for their lives at the hands of the Queen of the North Forest. In piecemeal phrases and signs, Lin asked Arben,

"Find out why they kidnapped me, Arben. Find out why they wanted to attack us. Then get them out of here. Alive."

Arben had a snarled discussion with the wounded warriors. They blurted words Lin did not understand, their frightened eyes swinging between their conquerors, a diminutive woman and a despised Pelluken. Finally, Arben let them struggle to their feet. Lin vision-shifted BeBe to send two bigbirds to escort them away. He did. The birds towered like titans over the hobbling Bandarken as they limped off.

With the Bandarken gone, Lin draped her arms over the necks of BeBe and Ida and hung between them, spent. The darrabin were content to have their little leader droop between them like a windless pennant. They were too weary to move anyway; BeBe in particular had been cavorting like a trick pony and his energy was sapped. The darrabin had a lot to take in. Mainly, though, they were grateful they were close to their goal. This creature from the North Forest had fought off all their enemies and got them here as they knew she would. It was always going to be.

The legend was right.

The living legend was exhausted, just happy to hang onto the shoulders of her massive mates and recover. Finally, she sighed in relief, straightened up and chuckled. She'd share the joke with Arben but it'd be too hard to explain. What were the chances of a modern girl standing on a prehistoric mega-creature in the distant past lecturing local people on moral responsibilities while getting support from an earth tremor and a falling tree? Really? *Yeah, right!* Would Arben understand it? Did she? He'd been a great support though. Lin wondered where that left Arben's people and the Bandarken. She didn't think the Bandarken would be back, ever. She couldn't say the same for the Pelluken.

Lin tried to get from Arben the reason the Bandarken kidnapped her and attacked the herd. He was clear on one thing. The herd wasn't the problem. They were. He'd stolen her and made the Bandarken look stupid, a foolish move. They wanted him dead. The Pelluken warrior showed that with mime and strangling motions across his throat.

The Bandarken told Arben what they wanted with Lin, but he struggled to explain it through the limited language they shared. But she got the rough drift and didn't like it. Darrabin were the Bandarken totem, their special animal symbol. The Bandarken had marvelled at the magic between the strange visitor and their totem, and they wanted to breed from her. That way the magic would rub off and they'd be one with the darrabin forever.

24

THE NORTH FOREST

Lin had thanking to do. First, her lieutenants for their courage in seeing off the Bandarken. DaJiao was first on the list. The huge kangaroo was grazing nearby, holding a tree branch and gnawing at the leaves. Lin smiled at him, and asked,

"DaJiao, do you ever do anything but eat? You stuff it down like a pen full of pigs! Trees are the only things in danger of extinction with you around."

Lin reached up and shook his long forepaw. He didn't pull away, just looked at her. He had no idea what she was saying or doing or why, but he didn't mind... they were pals. She patted his shoulder and did the same with the other king-sized kangaroo who looked even more bemused.

She stroked Yingjun's long nose and patted him. He didn't look ugly any more. Max, the koala king, was already up a tree, so were the kokatu; she'd deal with them later. Spike and the gang had nodded off on the pile of destroyed weapons. She wouldn't wake them. They were a grumpy bunch when disturbed, and she certainly wasn't going to pat them. They were the saviours today though. She'd let them nap.

BiZi? Where was BiZi? She found the little critter with his clan in a gully away from the main camp. He was quieter than usual, less exuberant, but he rubbed against her legs in his cat-like way. Lin always got happy vibes from BiZi. He 'told' her how he'd dealt with the Bandarken sentry and how they'd gathered and stored the weapons. Lin told him that without those brave acts they couldn't have done what they did today. He would go down in his family history forever.

Bigbirds! What to do for the feathered fighters? She couldn't high-five a creature with a wingspan the size of a small plane? She couldn't shake hands with a foot on a leg that was about as big as her. But they had to know how much they're valued, and those lovely, long necks should be decorated. Lin had seen small, yellow flowers with teeth-shaped petals growing on the flats by the river. Similar flowers blossomed in China and when she and Song were kids they'd made chains of them, threading one flower stem through another to make garlands for their hair.

Lin picked some and sat with her back to a tree, Arben by her side, their shoulders touching. It was a chance to relax, recover and let go the tension. Arben had no idea why she'd picked the flowers.

"Can you eat them?" he asked, pointing to them and his mouth.

"No," Lin laughed at the idea. "They're for decoration."

Arben didn't understand but watched on absorbed as his companion threaded five flower chains and looped them together. She picked up the garlands and, cradling them in one hand, beckoned Arben to follow. *He can trot after me for a change.*

The giant birds were moseying about, not feeding, just restless and out of sorts, not knowing what to do or what would happen next. They'd seen off the Bandarken, but they'd not got to the North Forest. Lin conveyed to BeBe that she would like the first bird to bend his head down to her level. BeBe relayed this and, somewhat warily, a bigbird complied, its neck trembling. The huge bird was like a small child holding out a hand to an adult who'd tickle their palm, then grab them. They were much in awe of this featherless figure, but they never knew what she'd do next.

Lin gave the garlands to Arben to hold, took the first one and slipped it over the bigbird's head. As he or she – Lin didn't know – lifted its head, the tribute slid down to settle as a golden wreath around the grey-brown breast. Bigbird was surprised but impressed; Lin could see that. She honoured him with a Buddhist salute, her hands clasped prayer-like and head bowed. The other three lined up and when Lin had decorated them all, and bowed, they nodded in unison and walked away proudly, golden garlands bouncing like jewels on the bosom of a dowager empress. The garlands wouldn't last but everyone knew what they meant and in what esteem the feathered fighters were held by the Queen of the North Forest.

Lin saved the last flower chain for Arben. He ducked when she tried to put it over his head. But Lin insisted and managed to kiss his cheek as she slipped the yello lei over his dark, wavy hair. He didn't jump. It did look good around his strong neck and shoulders.

*   *   *

Arben blushed. He couldn't understand why she'd want to honour him. This remarkable woman had done it all. He'd done nothing. She'd mustered and marched a herd of wildlife across a swathe of hostile territory to bring them to a haven. MeLin fought and killed a durakkan, a fearsome python – an act he considered incredible – and beaten off a dropcat, the land's premier predator. She'd outflanked and out-thought a band of warriors whose knowledge of this land was unsurpassed and then, somehow, caused the earth to shake and a tree to fall.

MeLin had taught koalas to ride darrabin, got murrabin into kangaroo pouches, put koorabin onto sleds pulled by tulangi and turned a mismatched bunch of beasts into a formidable force led by herself, a dumb darrabin, a tiny murrabin and four very large birds. She'd done all this by herself. Arben felt embarrassed that a woman with such energy, force, and will wanted to recognise him. He wasn't sure why she had done any of it, but he was in awe of her courage and determination and bewitched by her gentle charm.

*　　*　　*

Arben and Lin sat against a tree and watched the sun rise as the herd foraged for food. The day would be as fine and warm as they'd been since Lin arrived. She couldn't remember how many days she'd been here now; the long walk had blurred her memory. Breakfast was berries saved from their last meal, a few more of a type that Arben found nearby, and some chewy flower buds. They sat a while, saying little, both needed to recover from the battle with the Bandarken. It had taken its toll.

The adrenalin that drove Lin through the night had drained exposing the anxiety that sometimes showed on this long trek to safety. Her body was tired. But it was getting time to leave BeBe and the herd and head home. The corners of her mouth turned down as her eyes clouded. She'd miss them.

Lin's energy felt used and her mind empty, but she'd yet to get the herd to the North Forest. That was the deal. Time to get them going for their last walk together. She shook her shoulders and stood up.

"C'mon Arben," she said as she pushed to her feet.

It wasn't hard to round up the herd, they were keen to get moving. Max and the koalas would walk the last leg as would Spike and the gang. An end to the trek would energise their little legs, fire their enthusiasm and stifle any koala complaints. They'd make it okay. The murrabin would hop into kangaroo pouches as usual. Lin wasn't concerned to keep the herd together, the bigbirds would run sentry duty as always. Just a few more kilometres then she was done.

North Forest here we come.

Was it really the North Forest?

It'll just have to do.

The herd set off toward the short, steep peak that stood out on the near horizon. It wasn't far. The kokatu were already there squawking among the trees; Lin could hear their rasping cries as they neared. She'd never complain about that raucous racket again. She'd seen what those wonderful, white birds could do.

The mountain was small but craggy; bare rock faces dropped precipitously into ravines clogged with trees and shrubs of the same drab, olive colour. Large boulders scattered around the base of the mountain like clock hours telling time for the ancient peak. A broken ridge led down the north side ending in one of the tilted plateaus that made up most of the North Forest as far as Lin could see. They gave the forest a zigzag silhouette against the horizon.

The sky was clear, blue, and cloudless. The heat was building; a pair of large birds circled high on thermal currents. The country between the Bandarken camp and the North Forest was much the same as it'd always been, a flat, grassy plain with occasional lightly-forested and scrubby areas. The herd followed the waterway; water being their most treasured knowledge possessions. Their pace picked up as they neared their goal.

Lin and Arben walked side-by-side, comfortable in each other's company. Sometimes he'd point out something to her and say its name. She'd repeat what he'd said, and he'd nod or shake his head, smile, and try again. At other times they just walked easily, arms and shoulders touching occasionally, thoughts separate but interwoven.

*　　*　　*

Arben was lost in wonder. He thought about the wonderful woman who'd brought him alive, made his days shine like morning sun over a lake. What would life be like now that her task here seemed over? His world would never be the same. The life of the Pelluken – repeated rituals over timeless days – had never seen anything like MeLin. He doubted it would again and he, for one, would miss the adventure. She'd shown him so much; about how people treated each other and animals, how men and women shared work and worlds. He'd seen her bravery, watched her do things that would have challenged the greatest Pelluken warrior. She had the wisdom of an elder, the ease of an eagle, the lightness of a wren... and the cunning of a dropcat. She'd never faltered or wavered. And he was taken by her charm and beauty; her hair shone like dark river stones, her eyes as bright as the evening star. His thoughts got lost in the wonder.

*   *   *

Lin halted the herd at the side of the small mountain.

"Woohoo! Made it. This is it; last stop, the North Forest. The end."

She tripped lightly on her toes and smiled. The fast-vanishing herd didn't notice. *That'd be right.* Lin smiled. *The trek's over, the walking's done. Ignore me. Just like DaJiao and the snake.* BeBe and BiZi had asked her to get them here – to fulfil their prophecy – and she'd done it. They'd made it here together and safe. She wasn't sure how, but they'd done it.

Time for Lin to say goodbye, return to the disc, and home.

Lin would depart with Arben and the animals would go their separate ways, each to its favoured place. The kangaroos and darrabin would graze on the plains and seek the shade of the trees when needed. In front of them a flat valley floor disappeared into the distance between uptilted plateau peaks. It looked just right. The tulangi would seek out marshy places to wallow and wander. Max would lead the koalas into the trees. Bigbirds would make their way along valley floors, fern gullies and high hillsides alike. The murrabin would find the brush-filled gullies they knew, as would Spike and the gang. The latter were making for them now, their bristly bodies pitching and rolling like a stubby armada heading for harbour. Spike obviously wasn't one for long goodbyes, or goodbyes at all apparently. BiZi and BeBe and Ida were though, and if they were there, then so was Little Quilt, getting bigger and bolder every day.

Lin had wanted this journey to end from the time she'd muttered, 'Marsupials march' and 'rolled the wagons' out of BeBe's home valley. Now she wasn't sure. She'd led the animals because they wanted it, it had to be done, and it had to be her. There was no-one else. Now it was over, and she'd delivered them as promised. It was time to go. So why was she unhappy?

Part of it had to be the excitement. Life at home was never this sensational. The past days had been breath-taking, a roller-coaster ride so different to mundane maths homework, and the daily bus trip to college despite how much Song made it fun. There could be the occasional monster on the bus. Her old buddy Qinghua was a real pest, but he didn't drop off the luggage rack and claw her heart out like a dropcat. Or rear up from behind the back seat and sling a loop around her body like a python. Well, not so far, anyway.

Lin had gone through less demanding days and she'd welcomed them. They'd given her time to get her breath back, regain her poise, appreciate what she'd done and why. Life couldn't always be hyper-busy, and she liked it quiet sometimes. She wondered whether the difference lay in the purpose rather than the action.

What was the end of all this busyness, energy and excitement? What did it mean? Saving the threatened creatures even for a short time felt so good. Hearken to your heart, Granma said. Lin had done that, and Granma was right. These creatures had stolen her heart.

Lin cared for the herd in a way she hadn't thought possible when she first cast startled eyes on BeBe's frightful features. 'Marsupials march' had become 'marsupials mine'. And now she didn't want to let them go. They were such simple, loveable creatures, hanging in there, doing what they did, trying to survive and have more of their kind. That's it. Simple? Sure. Hard to do? Absolutely! And if she'd kept their lives going an extra day, an extra month, it was worth it.

Lin's thoughts turned to Arben. The days had brought them together, the years would drive them apart. He meant so much to her now, and she wondered how she'd cope with leaving him, because part they must. She so liked being together... walking, talking, laughing, sharing, playing house. She didn't want to lose him, but she had to go; Mum, Dad and Grampa would be frantic, her buddies would be beside themselves with worry.

Arben would take her to the disc, and she would leave. He would stay. As they'd walked together Lin had thought of what a picture it must present; she, a small, blue-clad woman with floppy hat, rolled-up cloak and bumbag; he, a tall, near-naked man with a spear and club. She, a child of the 21st century; he, a hunter-gatherer from a time before time. This saga had brought them together; its ending would drive them apart.

Lin had thought about taking Arben back to China. It might seem a fun thing to do but she doubted he'd fit in or want to stay. She imagined tumbling out of the spacepipe into her bedroom.

Mum, this is Arben, he's my new boyfriend. Arben, meet my mother. He comes from thousands of years ago, Mum, doesn't speak Chinese, doesn't wear clothes, doesn't go to school, never will. And, oh, he carries a spear and a club to kill things. But not you, he loves your dumplings.

Yeah, sure! As if that'd work. She'd reach for the big broom in two seconds flat.

Still, they had togetherness for a few days yet and she didn't want to think of leaving, and losing, Arben.

The kokatu were perched in the trees nearby when Lin asked BeBe if some could come closer so she could thank them. They all came – one in, all in – except for a sentinel up the tree. They scattered and squalled about her feet, yellow crests raised, black eyes shining, hooked beaks open, heads bobbing up and down. Lin laughed to herself as she thought of the possibilities for their talk: what might they be saying? *What's happening? Skraark! Dunno, what do you think? Squaawk! The little human wants us here! Maybe it's food! Skraairk!*

Lin had nothing to give them and they didn't respond to vision-shifting, so she placed her finger behind the crest of the nearest bird and stroked it as you would pet a cat. Lin didn't know it, but this was kokatu bliss; this was mooncakes and bubble tea, icecream and eclairs, cake and cream. They loved it.

In seconds kokatu were all around. Lin stood like a tourist feeding pigeons in a park. Kokatu were everywhere, bobbing up and down, squawking, pressing close to her, screeching for a rub. She had to use both hands and get

Arben's help otherwise they'd have been there until dark.

To Arben this was another example of the strange power of MeLin; to her it was not enough thanks for what these amazing wild creatures had done to get them to the North Forest.

Late in the afternoon when Arben went looking for food, Lin, BeBe and BiZi had time to be together, probably for the last time. They 'talked' of what they'd done. Lin didn't understand how vision-shifting worked. The best she could think of was that it was a gene tweak that triggered thought transfer between beings. Mind-reading in a way! It was hard to do but it worked for her, BeBe and the boys. BeBe showed her she was now in their visual annals, a small hat-topped figure walking in front of a herd of darrabin, performing extraordinary acts of bravery to bring them to their new home. She was their Queen of the North Forest.

Lin still wasn't sure, but BeBe and BiZi knew; they'd known that a strange creature would come through a new sun in one period of the moon. The sun appeared in the early days of the new moon, Lin had appeared after BiZi had gone through it and back a couple of times. That was all the proof they needed. The sun would disappear when the moon had waxed and waned. This was what they always knew, and it happened the way it had been foretold.

The sun would go. The disc disappear! What? When? Lin panicked. Why didn't she remember that? She had to get home. Was the disc still there? Where were they in the moon cycle now? How much longer did she have to get back to BiZi's home valley? The herd didn't care, but she did! Omigod, did she?

Details spun through Lin's head like marbles in a barrel. When she was taken by the Bandarken the moon was bright but not full, probably on the wane, and that was a few days ago. So there had to be time left, but how much? Numbers, dates. She had to get it right! When did the disc arrive? She remembered the day well, but what was the date? How many days had she waited while the disc sat in her room, how many days had she been here, met the darrabin, run into Arben and guided the herd north?

Lin crunched the numbers, settling her swirling mind with something she could do... count. She worked through the figures and dates. About twenty-four days seemed right. That meant three more nights to get back to the disc, including tonight. Three nights? *Omigod! Only three more days. Relax, that'll be okay.* She and Arben could walk faster than the herd, and for longer if they had to. Three days would do it. Easy. They'd leave tomorrow with the dawn. But first they'd mingle with the rapidly-dwindling herd and get to know the North Forest. Lin's tension left. She scratched the darrabin, stroked BiZi, and left them to their foraging as bigbirds clustered together by the stream.

25

ATOP THE BIGBIRDS

Bigbirds had been at the battle when Lin and Arben rode on the backs of the darrabin. They were impressed, and maybe a little envious. Perhaps carrying the humans for a short while might be possible for them. They were strong and powerful, not as strong as a darrabin but strong enough to carry a human, particularly a small one like the Queen of the North Forest and, yes, even her questionable companion. The birds conveyed this to BeBe and he relayed it to Lin.

I'm not so sure about that, Lin thought, although she liked the idea. *Wow, get on a bigbird*. Still, the idea of riding a bird no matter how large, seemed unfair. Birds were high fliers, not beasts of burden. Birds were cackling kokatu, cooing pigeons, soaring eagles, chirping sparrows... and you couldn't ride a sparrow.

Bigbirds insisted it would be fine and they'd be

honoured if the Queen of the North Forest and her consort would try it. Lin told Arben about the idea and his eyebrows arched in a personal best. He'd never done anything like it but, with MeLin, anything could happen, and usually did. So, he nodded, not really knowing what he'd agreed to.

When Lin and Arben said yes, they climbed on top of BeBe and Ida by way of a fallen tree and stood up on their broad backs. Two bigbirds walked alongside. Lin and Arben grasped the strong, feathered necks, tossed their right legs over and eased into a seat where neck met body. The riders' legs slid down in front of the stubby wings as though they were made for them. Lin fitted easily, as if she'd been born to be a bigbird jockey.

The birds weren't built like ostriches. They didn't have a horizontal body cage with a neck sticking straight up at one end. They were more the shape of an egret with a thicker, stronger body angled at about 30 degrees. They were a lot larger than your average wading bird, though.

Now that she was up close and personal, Lin spotted what might be a gender difference. It was most likely the males that had a slightly heavier tuft of feathers running from their heads down their necks to peter out among the body plumage. Two had this barely noticeable feature, two didn't.

The two that did were carrying Lin and Arben and seemed unworried with the weight. Aboard the giant creatures, the jockeys were puny passengers. Lin wrapped her arms around the bird's neck and pressed her cheek against the feathers. It felt like hugging a downy tree. She sat, legs hung over the sloping shoulders, heels against bigbird's chest. Even seated behind the neck, Lin's hat barely made it as high as the beak. She was a tiny rider astride a massive mount. Lin looked at Arben. He was smiling nervously; these steeds made him look little.

When they moved the riders hung on because bigbirds didn't walk for long; they jogged, then ran. Lin had never ridden a horse, neither had Arben. The closest either of them had been to riding was sitting on slow and cumbersome darrabin. BeBe could never make anything like the pace of bigbirds. They were sleek, speedy Formula One's to his old clunker. The birds loved to run. It was the way they chased and caught small prey; it was how they evaded predators. In the absence of flight, running was life. The giant creatures ran with necks bent forward, their wings lifted a little off their bodies. Lin and Arben tucked their lower legs back under the wings, which made riding easier.

The birds were powerfully-built creatures with sturdy legs. Each footfall sent a small tremor through the riders that became a vigorous shudder as the birds accelerated. The tremors shivered through Lin's thighs and groin, speeding her heartbeat and quickening her breath as she tightened her legs around the strong body. Colour flushed her face. Warm air buffeted her hair and swept over her skin in a heady stream.

The valley receded to a blur of green in the face of Lin's adrenalin high, her racing pulse and an electrifying spurt of energy. She was fearful at first, but the thrill of the galloping giants soon overcame anxiety and Lin revelled in the power and passion of the ride.

Arben had never experienced anything like it either as he raced MeLin along the valley floor with nothing to confine them; two high-spirited people on two fearsome, feathered chargers.

Bigbirds started together but the one carrying Lin got a little ahead and away from Arben. She wanted to be closer. She placed her hand on the left of the thick, feathered neck and pushed; bigbird went right. She put her hand around the front of his neck, pulled back a little and he slowed. In this way she made her way towards Arben and for a time the two pounded along side-by-side lost in the thrill of it.

Lin drew alongside her companion and held out her right hand. He grasped it with his left, a broad grin creasing his face, long hair streaming behind. Lin had no idea of how fast or where they were going but right then she didn't want it to end and could've gone on forever astride their mighty beasts, thundering onwards hand-in-hand.

It had to stop. Bigbirds separated to go either side of a tree on the valley floor and the riders' fingers slid apart. They came together again beyond the tree as the birds throttled back to trotting pace. They held hands again as their mounts slowed to a walk. The drop in speed gave them a chance to look around.

Arben didn't know this place and wanted to know

what it offered. The valley had narrowed behind them as they ran. After they passed through a small gap it opened out into a wide central plain ringed by the tree-clad walls of the North Forest range. The vegetation was thickening; just as many trees but clusters of a plant that Lin had not seen before spread in profusion. Dark, pencil-like shafts grew tall out of wide spreads of broad, thick leaves. Some of them would have been as tall as the bigbirds. The interior plain seemed drier, yet it fed into the river the herd had followed north for much of the way. Lin was looking at the scenery, Arben was looking for signs of life – human or otherwise – and food. There were no threats he could see.

The other two bigbirds, which had trailed in the wake of the speeding pair, eventually caught up. All four feathered giants walked together a while then simultaneously spun on their clawed feet to return the way they'd come... and dropped to the ground. They squatted on the valley floor as if nesting. All four looked at Lin and Arben. The riders turned to each other, eyebrows raised, then dismounted. What was happening? Lin's bigbird stood. So did Arben's. The other two remained squatting. This was changeover time. Bigbirds 1 and 2 weren't tired; bigbirds 3 and 4 wanted to carry the Queen of the North Forest and her companion.

Lin wasn't sure whether the new birds were female. They were equally as big and strong, though, and just as capable. The riders changed steeds and sped back the way they'd come, not quite as quickly as before if only because

Lin didn't want to go so fast. She wanted to revel in what might be the one and only experience like this she'd ever have.

The birds returned the riders to where they'd begun. Lin hugged her bigbird's neck in gratitude, slipped to the ground, walked to the other feathered runners and hugged them in turn. She could only reach around their chests, but the birds stood for it, swinging their heads to peer at her intently. Lin returned their gaze with a smile. What she'd once taken to be a very scary stare was now a good-natured gaze. She loved them. They liked her. She knew that, as she knew she'd never forget the ride with Arben.

Bigbirds mooched away to feed. The darrabin were foraging around the edges of the valley as the sun descended. Lin found BeBe and conveyed that she and Arben would leave in the morning. He dropped his head to acknowledge this and went back to gnawing on a shrub.

Lin picked up her cloak and she and Arben walked towards the mountain slope to find a campsite. They forded the stream and clambered up a rock overhang that Arben had seen from the valley floor. It was not large, maybe a couple of metres deep but with cover enough to protect them against rain should it ever fall. They were not the first residents. Rock paintings decorated the ceiling. There were pictures of darrabin and kangaroo and an outline of a serpent like the one she'd fought in the river. Maybe there was one like it here. The thought of it made Lin shiver. She touched Arben's shoulder, pointed at the snake outline and raised her eyebrows in question then pointed to the stream. He shook his head. Too much life flourished for there to be a durakkan here.

There was another drawing of a lizard-like creature similar to the one Lin had seen in an earlier cave. Lin pointed it out to Arben. He shrugged, shook his head, muttered, "Eskaven," and fluttered his hand away as if to suggest the creature was either long gone or far away. He knew this place as Bandarken territory, and they must've done the paintings, probably a long time ago. This was not Pelluken land. It was the reason he'd kept an eye out for life even though he was sure the Bandarken wouldn't return for a while.

Arben gathered material for a fire and motioned Lin to light it while he went to find food. He took his spear and club. Lin held his elbow to detain him, pointed to the kangaroo and the darrabin paintings, shook her head and said, "No." These were not to be hunted, nor the little creature she mimicked by flapping her hands for ears and pointing her nose.

He nodded unenthusiastically but Lin knew he understood. She hadn't brought the herd all this way to eat them. Bigbirds were safe; he wouldn't go near them after the time he'd just had. Lin lit the fire and sat back to watch the late afternoon sun set over the valley. The darrabin and the kangaroos were foraging. Bigbirds had gone off looking for food; the kokatu were scattered over the plain picking at grass seeds. They stood out like dandruff on a dark suit. Not for the first time Lin felt like the original woman looking out on this land. She knew she wasn't, so she contented herself thinking she must be the first Chinese woman.

It wasn't long before Arben returned with food. He was a good provider and more than just a hunter. He could gather as well. He'd collected a clutch of purple berries and a few eggs that he held in a broad leaf. And there were two large fleshy bulbs. They were peeled and Arben placed them onto the fire with small sticks as skewers so that they could be retrieved when cooked.

He'd also caught two small fish, a type that Lin didn't know. Maybe he'd speared them. Arben returned to the river to gut and clean the fish using an edge of sharpened stone he kept in his belt. The fish went on sticks held over the fire. The eggs cooked whole in the coals; this was indeed a meal. Lin was hungry. All this action in the open air was firing her appetite. But she really missed rice. For what's a meal without it? Still, she ate well and, when she was finished, washed her hands in the stream to clean off the fishy smell. Arben no longer commented upon her scent. It was the smell of clean, clear water and sunshine that surrounded her now.

From this point the sun descended swiftly; darkness covered the land like a cloak. Lin was taken by how simple life was when the things she used to rely on weren't around. No cars, houses, white goods, gas, electricity, laptops, iPods, iPads, TV and mobile phones cluttered Arben's world. Without them the need for food, water, warmth, togetherness and safety took priority. Looking for food didn't take a lot of time. Most of the day, Lin guessed, would be taken up with being together, looking after family, story-telling, and talking about the day... the things that gave life meaning. It was a far cry from her world in China.

Arben seemed to possess about six things and his life didn't seem to want for much. In his world, the future and things weren't as important as the present and the people. She reached for his hand and felt the reassuring touch of his fingers.

A fire was welcome, and essential. It gave light, warmth, security and a space for togetherness. Arben gathered more fuel. Dry wood lay everywhere. With the fire alight, they sat and shared the quiet of this broad valley that rose around them like a cathedral. Sometimes he'd hear or see something and give it its name. Mostly they sat and gazed into the fire and thought of the day just gone, the fight to save the herd and the ride on bigbirds.

Lin mused on the departure to come. Tomorrow she'd say goodbye to this wonderful lot of critters, head south with Arben and find the disc. Then they'd part; a farewell she didn't want but couldn't avoid. Lin swallowed and blinked, tears edged her eyes. She'd only known Arben a few days, but Lin felt she'd known her Pelluken companion forever. He meant so much to her now. She'd come to depend on him, to help, to provide.

Yet she knew he was so much a part of the time and place into which he was born. Arben lived wholly in this world, as much a part of it as trees and streams. He was so at home. Nothing could change that, and they couldn't escape it. Their lives were very different. Taking him home, providing he survived Wang Mei's broom, would be like those exotic people that were taken to China to amuse the old emperors. He'd be a one-off wonder, gawked at and prodded, then quickly forgotten in the world of the ten-minute news cycle. No, he'd be better off here in a world he understood. But would they be better off without each other? The question had no answer.

Twilight meant the departure of the daytime animals and the emergence of night prowlers. The interval held many mysteries. Brightly-coloured birds chose their roosting trees and settled for the night. Individuals flew in late to disturb the hard-won balance on boughs and branches. The small creatures pecked, squawked, and shuffled until the newcomer was settled and the tree-home stilled into silence. Large birds flew silently from tree to tree. Bright eyes glistening with firelight shone from tree limbs and shrub canopies as the nocturnal hunters bided their time.

Humans were creatures of the light and prepared for sleep not long after dark. Lin had her hide-coat to sleep under; Arben slept as he was. He'd collected an armful of bark, reeds and grasses and strewn them over the overhang's rock floor to soften the hardness and cut off the damp. Lin organised her hide cloak on the bark and grass and rolled herself into it, one arm and hand out, palm up and prepared for sleep. Arben put some more fuel on the fire so that it would stay alight into the night. Then he pushed the excess bark and grass close to Lin and lay down. He reached out his hand and their fingers clasped together gently.

*   *   *

Arben was in awe of MeLin. Life had never been anywhere near as exciting before he met her. The appearance of this small blue-clad creature had been amazing, and he didn't want the excitement to stop. But he feared he was about to lose her. She was about to return to her world, he could sense it.

*   *   *

The morning was bright. The sun rose behind the mountain and threw shortening shadows across the valley floor. Darrabin and kangaroo grazed together. In their midst – of no fuss or concern – stood a pair of leggy, slender grey birds. Nowhere near as large as bigbirds, they were maybe a metre and a half tall, with long, supple necks. They were like cranes in China, Lin thought, except this pair had red spots on their heads and black flaps under their chins. They were attractive creatures.

The two birds stood quietly side-by-side. Lin watched them, admiring their supple elegance until Arben stirred the fire and she left to fill her water bottle from the stream and have a quick wash. There were eggs left over from the previous evening. They cooked and shared them, laughing together as Lin tossed the hot ovals from hand to hand.

The remaining berries and a scrap of cold fish followed the eggs, and that was breakfast. *Okay, now to find BeBe and BiZi, say farewell, get back to the disc, and go home.*

Lin looked at Arben, her eyes misty as she strapped on her bumbag and put on her hat.

"Let's go," she murmured. "Before I decide to stay."

Lin picked up her cloak, descended to the valley floor and crossed the stream.

BeBe plodded over to greet them. He lowered his head. Lin did likewise. If she'd been expecting a band, fireworks and a farewell fanfare, it wasn't to be. BeBe, Ida, and Little Quilt made up the departure party. They showed no signs of sorrow, loss or emotion.

No other member of the herd showed up to farewell them except BiZi who came out of the brush and hopped up to Lin. It was BeBe and BiZi who'd brought her here; it was right and proper they should be here to say goodbye. BiZi brushed around Lin's legs and Lin bent down to scratch his ears and say farewell. It was then she noticed BiZi's fully loaded pouch. He'd been getting plumper of late, now she knew why. BiZi was carrying young! BiZi was so not a he. All this time Lin had thought BiZi to be male; she'd no way to know. This tiny creature that had endured so much, risked her life to fool the Bandarken with an audacious scam; this tiny, brave creature was female, and did most of this while pregnant and then nursing young. This place still had much to teach Lin about assumptions and expectations. Her eyes filled with tears Arben couldn't understand.

The darrabin dropped their heads in a show of respect and BiZi wound around Lin's legs one last time. The Queen of the North Forest went to both of the larger darrabin, stretched her arms around their necks, hugged them, scratched their backs and conveyed her affection and respect through vision-shifting as best she could. She didn't notice their smell. The pair shuffled and grunted and rubbed against her. It was all Lin could do. Nothing she could say or do would make half as much sense.

Lin knew how these creatures felt despite their lack of expression. Finally, she squatted down in front of Little Quilt, grasped his jowls and kissed him on his broad forehead. The little darrabin, bobbed his head and gently, ever so gently, butted Lin in the chest. She scratched his head.

"I just wish I could see you one day when you're a big Little Quilt. 'Cos you're going to be a giant. Bigger than your dad."

That was it, Lin turned to go.

Lin and Arben were about to walk when the two slender birds standing nearby began to dance. No curtain went up. No bell rang. Flapping their wings gently, carolling softly to each other and to the watching group the pair commenced a graceful minuet. They bowed and circled, bobbed and curtseyed, pirouetted and pranced, flapped their wings, spread their feathers and glided effortlessly back and forth, long necks swinging to and fro. It went on for two minutes, their keening cries echoing through the valley, the forlorn sound slipping down the crags and weaving through the trees mimicking Lin's blues as she watched the sweet swansong.

Lin didn't know whether the dance was arranged or spontaneous. It couldn't be arranged; she didn't think BeBe was big on dancing, unless it was the Stomp. It didn't matter. It was a farewell she'd never forget. Tears slid down her cheeks as the two graceful birds finished with a genuflect to each other and the departing duo.

Forget the fanfare and fireworks, nothing could better what she'd just seen. If that's thanks, then it was all she needed. Dropping to a crouch Lin stroked BiZi one last time, stood, and turned to the south, to home. She motioned to Arben, she dared not say anything through the tears, and they began to walk. After fifty metres or so she turned. They were still there, the darrabin with heads lowered, the tall birds oddly still. BiZi bobbed up and down. That was the last she saw of them as she and Arben turned again to begin their journey to the disc.

26

FIRE MOUNTAIN

Lin and Arben walked through the day, save for a couple of hours to escape the midday heat. Arben knew where they were going. It was to where he and Lin first met just a few days earlier. So much had happened since but that was where she wanted to return. From there, BeBe had shown her the way to the disc.

And home.

For the first hour Lin was quiet, her mind on the herd and its future. The triple-threat of drought, fire, and people still loomed. She worried for their survival but beating the Bandarken should keep that bad bunch away for a while. They'd left scared and running. There was nothing she could do about wildfires, earthquakes and drought, but the forest had plenty of water and food. They should be okay.

In the afternoon as they walked together, hands touching occasionally, Lin's spirits rose. The quest was over. Finished. She'd done everything the herd had asked, got them safely through a crazy trek. The North Forest was theirs. The future was in their hands... or feet... or feathers. Whatever. She just wanted to be with Arben. For they didn't have long.

The country they walked across was no-man's land, a contested space between Pelluken and Bandarken. Both groups were wary of it, a chance meeting could mean violence, even death. A young Arben had been told of a Pelluken boy who'd tracked a wounded kangaroo into this area and been caught and killed by the Bandarken. All his people knew the story and heeded its warning.

Arben knew the area, but not well. He'd chosen this way because it was quicker, and Lin had to get back to where they'd met within three days. He thought it likely the Bandarken would keep out of the North Forest for a while. But he couldn't be sure. They were an unpredictable lot. So, he kept a watchful eye. The other he kept on his companion.

They walked over flat land. Nothing new in that. Except for the North Forest, the country had been flat and boring since Lin had arrived. They made good time. Soon the forest shrunk to a dark, raised line of trees and a craggy bump behind them. A long way ahead two humps rose out of the plain, like the two where they'd fought the dropcat, but these two bumps were bigger. She pointed them out to Arben who gave them a name and signed they'd walk around them on their way to the disc.

Lin needed Arben's knowledge to get her home. They weren't following the river; the herd had because they needed the water. But she and Arben weren't bound by that. He knew where to find water; it was part of his people's lore, even if they weren't in Pelluken territory. Lin filled her flask whenever she could, and food was to be found most anywhere – you just had to know where to look. And Arben knew. The walking was easy and Arben was delighted to share more of his language and life, so pleased to spend more time with MeLin, the woman who had upended his existence.

They walked into the evening, no longer restrained by the plodding foot speed of the herd. The surface grew rougher as they went. They walked around and over clumped grass and splashed through rivulets that etched the surface. Lin's sneakers were wet and dirty from squelching through the damp. Arben splashed through it barefoot. As the sun touched the horizon, the pair stopped in a narrow gully that led to the main stream now many kilometres away. Arben gathered wood and went looking for food. Lin lit the fire and tended it.

Arben was gone a long time; twilight was passing, the night closing in. A long, thin cloud passed across the setting sun, splitting it like a dagger drawn across a blood orange. Trees cast their last shadows over the rock walls. Lin watched a cat-like creature run along a branch and launch itself into the next tree. The limb bent under its weight. The animal swung precariously over a long drop before scrambling to safety. Flickering shadows from the fire cast long silhouettes across the valley. An unseen bird piped a mournful goodnight. There was no reply.

Lin heard odd sounds, saw unknown movements. Something scrabbled in the shadows. *What was that?* Goosebumps rose on her arms as the grass in front of her parted to let some creature pass. It made no sound. Was it a snake? *Omigod, no!* Without Arben she was on her own, exposed and vulnerable to this land's dangers. She hoped he was okay. Maybe he's hurt. Maybe the Bandarken had killed him. *No, don't be silly. Relax, girl! It's gonna be okay. Be strong. He'll be back. Just wait. Wait.* Long moments passed. Lin's heart beat harder as she struggled to calm her growing panic. What could've happened?

A twig snapped behind her. She swung in fright. *Arben.* His smile broadened when he saw her. Lin breathed out loudly as her body shed its tension. Arben put down food he'd brought and nudged the fire into action. A cascade of sparks spat and crackled; glowing points of light fluttered like fireflies. Bright licks of flame sent off the shadows as the campsite lightened. He tossed another branch on the dancing flames and sat to prepare the meal. Firelight gleamed on his face. Lin relaxed. It was so good to see him. She didn't know she could miss him so much.

Dinner was an eel. Trapping it took time. The slippery creatures were often on Chinese menus, and Lin liked them. Arben had also picked fruit and some larger berries, ones she'd eaten before and liked. He tried to indicate in words and gestures that he'd trapped the slippery fish in one of the narrow rivulets. This was a damp area favoured by eels and people alike. The Pelluken camped at sites like this to trap the fish as they slithered through the shallows.

Arben cleaned the eel then placed forked twigs either side of the smoky fire. He threaded the eel onto a long stick and suspended it over the smoke. They shared some berries while they waited, laughing and ducking as the light, shifting breeze swung the smoke towards them wherever they sat. Lin remembered a time with her granma – campfires were like that, she'd said. Smoke chases you like a debt collector.

Both Lin and Arben were hungry; it had been a long day. They ate without talking and had barely finished the meal when the earth stirred again, not much, just enough to let them know something moved underfoot. The pair exchanged glances, eyebrows raised. Arben smiled; they were okay. There'd been worse. The worst quake saw off the Bandarken.

Meal over, they talked awhile then arranged their beds under the trees. Lin watched the stars come out, myriad pinpoints of light sparkling in the vast black cavern of space. She held Arben's hand and wondered again at the magic, the providence that had brought her here, to this time, this place, and this special man.

Lin had thought more than once about the chain of chance that drew her to this land. It didn't make sense. Any of it. Too many coincidences, too many unexplained events. The story had more loose ends than her mother's sewing basket. Why her room of all places? Why her? Why not in the Summer Palace or the Great Hall of the People? *That'd really give them something to gab about!* There was no reason for it to be in her room. It had to be chance. Some oddball oddity dropped the disc next to her bed. It could've popped up next to any of the eight billion people in the world. It just chose her room, because she was so special. *Yeah, right.* Or maybe she had nothing to do with it, and it was the place and space. She hoped the disc was still comfy and quiet in Granma's closet.

The spacepipe might be a wormhole. Lin had heard of such things, spatial oddities that thread through gaps in the galaxy to find other places, other times, even other universes. That's what might have happened to her. She didn't know. But it was the only explanation she had.

Lin had heard her nerdy pals at college talking about wormholes once. She hadn't listened much, partly because the idea seemed fanciful, mainly because that lunchbreak she and Song were still gossiping about their pal Zhou and a possible romance. But if what she overheard was correct and a wormhole had an entry point at both ends, then she might have gone through a wormhole. It hadn't been much fun. Might be easier for worms. She'd talk with those boys when she got home.

But the real riddle, the mind-bender Lin couldn't get her head around was why those weird and wonderful animals – who were expecting some special saviour – picked her? And how come she had this strange power of vision-shifting that was so important to getting the herd north. And then, to add to it all, it just so happened that one way of saying her name comes out as North Forest. *That's crazy. What if my name had meant Sweet Peach? Would the disc have been by my bed or in the fruit section at the supermarket?*

Too many coincidences, not enough explanations. Lin was not religious. Like her parents she thought men invented gods, not the other way around. She'd little regard for faith-based views of the world and held to her father's view that one day science would explain all things. But she didn't dismiss other possibilities. She couldn't, because right now there was no rational explanation for what she'd gone through. Forget it. None of it made sense. *Gotta be like Arben. Make the most of now.*

Just one more day to share with him. One more sleep and she'd be back at the disc, and home. *I don't want to go. But I have to.* Such were Lin's contrary thoughts as she woke with the dawn and opened her eyes to a riot of colour. Arben had disturbed her when he'd prodded the fire alight and gone to find food. The night had been cold, even her cloak couldn't keep out all the chill, but the first rays of dawn were brilliant. Pale blue, dark blue, pink, gold, orange and red layers tried to better each other in a vivid parade of merging, moving colour backlit by the golden-orange sun lifting off the still-dark horizon. It was superb... and sad.

Lin lay under her cloak, watching sparkling shafts of sunlight flicker and flash – black and white, light and shade, bright and dull – through a twisting spray of leaves at the gully's edge. The last day and it was beautiful. The last day with Arben in this world and her heart hurt. She would soon return home to her friends and family.

She would lose Arben.

The days often started with sunlit splendour and

bird calls but this morning the dawning glory was to be especially celebrated. Two large, grey-brown, long-beaked birds flew in to a tree above their camp. Lin saw their arrival and ignored them. She'd seen their like before. Suddenly that changed. For after a subtle, melodious warbling, the birds erupted into raucous laughter, a mighty mirth that exploded over the plains welcoming and encouraging the arriving day. The pair dueted noisily, heads thrown back, one hooting a steady bass guffaw the other cackling a rising-falling chortle that swooped and whooped across the grassland and echoed through the small valley, a happy welcome to the soaring sun.

Lin loved it. For a few seconds the joyous sounds swept her up and she was at one with the sun, the life and the land. If this was ancient Australia then, in her last hours here, she was at home and happy. The dawn chorus chortled up and down to end in a fiendish, staccato chuckle... then silence.

The birds flew off when Arben returned. Once the sun broke over the horizon, life and movement began in earnest for him. Lin smiled and shook her head. If there was such a thing as a sleep-in, Arben hadn't heard of it. Come the dawn and he was up and about, looking for food. Lin's purpose was clear too. Keep walking. So, with breakfast over, the rising sun and the memory of birds' laughter fresh in her mind, Lin and Arben continued their long walk south to the disc... and parting.

Some days there had been creatures, big and small, foraging on the plain. Not today. Except for the distant hills the plain stretched wide, flat and deserted. They had it to themselves, no birds, bees or beasts. Not a thing. Not even the raptors that had been circling high in the sky since Lin arrived were to be seen. She noticed the emptiness. Maybe they weren't the only people on this earth. But today it seemed right. They had it to themselves.

The pair walked for some hours, a cloudless canopy of blue arched above them. Apart from the sunrise laughter of the birds, they heard no more calls or sounds. The world was quiet. Only the faintest of zephyrs ruffled the heads of long grass as they passed.

The herd and their trek to the North Forst seemed well behind Lin this blue-bright morning. Arben was always watchful for dropcats but since the first and only one Lin had dispatched, there had been no others. There were few trees around anyway, and they avoided those that were. The late morning saw the pair closing on the two hills that grew larger on the horizon as they walked. Arben was using them as a trip marker of sorts. He meant to walk around their edge.

Lin had brightened with the morning. Her mood was usually light with Arben but today was different. She was going home tomorrow. Woohoo! She'd see her buddies, listen to Mum, phone Dad, text Song, eat a real meal and be a normal Chinese girl. She wouldn't have to be some Xena-type warrior woman hellbent on saving the planet. Lin smiled at the thought. That'd be so good. Yet her face drooped as she thought of leaving Arben. *But we still have time.*

As they walked, Lin talked of the trek and what they'd done together. Some of it was in his language as she'd developed a basic, baby grasp of it, all nouns, simple verbs with not much holding them together. But with signs, smiles and a limited fund of shared words they could make each other understand. He asked her where she was from and who she was; Lin attempted to answer. The gulf between their lives was so vast, however, that it was impossible for her to put into words where she'd come from and have him understand its reality.

Arben knew so much about this world, the people and things that lived in it, the land, trees, the animals. He was part of it and could survive here, living on his wits and working with his family. But she couldn't. She was a city girl from a so, so different world. Survival for Lin meant working hard at whatever job she could get, improving her education and training, finding a place to live and helping support her parents. Survival meant working with the huge, messy bureaucracy that was modern China. The skillsets were not even close. Some of this she could make clear to Arben, but it was difficult for him to grasp words that conveyed buildings and cars when all he knew were lean-tos and legs.

Still, Lin told Arben about the little things; about pandas, Song Qili, her family, college, about being called 'baby' by her father, what she wanted to do after college. She told him about her mother and the brooms, about Granma and the red vase, the spacepipe, the reason she was here. She knew a lot of it was silly. She knew she was burbling on but couldn't stop. He wouldn't understand much. But she nattered away, chatting aimlessly, her spirits buoyant, happy to be walking and talking with a marvellous man on a glorious morning in a primeval world.

The pair stopped for food and water in the early afternoon and rested in the shade. By mid-afternoon they were past the small hills, still deep in happy chat, faces alive, voices animated, arms and hands waving. They took little notice of what lay around them, so delighted were they in each other's company.

There'd been no bird cries, no insects chirping, no animal sounds at all throughout the morning, just a spreading hush. Arben had noted the absence of wildlife but he was lost in the charm of the wonderful woman walking with him. So, while he thought it unusual, he didn't worry. Everything had been different for days.

When steam and smoke vented from a fissure that split the nearest of the hills, they didn't notice. The first warning was a massive rumble that shook the ground beneath their feet... and didn't quit. The once-solid earth shuddered and shook.

The idyll was over.

The world tilted; the horizon dipped. Lin lost her balance. Her eyes wide with fright, she looked at Arben and gripped his shoulder for support and reassurance. They huddled together, shocked and scared, frightened actors on a shaky stage.

There was no chasm yawning beneath their feet, no toppling trees, just a wobbly horizon and a gut-clenching roar that shattered any idea the world would ever be the same. All thoughts of normal were destroyed by a scarlet rupture that slashed the hill's crown. Bright-red magma oozed like blood from a gaping wound. Smoke and debris blasted into the sky and a cloud of ash spread over the sun like a dusky shroud. Eerie shadows covered the plains. The sun turned from gold to dull red through the smoke and the light took on a greenish tinge. Lava seared down the hillside like scorching treacle. Pushed by the breeze, a fire stormed across the grassland. What moments before had been placid and pastoral was now a fiery hell.

Lin and Arben stood transfixed. Fight or flight became freeze.

"Oh. My. God!"

The words came separately, slowly, Lin's voice barely audible. Unable to look away, stunned by the ferocity, the pair watched on, mouths agape, as their once-stable world blew apart.

Massive underground forces hurled heated debris into the sky like a venting pressure cooker. It fell back as a hellish rain of rock. A boulder the size of a motorbike crashed to earth and lay smouldering in the grass, tendrils of fire flicking around its edge like snakes' tongues. Sizzling stones thudded into the grass, igniting grassfires that flamed and flared. A wave of reeking sulphur sucked away the oxygen leaving the pair gasping and gagging. A molten rock, flame-red and hissing fire, thumped into the earth some thirty metres away and rolled towards them, breaking their trance. Another hot rock caromed off the first and fizzled past the petrified pair like a burning billiard ball.

Then the suffocating ash settled.

Lin and Arben looked at the chaos, then each other.

"Run, MeLin, run," Arben screamed.

Lin was already moving. Only good luck and speed could protect them from the incendiary barrage that exploded around them. No shelter offered, no protection loomed; all about them an open plain fizzed with hissing missiles. The smell of sulphur, burning grass and molten rock reached deep into Lin's lungs. She gagged. The pair ran in the same direction, Lin's panic replaced by purpose. She moved a little away from Arben so they didn't get taken out together. He'd know why. A large, glowing rock thudded to a fiery halt a metre away.

"Shit!"

She screamed, jumped sideways, and ran on, the acrid smell of singed hair scorched into her senses.

The runners sought a place where the sky wasn't raining molten missiles. Lin's mind steadied. There had to be an end to this fall of fire somewhere. They ran to find it, they ran in hope, they ran to live.

Small and large rocks fell around. A hot stone bounced off Lin's shoulder, but she couldn't stop running. If there were an end to this molten torrent, it wasn't close.

Ash coated the runners' bodies. Sweat and cinders matted their hair and trickled down their faces. Dust caught in Lin's eyes and seeped into her mouth. She stopped and bent over to spit grey muck. A rolling piece of fiery debris moved her on. She would have taken off her top and wrapped it round her face to protect her breathing from the ash, but she couldn't. The cinders would burn her skin. She clutched her hat over her face instead, baring her head to the shower of ash. Lin could see Arben brushing ash off his body as he ran.

Superheated lava oozed from the crater mouth and flowed hot and slow through troughs and channels. The runners dashed along any ridge they could find, putting space between them and the violent volcano. It took time Lin couldn't judge before she sensed they were out of the range of raining rock. She breathed easier. *Maybe we'll get out of this.*

Arben waved at her and pointed right as they ran. He changed direction; she went with him. Their hearts raced but their legs slowed. The pair moved closer to each other and jogged on. Lin had seen earthquakes in China, but she'd never been up close with a molten mountain. Eventually, they tired into a fast walk. Ash still fell but not as thickly now. Lin looked over her shoulder. The two hills were twin grey humps through a heavy haze. Everything was grey, the foul air choking their lungs as they searched for clear air and safety.

Arben found what he was looking for – a long gully that held another of the tributaries to the main stream. The pair dropped over the edge where the gully swung through a long bend. On the side closest to the volcano the grassy slope led up to a rock undercut. The overhang was about three metres front to back, the floor clear of debris and ash. The roof angled steeply but it provided protection as the rear of the cavern was towards the volcano. Rocks were unlikely to roll in and the ash would settle outside. It already had. The two sought shelter under the ledge and bent over, gasping, spitting, their bodies grimed with ash and sweat.

Arben gestured to Lin that he wanted her water bottle. She handed it to him. He ran to the stream to fill it, reaching deep into a pool after brushing away the slick of ash that smeared the surface. Lin looked skyward from the edge of the shelter. The flying rocks mightn't make it this far, but ash would. They'd need clean water now, and later. Arben brought the bottle back and they drank their fill after rinsing their mouths of grey, sooty muck. Arben filled the bottle once more. Food of any sort would be hard to find and right now he didn't want to venture far. The risk was too great.

They collapsed under the shelter and looked at each other, two forlorn figures in a dim, grey cave. After a while Arben laughed. At first it was a chuckle but then he laid back, slapped his legs and guffawed. Lin didn't know what to make of it. She squinted at him suspiciously. Maybe the stress had got to him and he'd lost it. She'd heard of such things happening.

Finally, he explained in words and mime that she looked like a grey-haired, old crone. She had to agree; everything and every part of her from the crown of her head to the tops of her sneakers had come up grey. She told him he looked older too, the grey soot aging him beyond his years. Lin reached over and made streaks on his face with her fingers. Grey, the dreary shade broken by lines of sweat running down their faces and onto their chests, spread everywhere. They lay under the overhang and laughed, as much from relief as from the absurdity of the murky disaster that engulfed them.

Lin rolled over, put her head on Arben's chest and hugged him, in gratitude and solidarity. He wrapped his arms around her and they lay locked in a quiet embrace; a happy if forsaken couple in a desolate landscape. Outside their rock canopy the grey haze swelled and fell around them as the landscape shrugged on a robe of cinders.

27

LIN AND ARBEN

What to do? The tired travellers considered their options. There were two: stay under the overhang protected from the rain of ash and rock or venture out and be killed. No contest. They would stay until the morning. The sun was descending, turning the grey haze to black. Soon it would be night. Beneath their feet the earth had stopped shuddering but, for Lin, nothing would feel quite right again. The ground was supposed to be solid, not shaky. It was as if she'd been double-crossed, like when a one-time buddy broke her trust and spread a secret she'd shared. She'd never forgotten. Same with the ground. For Lin, the earth's shattered stability would take time to heal, if ever.

When the sky quit raining danger, Arben went to look for food. He kept to whatever shelter the trees offered, just in case. Water-edge bulbs pried out with a stick were all he could find. They were edible and not covered in ash. Arben told Lin that such food was usually cooked but could be eaten raw. That they did, chewing their share of grit. The last of the berries in Lin's foodbox were rinsed and gulped down.

Grey dust was everywhere and in everything. Arben found a small pool under an overhanging branch that had missed most of the rain of ash. Their water supply was okay for the moment. Lin rinsed the ash from Arben's shoulders and torso. He splashed it on her arms and hands. They sat for a long time, looking out at the gathering gloom, talking and gesturing about the day, the volcano and how lucky they were to be alive.

Arben talked about volcanoes in words and gestures.

"My people came from over the water, MeLin. They came from up there."

He waved his arm in a direction Lin took to be north.

"They lived on a warm, wet island where fruit and fish were plentiful. But one day a huge fire mountain roared and scattered ash and rock as far as they could see. Just like today, only bigger. The skies turned grey and nothing grew as cold days followed the warm. Many of my people perished from hunger. The rest moved on."

Lin thought this sounded a lot like BeBe's story. Arben continued.

"They finally made it to an island where they could go no further. But a small boy watching from the shore saw birds flying away over the ocean, birds that lived on the land. The Old People took this as a sign that a land existed beyond the water. They tied trees together, like we made for the tulangi to pull, only much bigger. They got on them and pushed over the ocean to get here. A fire mountain drove us here, MeLin. My people honour and fear fire mountains."

Lin hadn't heard Arben talk about the legends of his people. *He must know a lot of stories.* She'd liked to have heard more but she was worried for her future, and Arben's. If they made it through tomorrow, if they survived this place, she'd get to the disc and go home. Arben would stay. How much further did they have to go?

Lin had only a rough idea of their current location; maps and navigation weren't her strengths. She sought Arben's advice. A mud map scratched on the floor of the overhang helped explain. The valley they were in was a tributary of the main stream, the one she knew and had followed. Arben indicated they'd follow this small stream a while. When it straightened to flow towards the larger waterway they'd save time going overland to the place where they'd met.

Arben remembered the place well. With the rock canopy as a backdrop he acted out his shock at seeing her for the first time. Lin knew exactly where he was and what he meant. First, the swivelling ears and large feet of the kangaroos; then an image of herself, a screaming banshee. He even reprised his own terror. It was convincing. Lin was delighted. He was such a good mime. Seeing her was a greater shock to him than he was to her. Arben would've agreed. Nothing like Lin had been seen in this land and the place of their encounter was etched into his brain like carving on stone. BeBe had shared with Lin how to get back to the disc from where they'd met, and she knew she could find it. Lin guessed the remainder of the trip to be an afternoon's walk. She had to get back tomorrow, or the disc might disappear and she'd be stuck here.

Would that be such a bad thing? Lin looked at the well-built, young man squatting on the other side of the overhang. He caught her gaze, their eyes held in a moment of togetherness, and he smiled, the depth of feeling glowing in his eyes and softening his face. Lin overflowed with emotion. She was caught between weeping and wanting. But she'd been through this before. Would it really be that hard to share her life with Arben, going wherever he and his clan went, wandering hand-in-hand through the wilderness together? They could share their lives. He would look after her, she knew that, and she'd care for him. Maybe they could have a child, a little Arben or Beibei. Maybe both; this land probably didn't have a one-child policy. Certainly, there'd be lots of pure air, clean food and water as well as no pollution, traffic jams nor continual crowds and noise.

But then, she'd never see Mum, Dad or Grampa again, never giggle and gossip with Song over a Coke. Her dreams of a career would come to nothing. And what'd happen when Grampa's cigarette lighter ran out of fuel? Who would she be when her magic tricks ran out? When she got old? She hadn't seen any older women.

Seriously, would she be happy with hides and skins for clothes when hers wore out? Could she really survive without her mum's dumplings, a soft bed, new clothes, cosmetics, toilet paper, tampons, a mobile phone, and shopping? She'd like to think so, but probably not.

This had been a wild ride. She came for Granma's vase and she'd take it back full of memories. She'd never forget her travels with Arben and the herd. But this was a harsh land. There was no choice. She had to go, and Arben would stay. And that would be tomorrow, their last day together.

Lin sighed, and got ready for rest. She couldn't remember carrying her hide cloak in the run from the volcano. Yet it was with her. Carrying it was almost second nature now. But like everything else, it was covered in grey. She unrolled it and found the inside dust-free. What a warm and thoughtful boon it had been. She tossed it over Arben, cuddled up to him under it and they lay together through her final night in this weird and wonderful world.

*   *   *

The last morning broke bright and fine. Grey dust covered the earth like flour on a floor. A breeze from the south had scattered the ash from the trees and sent some of it scudding back towards the volcano. The air was transparent, the way to the south open and clear. When they reached the top of the gully wall and stepped out onto the plain, Lin and Arben looked back. The two hills had receded into the distance, one much larger than the other. Smoke and ash spewed sporadically from the crater, a line of hardening lava crusted its edge like a scab. The horizon lay blanketed in a pall of grey.

They looked at each other, and Lin sighed. God, they'd been lucky. That was an awesome explosion. Her shoulders shivered at the thought. Even well to the south of the volcano stray rocks lay about, dark and dust free, aliens in the grey, grass world around them. Lin touched one cautiously. It still held the heat of its molten birthplace, the fiery furnace that had shot it skyward. Getting hit by any of those could've killed them. All she'd got was a small bruise on her shoulder. It didn't bear thinking about. They both got on with walking, following the smaller stream Arben had pointed out the night before.

The breeze whipped the long tussocks of grass around their legs. The ground was firm underfoot cushioned by a thick layer of moss. The ash layer was thinner; occasional wind-drifts of soot lay caught among the grass clumps. Long-legged insects that had survived the rain of death sprang out of their path, catapulting clumsily to land any which way and peer goggle-eyed at the passers-by. A black beetle toiled laboriously across a patch of ash as a lizard slid into a crack in the earth. Two large birds circled high overhead once more. Little other life showed.

Lin pondered the absence of the larger animals. Maybe the big wildlife had gone until the volcano was done. Animals seemed to know more about these things. God, she hoped there were no more lava bombs.

The morning was good for walking and Lin was used to these daily treks. Her legs were strong and fit, her lungs healthy. They walked steadily and purposefully, following the line of the stream but keeping to the plain where the walking was better, except when they needed water. Nothing strange or sinister hindered their progress and the breeze kept the heat down as the sun lifted.

It wasn't long before Arben detoured from the route they'd been taking. He beckoned to Lin.

"Not again with the 'Follow me, Girlie', routine," she muttered to herself.

"I've got to straighten that boy out before I leave."

The thought of leaving brought sudden tears. Lin choked them back. *Can't let him see me like this.* She hesitated a few seconds, faking a shoelace problem, then caught up with Arben, her eyes red. Maybe he wouldn't notice. Her companion had stopped by several rocks erupting through the surface of the plain.

*   *   *

Arben saw her sad state but said nothing. Lin bent over to peer at the rocks and Arben pointed out marks carved in the surfaces; straight and wavy lines connected at angles, others ran into each other or formed circles and squares. Arben explained it as a drawing of the country they were walking through. Old People had etched it when they first arrived. It outlined the streams and mapped the waterholes and food places. It pictured the sacred places of his people as well, although Arben didn't say as much.

There was only so much male tradition he could break for this beautiful stranger, the one who gazed intently at the rock markings while he gazed intently at her. The country lived in the carved marks and word poems that Pelluken passed on from one generation to the next. The chanted verses helped them navigate the vast spaces of this land. It was here that the waterway they were following stopped its winding path and flowed directly to join the bigger stream. Arben pointed to it on the 'map'. It was here they were to turn away and head across country to the place they'd met.

Arben thought about the changes MeLin had wrought on his life and wondered how he would survive without her bravery, warmth and fun. His heart was lost. She would be with him always, whatever happened. They trudged on glumly, wrapped in worlds that were joined in a way neither could acknowledge nor escape.

*   *   *

Unlike yesterday, Lin and Arben hadn't spoken much on the morning's walk. Both were aware that this day would separate them, probably forever. Neither wanted it, neither could avoid it. The melancholy of parting kept them silent. Lin was not sure she could speak without tears betraying her misery. Her face maintained a stoic calm.

It took most of the morning to return to where they'd met. Arben recycled his miming repertoire and their gloom lifted. He mimicked the kangaroos, Lin's arrival and his own shocked response. He leapt, danced and cavorted through a routine. Lin reprised her mad, yelling attack on him. They laughed and giggled like schoolkids on an excursion. The lightheartedness freed their hearts and let them reflect on the amazing journey they'd gone through... and survived. Not for the first time Lin thought about the remarkable creatures that had occupied this space not so long ago, the ones that had connived to bring her here. It was their loyalty and love of kind that brought her to this land. Well, they were as safe as she could make them now.

BeBe, BiZi, and the herd had been on Lin's mind. She'd done what they wanted but it wasn't enough. It never could be. None of these supersized creatures lived through to her China time. They'd disappeared, gone, lost out to whatever fires, drought or hunting did away with them. She'd never know which one would be the last. It wouldn't have been any of her buddies. Lin thought the herd would live out normal lives and their offspring might flourish too. But sometime, somehow, one of their descendants would fall to hunger, fire, or a brutal club strike, the last of their species gone forever, never to be seen again. Only their brittle bones would be left to tantalise some latter-day anthropologist. Was she crazy to take them to the North Forest? Did she put her life on the line for nothing?

Such reality sobered Lin. How could there be a world in which the colossal cuteness of BeBe and his kind didn't exist, where bigbirds couldn't strut proudly, where Spike's rolling gait couldn't be seen bearing his bristly body across the land? They were unique, and so much a product of this country, at home in its dry desolation and danger. Even the dreadful dropcat had a true place here; efficient, savage killer that it was. He and his like were gone too. But Lin knew extinctions were happening all the time in her world. Day by day, creatures big and small were falling to the relentless expansion of mankind and its demands.

Lin shook her head to free herself from such sad foreboding. *Stop the nonsense, girl. If I can make a difference it'll be in China where I can do something.* That meant home and finding the disc. She filled her water bottle from the spring she'd found in those eventful early hours. Arben collected food. Together they headed out onto the plain in the direction BeBe had shown. Lin's steps lightened. Her smile broadened. *I'll be home soon.*

She'd never see Arben again.

Her face sagged, and her shoulders drooped.

It was but an hour to find the valley of the disc. Going the other way, Lin had followed BeBe's swaying rump and he was a slow walker. This time, side by side with Arben, they kept a fast pace through the grassland, past the tree clump where BeBe had signalled the existence of dropcats, towards BiZi's one-time home valley and the disc.

The time went quickly. It did when Lin was with Arben. They needed to know each other, and their togetherness was drawing to an end. This hour they talked, about him, her, their families, their hopes and dreams although Lin knew much of this was absurd. How could Arben know what her world was like; she could hardly grasp the life and death simplicity of his.

Lin felt smug about her pathfinding abilities when she brought them back to where the disc was located. Okay. Not quite. But she knew where they were; just downstream from the disc. Not exactly the point where she first met BeBe and BiZi, but it wasn't far. *I'm getting better at this.* This was where she stopped and turned back on her first walk. Just upstream was the pond with the tadpoles. Her directions and bush skills were improving. Arben looked at her, smiled, and nodded his approval.

Lin beckoned to Arben and they walked alongside the rivulet. The small pool came into sight and although she was anxious to find the disc, Lin was desperate for a bath. She had to get the ash and crap out of her hair. She might be going home but she wasn't returning as the grey-haired old lady Arben had laughed at. This was the only place she knew to rinse off the muck. Lin signed her bathing needs to Arben. He looked alarmed but checked the pool and its surrounds carefully and could see no threat. Lin stripped to her bra and pants, shook the ash and dust from her clothes and placed them over a bush. She didn't have time to wash and dry them now.

Lin and Arben eased into the cool water. The pool had a sandy bottom, which made for firm footing. The water level was up to Lin's breasts. She washed her body, splashed water into her hair and, after a second or two, ducked her head under the surface to rinse the ash away. Her mane of hair swung lazily in the water and as her head broke the surface, the current flushed the grit over the edge of the pool to drift away downstream.

It was good to feel clean again. Lin reached for her bumbag and got the small hand-soap bottle. There was a tiny bit left; it'd be enough. She'd have more soon.

Lin got out of the pool and stood on a wet rock by the pool's edge while she lathered her body with the remnant soap. Lin offered Arben the few drops still in the bottle, but he shook his head. He looked at her appreciatively. She was a beautiful creature standing there with the warm sunlight caressing her near-naked body and highlighting the wet tints in her dark hair.

Lin stood on the edge of the pool. Her graceful stance was upended when her foot slipped on the soapy surface and, in a move more pratfall than poise, she plunged into the water. Arben caught and held her flailing body as she fell. They stumbled together laughing, water cascading wildly, until Arben's back found support against the wall of the pool and he stopped, clutching Lin's body to his in a tight, wet embrace.

There was a tender pause. The water, the warmth, the air and the situation all called for it. Lin reached her hand behind Arben's head, pulled his mouth down to hers and kissed him.

Arben's people did not kiss, it was not their way. But he felt the primitive urgency in her unusual wet embrace.

Lin felt his strong body respond and she drew him closer to her. With some shy giggling and some equally wild and wet ardour they were drawn to do what both had wanted for some time. They made love; in the water, on the bank, against a tree. It was sweet, it was slow; it was caring, it was kind. It was everything and all they could draw from each other and the world right then. This was their time of togetherness; if they had to part, then this was what they'd remember... an ecstatic embrace under a brilliant arc of blue, in a stream, in a glade, in a land as old as time with a couple as new as tomorrow.

Finally, they rested on Lin's hide cloak, their bodies touching, warm and sated, by the edge of the pool. Lin ran her fingers gently over the scars on Arben's chest as she lay by his side, her head on his shoulder. He had one arm around her, the other hand touching her cheek and neck.

Arben was an initiated man of his clan; this was not the first time he'd made love. It was without doubt the first time he'd made love in a stream in the afternoon with a partner as unreserved and willing as Lin. He would never look at a woman or a waterhole the same way again. His eyes and mind were filled with awe. This young woman addled his brain and messed with his senses. Her body lingered on his skin, in his nose, his mouth, his ears, and he wanted her there forever. There was nothing he would not do for her. And she was leaving.

Arben tried to talk about the separation and encourage this enchanting creature to stay. He inwardly cursed his inability to find the words that would persuade her. She said she had to return home through a little sun, but if ever the time came when she was needed, she would return. The sun would be there. He didn't know what she was talking about; he wasn't convinced. But, if she were to return, he hoped it would be soon. And he told her so.

Lin lay quiet and content. She had no need to say anything. She'd expressed how she felt and needed no reassurance about who she was or what she could do. She'd made love to a man with an abandon heightened by their soon-to-be separation. She'd finally met a brave and worthy man whose commitment was to her, not basketball, Weibo or the latest app on his iPhone. Yet they had to part, and soon. But Lin knew if they were to lose each other it was because they loved each other. The softness in his eyes and funny, quirky smile told her all she needed to know.

Lin had come to this country a schoolgirl looking for a vase; she was leaving it a wiser, smarter and stronger woman. She'd led a troupe of ill-assorted creatures to safety in the North Forest, battled serpents and a dropcat, fought off kidnappers, ridden the wind on the back of a bigbird, suffered through a volcano, made it through a desolate world, met and loved a strong, noble man... and survived a spacepipe.

28

BEIBEI AND THE BEAST

The spacepipe! What time is it? Gotta find the disc! How much longer did she have? Panic beat up Lin's brain. She broke from Arben's embrace, leapt to her feet and had her gear together in seconds while urging her drowsy companion, "Move, Arben, move. We've gotta find the disc."

Arben understood her anxiety if not the words and soon they were walking alongside the stream, Lin with her bumbag, cloak and hat, Arben with his clutch of spears and small axe at his waist, their lovemaking a warm and gentle memory.

Lin's panic ebbed, and she relaxed. They had time. Sunset was at least an hour away and the disc was close. Her first foray to this now-unforgettable pool had been quick so the return to the disc would be minutes not hours.

They skirted the fallen trees and walked by the place where Lin almost stepped on a snake. She could speak

Arben's language well enough to tell him the story of this once-scary encounter. Arben smiled at her attempts to 'shoo' the snake by tossing a small branch at it.

"But you killed a durakkan, MeLin. That took more than a funny noise and a tree branch."

"I destroyed it before it killed me, Arben. I'd no choice. I've learned a lot in your land. I've had to."

Their attention was on each other, the rocks and the stream, but mainly each other. If Arben had not been so rapt in his companion he might have seen it first. As it was, Lin did. She stopped walking, eyes wide and jaw slack, her usual cool seriously shaken.

Arben saw her face stiffen. "What is it, MeLin? What's wrong?"

"Look, Arben, look," she whispered, knuckle to her mouth while the other hand gripped his forearm.

"What is that?"

Arben followed her gaze. His face tightened as his body tensed. One hand went to the axe at his waist, the other clenched the spears as he edged between Lin and the evil that confronted them. Both stood transfixed, all warmth and contentment gone and suddenly very afraid. For twenty metres away skulked the creature of the cave walls, the red-eyed monster that glared from the black pit of every Pelluken nightmare, the most terrifying predator either of them would ever see... a massive, murderous lizard.

"An eskaven. Alive. An eskaven?" breathed Arben, fear choking his voice.

They watched with fascinated horror as the dragon-like creature lurched low along the valley. Each shoulder hauled one side of the monster forward in turn, its body advancing in a series of slow, swinging arcs while the huge head stayed steady. This was no faded image on a cave wall. The eskaven was six metres long and a metre high. It crawled on four short, bent legs – thick and heavy like flexible tree trunks – tipped with heavy claws. The broad tail switched slowly, brushing aside small bushes and scrub. A grey, scaly hide protected the massive frame, flaps like sagging chain-mail shielded its flanks.

The reptile's head was huge; the broad muzzle tapered to a rounded tip over racks of dull yellow teeth. A forked tongue flicked side-to-side. A ragged ridge of heavy scale ran like armour down the lizard's back, starting behind its hooded eyes and finishing at the tip of the tail. Lin had seen photos of Komodo dragons; this could have been their primeval ancestor, a Godzilla-like creature looking for a meal. The beast appeared in no hurry, it had no need to worry about enemies; even dropcats stayed clear. As yet, it hadn't seen them. While its senses were sharp, it didn't see what didn't move. And Lin and Arben were like statues.

Arben had never seen such a creature. Neither had his family. They'd heard of them, everyone had. The beast terrified his ancestors when they arrived in this land. Those who challenged it died in agony, to be torn apart and eaten. The Pelluken gave it the name eskaven – 'poison fang' – and learned their lesson well. They avoided the beast, and its ferocity slipped into folklore, used to scare children into obedience. But the Pelluken thought eskaven had died out. No-one had seen one for many seasons. Only Arben's father's father could recall a live one. Maybe this was the last of its kind, disturbed, out-of-sorts and pushed out-of-place by the volcano.

Pelluken legend knew these creatures to be deadly. Slow and clumsy they might appear, but they could lift and sprint for a short distance. That's all it took. One gash from their toxic teeth, one slash, and victims, large and small, hobbled away to die of blood loss, paralysis, or both. Either way, dead or alive, they became easy meat for this lethal lizard. Chatter about that could take place later... if they survived. For the eskaven had caught their scent; it swung its huge head towards them like a snake sizing up a snack. It had seen them. There was nothing else for it; get up a tree. It might be their only chance. Running wouldn't save them.

Arben shoved Lin towards the valley bank and screamed at her to climb a tree. She needed no second telling. She ran. The lizard reared and charged.

Family folklore was right, Arben thought, the reptile could run. The Pelluken hunter bolted across the line of the charging beast to give Lin time. He leapt high over the creature's head as it reared to seize him. The sticky saliva slapped against his skin as the snapping jaws missed his flying feet by centimetres. Turning wasn't easy. The beast was big, but it spun deftly, demolishing small saplings in the dust as it scrabbled after Arben, hissing hostility. By this time Lin was in a tree. Arben screamed at her to climb it as high as she could.

Lin was smart enough to know that. She scrambled six or seven metres up the tree and sat protected in its lofty branches.

Arben cut back to the bank and ran into a thick copse, a ploy to retard the bulky creature, which preferred open spaces to tight places. It worked. The beast couldn't find an easy way through the scrub. But its senses were powerful. It tracked Arben on the other side of the copse as he crept towards the tree where a horror-struck Lin hunched high up, her breath ragged and her heart pounding as she watched the deadly drama below. A clear space opened within the scrub. The lizard charged. Lin screamed a warning. Arben dropped his spears, leapt up, grasped a branch and heaved his body clear as the venomous jaws snapped behind his leaping frame. The creature spun around, reared off the ground and tried to drag Arben down.

In the seconds before he scrambled to a higher branch, the young Pelluken looked upon the lizard's fierce face, saw its gaping, fang-filled jaws, heard the roaring wheeze of its lungs, smelled the acid-venom stench of its breath and stared into red reptilian eyes that offered an infinity of nothing – no sympathy, no fear, no feeling, just the bleak awareness that he was food and it was hungry. For the first time in his life Arben knew the hapless feeling of being the hunted not the hunter. He was to die so this lizard could live. But not today if he could help it.

Holding its huge weight off the ground took toll of the eskaven. The hostile creature dropped to earth, hissing and snarling, and vented its rage on the base of the tree, ripping out its frustration on the roots and bark. Arben and Lin swapped anxious glances but could do little else. They were lucky to be alive. After a few tense minutes the hissing and scrabbling stopped. The monster halted between the two trees. Arben climbed swiftly up until he was level with Lin. As they watched, the creature settled down to wait. Nothing in this world threatened it. The beast could wait. Sooner or later its prey would make a mistake and the slightest scratch of its poisonous fangs was enough. Death was inevitable.

Minutes went by, minutes Lin couldn't count but knew each one to be critical in her fast-diminishing day. She had to find the disc, lizard or no lizard. She had to get past it and go home. Every now and then the huge creature lifted its head to stare into the branches and check by scent and sight that its food was still there.

The foodstuffs turned to talk. Lin was so grateful that Arben had risked his life for her, and she told him over and over, her tongue babbling beyond her brain. She scolded him for risking his life; she wanted him alive, whatever happened. Arben, for his part, would have laid in front of the beast if she'd asked.

Finally, Lin asked, "What can we do, Arben? If we stay quiet might it forget us and go away?"

"Maybe," Arben whispered and signed.

"But the volcano must've wrecked its food supply and

forced it from its lair. Eskaven haven't been seen for many seasons. We thought they were dead. It's probably hungry and looking for lunch. We're it."

Lin shuddered at the thought of such an end. Her anxiety increased as the sun slid behind the trees. Night was coming. If BeBe was right, the spacepipe could disappear. She wouldn't be able to get home. Maybe that wasn't such a bad thing. She'd found someone to share her life with. Lin longed to be held and loved again. She wanted to hold Arben, to embrace his warmth and passion. He was such a beautiful, brave man. But she had gone through all this before; she couldn't stay. Even the so-sweet time with him at the pond couldn't change that.

It was Lin's obligations to her parents, friends, school, society and her future – and to Arben – that tortured her mind. Desire was less difficult; *I want him.* But he couldn't live in her world and she couldn't stay in his. He was a warrior and a hunter, she was a student. *But I love him.* The agony went back and forth between her head and heart... yes and no, to and fro. Fighting serpents and dropcats was simpler than this. Finally, Lin knew she had to get by the lizard, locate the disc, and leave. Arben would help.

Lin descended slowly, quietly, holding her breath, moving deliberately, making each step steady and sure. The lizard stayed inert, its eyes shut. Perhaps it was asleep or generating energy in the sun? Lin didn't know. She could see its flanks flexing as it drew slow, steady breaths. But it wasn't otherwise moving. Arben cautioned Lin with signals not to move quickly as any movement or sound could stir the resting reptile.

Moving silently and slowly in a tree was tricky, but Lin was doing okay, working her way down branch by branch on the side closest to Arben. He moved down the tree he was in too. Lin put her weight onto a patch of sap and slipped. She fell but grabbed a branch while her body swung underneath. The lizard lifted its head.

Arben gasped and screamed, "No!"

In a heartbeat the beast reared up roaring to drag Lin to her death. It swung a massive clawed foot at her sneakers as she lifted her legs. The blow missed. Lin swung close to the tree her feet pawing at the bark. She had to get back up the trunk but couldn't get a foothold and hung there, lifting her legs, her hide-coat dangling while the monster reared and clawed at her, its massive feet and fangs just missing her swinging body. Swiftly, the creature moved to the trunk of the tree and clawed its way up so that its front legs could reach further along to Lin.

She scrambled hand over hand along the branch towards the tree Arben was in. But she couldn't hold on, her fingers shredded the rotted bark and she fell. The fall didn't hurt. That was the least of her problems as the lizard swung away from the tree, dropped, and charged.

Lin darted behind the trunk of Arben's tree. Maybe it'd be too big to twist around and get her. She played dodgem with the devil, ducking from one side of the tree to the other. It worked, briefly. But this top predator had chased small prey and knew what they'd do. The eskaven stayed at the base of the tree watching, waiting for Lin's next move to be her last. She froze.

Arben took his chance. The young warrior screamed, "Run, MeLin, run", and plummeted from the tree, body in line with the lizard, his stone axe raised to strike a double-handed blow at the reptile's skull. Arben slammed into the creature's back and drove his axe at its head. The axe shattered. The lizard shook, roared and reared as Arben screamed to Lin. "Go now. Run!"

She did.

The blow didn't even stun the creature. It couldn't. Its skin was thick, leathery scale and the skull was dense bone covered with a ridged horn of hide. But the monster was distracted and while it dealt with Arben, Lin dashed to the edge of the valley, turned past the copse of trees and raced upstream towards the disc. She turned her head just in time to see Arben thrown from the creature's back as a rodeo bull tosses a cowboy. He landed against a tree trunk and the lizard approached his inert body.

She screamed, "No! Arben, no!"

That was the last Lin saw of him.

*   *   *

Arben never knew why the lizard didn't kill him. It tossed him against a tree where he hit his head and lay stunned. Maybe it didn't see him in the long grass because he didn't move; perhaps the axe blow disrupted its thinking for the beast didn't take him. It approached a step, jaws gaping, tongue flicking, looking for his body, but it didn't finish him.

Lin's scream took the monster's attention.

The armoured head swung to look for her. With its attention elsewhere, a now-alert Arben was up a tree in seconds, as far from those toxic teeth as he could get. With no satisfaction from one food source, the lizard lumbered after the other. It followed Lin's scent, noise and movement. The creature's speed had slowed but it lurched after Lin almost as fast as she could run. Arben watched it disappear before he dropped out of the tree, picked up the bits of his broken axe, and spears, and set off after MeLin and the dragon.

✶   ✶   ✶

Lin ran wildly. She sought to shorten the distance by running along the stream. Fear gripped her mind as she heard the lizard's roar; grief gripped her heart as she remembered Arben.

"Arben, noo!"

She ran recklessly, sobbing and gasping, her lungs heaving.

"I've gotta find the disc."

The shrubs and trees tore at her body; rough branches scratched at her arms and legs as she splashed along the muddy waterway, stumbling over rocks and scrambling through the bush. Spider webs clung to her face and hair. She brushed them away, but the sticky threads clung to her skin. Something crawled across her forehead. She clawed it off. An exposed root hooked her foot and she sprawled headlong, bruising her hands and skinning her knee. The fall seized her with pain. She slowed, only to limp on spurred by the snarling lizard on her trail.

Desperate to find the disc, Lin searched for the broom handle she'd left to mark its place. *Where is it? Where is it?* The drab landscape looked the same everywhere, the next tree just like the one before. The small bend where she'd first seen BeBe was nowhere, and everywhere. *Where's the disc? Please! Where's the disc?*

Lin struggled on, more frantic with each moment. The disc, the dying sun and the murderous saurian competed for attention. The disc could shut with the sunset; she would be lost, and she'd lost Arben. Pain contorted her face as she gasped for air and grasped for self-control.

She could hear the monster wheezing as it crashed after her through the valley. The sun was dipping into the horizon. The light was fading, the disc nowhere to be seen and the lizard almost upon her. *But the bastard hasn't got me yet.*

Lin scrambled up a tree and sat hidden by leaves, hoping the creature would pass by and give her more time. As she watched, the big lizard lurched through the scrub at the edge of the clearing and paused. The beast's head swung around, searching, its tongue flicking, and for an instant the red-eyed gaze fixed on Lin's tree. She froze.

The lizard saw nothing.

Satisfied its prey wasn't there the creature lurched through the clearing, climbed a small ridge and scuttled into the gathering gloom. Lin watched it go. *It's gone, now please, where is the disc?*

As if in answer to her frantic thoughts, a shaft of setting sunlight evaded the clouds and flashed across the valley floor bathing the streambed in the last light of day. Instantly, from the base of the trees at the top of a low ridge, a small sun exploded, piercing the gloom and coating the clearing in lustrous light. In the sun's centre hung the familiar form of the disc, all of ten metres away from where Lin sat. The small, dull disc looked as desirable as diamonds.

"The disc... It's still there," she whispered.

Lin dropped from the tree and hid behind the trunk looking at where the dragon-like creature had departed. Where was the eskaven? *Gone, I hope.* She ran to the disc and found the broom lying in front of it. Lin then spied the crimson vase lying undamaged under the shrub where she'd left it.

"The vase is here. And so are you, Granma," Lin whispered as she picked up the small vial, held it to her breast and looked to the sky.

"Granma?"

The vase affected her powerfully. It always did. It was as if Granma's lifeblood blended with her own, their lives pulsing together through this crystal cup. As Lin stood by the disc clutching the vase, Granma's presence came upon her, kind and reassuring like a hand laid upon her shoulder.

Lin suddenly remembered what the dear, dying woman had said, 'Be like this crystal vase, Lin Beibei, be beautiful, strong and clear but don't ever be afraid to break.'

Standing alone, frightened, bloodied and bereft in an alien world, Lin's body shook with grief for Arben, for Granma, this world and the animals she was leaving. She was breaking now; her heart lay in pieces. The man she'd met and loved, the man who'd given her life meaning had died to save her. It was a life and loss she could not recover. Granma's vase stored memories that could never be redeemed.

With her possessions together, Lin turned to look upon this land of love and memory and say goodbye. She was overwhelmed; tears flowed for Arben and the threatened lives of her sweet mega-friends. *I have to leave.*

Lin placed the vase in her bumbag and the handle of the broom into the disc. The now-comforting traction began. *Should I go, or should I stay?* The broom slipped easily into the disc. She could pull it back or let it go. Maybe Arben's still alive; maybe she could find him, and they could be together still. Lin had eased her bumbag and hide-coat behind her and relaxed her grip on the broom when the lethal lizard re-entered the clearing.

Lin saw it as it spied her. The creature paused, then charged. *I've got to go.* It was leave or die. Lin grasped the broomhead and let it take her headfirst into the disc. In the rush to escape, her sunhat fell to the ground. The disc engulfed her in clinging, choking blackness. Would her feet disappear before the lizard got here? No, no. She couldn't move her legs. She had tried that before. It couldn't be done.

The wait and fear were excruciating. *No, no, please.*

Lin flexed her sneakered feet, waiting for lethal fangs to lacerate her flesh. She'd die alone in the pod. But in seconds it was over. She was sucked safely through the disc and pushed sobbing and distraught onto the capsule's floor.

29

FAREWELL

Arben arrived to see the lizard charging across the clearing at MeLin's legs disappearing into the middle of a small sun. He reared back and heaved his spear at the monster. The throw seemed futile – a sliver of wood against hardened hide – but it was all he could do. The blow didn't damage the creature, but it did divert it. The lizard paused then swung around, tail switching agitatedly, and stormed off the ridge after its assailant.

Arben clambered up a tree as soon as he threw the spear. The eskaven couldn't reach him. He sat among the branches watching the place where his companion had disappeared... a small sun. Just as she'd said. The young warrior climbed higher as the sunlight left the valley taking the brilliant, radiant net with it. Only a dull, faded shape remained within the scrub. For Arben the light had departed too; MeLin had gone. The lizard prowled the valley floor, circling, snarling, stopping occasionally to tear the ground with massive claws. Arben watched and waited; maybe he'd be up here all night.

With MeLin's departure scarred on his heart, Arben's thoughts turned to how they'd met. He was carrying a spear and a club then. When she'd left him, he still held a weapon. That first time – the one he acted out to hear her laugh – she'd stopped him throwing a club to kill a small kangaroo. It seemed so long ago now. When she left him, a few heartbeats back, he'd thrown a weapon to stop her being killed. There was a meaning Arben could sense, but not completely grasp. MeLin would understand. He sat in the same tree she'd perched in seconds before and waited as the eskaven tore up the valley floor in frustration. He felt safe from the rampaging lizard, but not from the pain of loneliness and loss.

The sorry warrior gazed at the place where MeLin left long after the sun had set and the twilight descended into darkness akin to his mood. There was nothing much to see, just the scrub and a dull outline, barely visible among the leaves. But it was where he'd seen her last and he wanted to remember, to hope she might return.

When nothing more than a vague outline could be seen in the starlight, the disc began to glow. At first a pale, clear glow spread from the centre, casting soft light over the surrounding scrub. The light changed to cream, pale yellow and, finally, an intense burnished bronze that grew richer and more iridescent until the light surged out around a fretwork of filaments, lighting up the valley floor in a pulsating web of gold. Finally, it blew out three times in a cataract of colour, an exploding rose of radiance that blossomed from bright to brilliant, and suddenly disappeared. As did the huge actor patrolling the arena. The brilliance was too much for the eskaven, and it departed.

Arben stayed crouched in the tree until dawn, his eyes fixed on the place where the disc had disappeared. Tears streaked his face. When the day broke and the birdsong had died, Arben stayed watching to be sure the monster wasn't coming back. When he was certain he was safe, he dropped from his perch and ran to the place he'd seen her last. There was nothing. As he turned to walk away he spied the crumpled sun hat lying behind a tussock.

"It's hers," he said, and picked it up. "It's MeLin's."

The young Pelluken touched the battered remnant to his cheek and drew in the familiar scent. The memories stored these many days flooded afresh through his mind. Tears coursed anew.

"MeLin," he said to himself, smiling wryly through tears at the mistake he'd made with her name.

"MeLin?" he asked loudly of the silent, brooding bush.

Then, holding the hat to his face as you'd cuddle a kitten, he turned and walked away.

✽ ✽ ✽

Lin sank into the spongy support of the pod, shoulders heaving, her face bloodied and swollen with sorrow. Her knee ached, her heart hurt even more. The pod began its rapid acceleration through time and space but not even the mysteries of the universe could rouse her. She didn't care. *Arben is dead and he died to save me.*

Lin lay like a discarded doll as the journey through ocean, land and heavens rewound. Unseen by its lone occupant the pod soared over a massive ocean studded with islands, then circled high in the void before descending through old but urban areas of what looked like modern China.

During the celestial voyage, Lin's better judgment revived. Her thoughts turned to Arben then to BiZi. Maybe it was because the little creature had once huddled frightened in this very place, a tiny mite trapped in white infinity, forcing herself on, enduring danger to help her kind survive. Lin found solace in the memory of the little marsupial. There was no real risk for Lin now. She was going home where she'd be safe. But BiZi and her brood, the myriad creatures in the world she'd left, were always at risk. She'd given some of them a new home, but they were endangered, and always in danger. Yet, so were millions of inconspicuous creatures in her world.

The pod's deceleration brought Lin back to earth and action. *Got to face the folks. This'll be fun. Not. Be strong, girl.* She drained the last vestiges of water from her bottle and with a remnant of tissue and a lick of spit cleaned the cuts on her face and knee. She pulled the comb through her hair and stood up ready to re-enter her room. *It'll be the same as I left it, I hope. Just the girl returning is different.*

Lin stowed everything in her bumbag. Granma's vase was packed safely away. It'd be too much to lose it now. She looked at the broom and the hide coat and wondered, not for the first time, why and how the coat was still with her, why she hadn't dropped it, or had it torn from her. It was a constant reminder of a journey she'd never forget and of the man who'd shared it with her. With bumbag secure and the hide coat fastened, Lin edged towards the disc, placed the broom handle into its line of creases and let it commence her final journey home.

Lin knocked her head on the closet as she pitched onto the bedroom floor.

"Ouch! Welcome home."

Rubbing her head, Lin picked herself up and looked around. *Nothing's changed and there's no-one here.* The room looked just as she'd left it.

Lin took time to take this in. Her eyes sought out detail just to make sure: bed, table, chest of drawers, chair, closet, the plinth for Granma's vase, all there. She was home. No doubt about it. And there were no weird creatures looking at her from the closet, or anywhere else. There was nothing under the bed. Everything was as she'd left it... how long ago?

The clock by her bed read 10.22 pm. If that was right, she'd been away two minutes. *Don't be silly. That can't be. I've been gone at least two weeks.* But a check of her bedside radio confirmed the time and date. 10.22 pm. It was two minutes since she'd departed. A lifetime in two minutes; a wild and wonderful ride, strange new mega-friends, a series of wild adventures and the love of a life gained and lost in one hundred and twenty seconds.

Come on! Lin couldn't believe it. Was it a dream? Or had she really been in ancient Australia with a bunch of odd megafauna and a wonderful man? Her mind struggled with the contradictions. Finally, the scratches on her arms said she'd run through streamside bush escaping the lizard. The bloodied bruise on her knee confirmed it. The memory of Arben's bright smile supplied any additional proof she needed. The hide cloak lay on the floor. She picked it up and held it gently to her face. The warm scent brought instant memories, and tears.

"Arben," she whispered to the cloak.

"Arben?" she said huskily to the wall.

The only answer was an echo in her heart that would reverberate long after his smiling image blurred. Wiping tears away, Lin wrapped the coat in string and reminiscences, tucked it into Granma's closet behind the now-faded disc, and closed the doors.

ACKNOWLEDGEMENTS

This book has been a long time in the making. It would not have turned a page without assistance from Kati Berinson and encouragement from Sunny Farrant and other family and friends. Thanks to the members of a Victoria University writing class who suffered through listening to early drafts of the manuscript. Self-publication is a complex task. My gratitude goes to Julie Postance for helping me over the hurdles. Without her guidance this book wouldn't be in print. Amanda Spedding helped edit the manuscript into an acceptable whole, Sophie White made the book presentable and Alfred Obare was responsible for the great cover art.

ABOUT THE AUTHOR

Robb Mason grew up in suburban Australia listening to radio serials and reading Marvel comics, *The Magic Pudding*, Henry Lawson, Jules Verne, Edgar Rice Burroughs, Carter Brown, Steele Rudd, state school readers and anything they'd let him borrow from the local library.

He read *Lord of the Rings* when he should have been studying, which accounts for his poor high school results and a fascination with trek and quest novels.

Robb has variously been a lecturer, writer, teacher, personnel manager, educational administrator, scholar, fruit picker, labourer and bulldozer salesman. He has lived in North America and Denmark and taught English in China. He lives in Melbourne where he follows 'the footy', loves 'Star Wars', enjoys cooking and maintains a tea addiction.

Queen of the North Forest is his first novel. He hopes it won't be his last.

www.ingramcontent.com/pod-product-compliance
Lightning Source LLC
Chambersburg PA
CBHW020702110726
47901CB00001B/268